Praise for

House of Milk and Cheese

"Mars D. Gill brings to attention the dynamics of racism and the process of grief and hatred that haunts the decisions her characters are faced with in the aftermath of a tragedy that many can relate to in our current state. Her characters speak with shocking sincerity as to what drives a person to negatively impact not only the victims of hate crimes and their families but also their own loved ones that they leave behind in their choices. *House of Milk and Cheese* will stay in your mind as the narrative of our times for many immigrant families and their tumultuous journey in finding their own success within American landscape."

–Navraaz Basati, Writer, Documentarian, Previous Creative Director at Prima Films and Radio Producer for Vocalo, Chicago Public Radio.

"Siana Singh will grab your heart as she struggles to make sense of tragedy and fights to make her father's dream, and her own, come true."

–Ilene Goldman, Short Story Author

"Beautifully and poetically written. Full of subtle nuances and story twists. How one incident alters the trajectory of multiple lives has been captured with empathy in this heartwarming story of Siana Singh. I found enough drama and suspense in *House of Milk and Cheese* to keep me entertainingly engaged till the end."

–Rosamin Bhanpuri, Lincolnwood Multicultural Task Force, Retired Community Relations Professional

ALSO BY MARS D. GILL

Letters from the Queen

House of Milk and Cheese

A Novel

MARS D. GILL

Book of Dreams, Inc

Copyright © 2021 by Mars D. Gill

Publisher Book of Dreams, Inc

South Barrington, IL

www.bookofdreams.us

ISBN 978-1-7349423-4-7

Printed in the United States of America

Book cover design by Covers and Cupcakes.

https://coversandcupcakes.com/

To *Bapuji*

Introduction

"The woods are lovely, dark and deep.
But I have promises to keep.
And miles to go before I sleep.
And miles to go before I sleep."

ROBERT FROST, STOPPING BY WOODS ON A SNOWY EVENING

Papa

FREMONT, CALIFORNIA. AUGUST 9, 2015

CLOUDS CLING to the buildings, the factory fumes pave a pebbly gray roof, a car honks, *ah* San Francisco. His solitary Sunday trek for the groceries, a long-time favorite, is in play, and he is not happy. He is slugging along Mathis Street with the grocery bags as he should. His mind is firing off images that are new and old. His daughter is upset at home, acting like a losing politician, her judgment final, her loss final. By now, her coffee must be steamy. Relief.

When he had first held her at the hospital, stars and fleeting clouds had blanketed the night sky, the outdoorsy, oily wafts of sunflowers had overwhelmed the crab-odor from the nearby fish market, the burning desert winds had moistened to a water cooler draft, not for nothing. For once, he was more than just a security guard or a cashier. He became a father to a girl. The magical ambiance wasn't a figment of his irrational imagination, the symptom of his boundless and sometimes misplaced happiness: it was real. Siana sleeping in his arms was more real than real. He'd arrived.

The entire night at the hospital, he had rested by the window with her in his arms.

Oh, her shut eyes, her wrinkly forehead, her curled fists, and her coos. His life had transformed with the meaning of altering their future, her future, forever. She would never tend the cash register as he did. Or follow a man.

But twenty-four years can unmake a soul. Siana has tended the cash register. Content with the ordinary, she hasn't learned to dream—the dreams he once saw under the shooting stars when she was born.

Why?

Just then, he crashes into a boy. Accident. He stutters a sorry. But the boy with moist orange lips and freckled cheeks flares his nostrils and draws out a gun.

Tejpal Singh doesn't have time to hear his words. In seconds, bullets tear holes. Two holes. The groceries fall and sprawl along the sidewalk before he hits the ground, lying face down in a puddle of his warm blood.

"Siana," he whispers for the last time.

The Beautiful Blond and Blue-Eyed

"We are all islands shouting lies at each other across seas of misunderstandings."

RUDYARD KIPLING, THE LIGHT THAT FAILED

One

PAPA named me Siana, meaning obedient and wise; I was anything but that. Outside of my family, I was better known as Sia, which freed me, shedding the world behind Siana, shedding the bondage of the gift of a name, like a nameless stray dog who is free until an entity claims her, slaps a band around her neck, and calls her theirs. Stray, okay. Owned, no.

Chaos like this had brewed in me, pushing me to question every truth: my origin, my purpose, and my identity. Most of all, I was angry at God for placing me in a Punjabi family, close like conjoined twins—except not twins, more like five connected people who smothered me with their love. The only liberating "me" part of my day was when I ran. Sweating and panting helped ease my anxieties, shed my fears, and silence the anger.

Had it not been for Dr. Silverstone, my therapist, I wouldn't have realized I had a purpose in life beyond crying in a corner over my cares.

I wondered what she thought about me though. Maybe, she pitied me because I had come to her drunk during my first therapy visit. Or maybe, my folding into a fetal position and sleeping on her plush velvet couch the entire first session was unusual for her patients. She had to wake me when the hour had passed. Her gentle smile showed no sign of frustration or feedback if I had snored—soft or loud.

She had said, "Time's up. See you in one week."

These words resulted into the most meaningful conversation I'd had in weeks: "Time's up" and a promise of meeting again. A week later, I sat upright—sober and awake, returning to her again and again and again.

It would add gloss to my impression of myself if I admitted that Dr. Silverstone was too sweet of a person. Her sweetness was the nectar that glued me to the couch across from her, and her simplicity was a rarity in this complex world.

I couldn't manage a meal, but this one-hour weekly session alone kept me afloat. And although I called Dr. Silverstone's office the Talking Room, I studied her more than I talked. The broken child in me hungered for her whole, from her laughter that resembled a well-oiled, luxury car's buzz to her calmness that assured me all was okay—for now. And like this, months had passed leading to today.

The Talking Room was situated at the front of her home. Inside, a rocking chair, where she sat, lay separated by a table from the green velvet couch for her patients. All empty spaces, the middle table, the side ottomans, the shelves, and the windowsills, graced plants and books. Away from the seating area, I waited for her, facing the wall with canvases of cheerful images: The sun rising above the mountain peaks. A wave cresting over an ocean. A grandmother setting a turkey platter on the table while her family laughed. They were so happy.

Gliding my hand across the wall, I jumped back when a dark face flashed in front of me. My keen eye had missed the newly added mirror, the size of a fist, between the Thanksgiving canvas and the mountain peaks. And nothing escaped my attention. Never. I counted my breaths, but it didn't calm my nerves. While I glared at my reflection, a sudden awareness gripped my heart. I didn't belong here. Rather, I should never have come.

I swung away from the mirror when the familiar sweet, chocolaty aroma of warm cookies wafted into the room. At last! Such breezes were all I received of Dr. Silverstone's life. It momentarily answered my hunger to learn more about her world beyond these impenetrable office walls.

When a faucet turned on in the adjoining bathroom, I rested my ear against the wall. As always, she washed her hands either because she was a germophobe or Dr. Silverstone removed bias, so only our shared stories hung between us. Whatever her reasons may be, I welcomed the swish of the water. It prepared me to begin the session, too. When the tap stopped, I rushed to the couch.

She entered the room, but her usual smile was absent. Mine disappeared, too. Tied in a messy braid, her blend of blond and gray hair rested on one shoulder. She wore a long skirt under her wrinkled cotton shirt and a sleeveless jacket, all too loose. Her usual polished business outfits came to mind.

She sank into her seat and adjusted the glasses on her nose. "Good evening, Sia."

"Are you okay?"

She chuckled. The sound sent warmth down my chest. But then she did something she had never done before. She gave me a glimpse into her life.

"*Oh,* it's been a terrible day. But don't worry about me. Tell me about your practice sessions."

I grabbed my phone from the couch. May 31, 2016. "Terrible day" sounded about right. "Practice is fine, doc." Why did my heart sink? I wanted to talk about her day, nothing else. "I'm ready for the IAAF World Championship."

"IAAF?"

"The International Association of Athletic Federation. I told you it takes place every four years like the Olympics. This year it's in London."

"That's fantastic, Sia. When do you leave?"

"I fly tonight."

"Hmm." Her glasses had dropped on her nose as she leafed through her notebook.

Dr. Silverstone had a calm, motherlike quality about her, but an occasional hand tremor or a head scratch never escaped my attention. Her "terrible day" was a milestone in my life even though I ached for her. She continued to flip pages.

Okay, Sia, do it now.

Today, I came with a purpose called the truth. Like the stories I had shared with her in the past—except true—well, define "truth." Does something have to happen for it to be real? The problem with my stories was . . . they were aspirational. Milk and cheese.

But the time had arrived when I had to speak a language which the world considered being "true."

I'd to prepare myself. My fingers clung together into a tight knot, and I heard myself from inside my shut eyes. "My first crush was on a boy named Brian. He had blond hair and blue eyes." When I opened my eyes, she wrote a sentence longer than the one I had spoken. I squinted but couldn't read her words from where I was sitting.

"Where is he now?"

"Stanford." A loose hair strand tickled my neck, and I slapped it. "A-although, I'm not sure, to be honest."

She stirred ever so slowly in her seat. "Are you still in touch with him?"

"Yes—No. It's complicated." *Oh,* I'd lost control of the conversation already.

"Why?"

Unlike my impulsive nature, Dr. Silverstone reacted to my stories in the following session. Rarely had she challenged me in the middle of the moment, but she never forgot our conversation, always returning with more probing inquiries. If I for once inhaled in her notes, I would dissect her brain and find out what she "really" thought about me.

"He wasn't interested in someone like me," I whispered.

Her eyes flickered. "Someone like you? What do you mean?"

My heart pounded as the clock's pit-a-pat drummed. Reflections from a car's headlights on the street traveled across the room while our gazes tied like a battle of wizards' wands.

"Think about this." She placed her pencil on the notebook. "If you had 'the blond hair or the blue eyes', would things be different?"

I smiled while my attention drifted to the girl seated next to the grandmother in the Thanksgiving canvas. The girl's swimming-pool-colored eyes twinkled.

"I don't know, doc. That's not the only reason why we aren't together."

Chains of rules bounded my teenage life. My classmates' bare necessities like cell phones were a luxury I couldn't afford; their pleasures were boundaries I couldn't cross like dating or going to prom. I grew up in the shelter of a bubble, the jail my parents constructed.

Our humble lifestyle flowed in my veins. My parents were laborers. Day and night. Work and rest, not for Papa. His feet bore the brunt of his body and his family: during the day, at the gas station, and night, as a security guard. To top that, he had depended on occasional truck driving opportunities. Mamma, too, stocked boxes at the local Target store. But lately, her hours had dwindled. We never ate out at restaurants. Our recreation involved Sunday visits to worship at the *Gurudwara*. My world was so different from my classmates' and arguably my shrink's, it would take me months to explain to the doctor why I couldn't date Brian.

Her head lifted and descended in a slow-motion nod. She turned another page. "What do you want to talk about today?"

Didn't I just bring up the blond hair and blue eyes? Why was that topic not good? I couldn't repeat the rehearsed words, risking exposing my deliberation. "I don't know."

"Let me see my notes."

Dr. Silverstone perused my file, her finger tracing the words, my back and neck the most straight they had ever been in the Talking Room.

Suddenly, my hands became limp, my mouth opened, and my eyes shut.

I pictured: Mamma whispering a prayer while cooking in the kitchen, her head covered with a scarf, her nails cut too deep; Papa kneeling and holding his sprained back while wearing his blue security guard uniform, his eyes shut in pain. He was unable to utter any words. And then he rose, adjusted his turban, and disappeared into the moonlight. He just went about his business. They were the people I didn't bring to Dr. Silverstone. Family secrets.

When I raised my head, she had brought the file closer to her eyes.

"How's your father doing? Has he recovered?" she said.

Strings of clumsy chuckles knitted out of my throat. "Yes, he is feisty. Much better now."

In the Talking Room, Papa upgraded to having a sprained back, or a headache, or a fever but not dead. Always alive. Never shot. I swallowed, sinking into the depths of her watery, emerald eyes.

She returned to her notes. "You were raised in—"

A shrill pitch mixed with my words. "There was a boy named Vikram."

"Who?"

"D-did I tell you about Vikram?"

Dr. Silverstone studied her notes. "No, who is Vikram?"

Speaking truth was hard after masquerading for months. But I tried. My head rested on my hands as I saw my beige, stucco home, indistinguishable from the neighbors': same polish, same windows, same doors, same landscaping, blending into a strange, concocted harmony and hiding the distinctions between those who lived inside—except for one visible difference, one piece of Papa on the front entrance: an American flag. A memory prickled me: Sweat sliding off my arms; my saluting the swinging flag; my marching inside, the music ringing through my headphones.

Dr. Silverstone's chair creaked as she shifted her body. "Are you with me?" Her shape reformed, the red nail polish shining on her hands.

Plowing down my cheek, a bead of sweat tickled my face. "Y-yes. Back in 2009. I think it was August—no—September. Maybe in August. I—"

"You don't have to be exact." She smiled.

"Sure. I'd just returned from my run. Vikram and his parents sat in a row as though watching a TV show." A hidden chuckle inside found my voice. "They passed for statues at Madame Tussauds of our living room. And my mom had neatly laid an Indian outfit on my bed." My clasped hands filled with sweat.

"So why did Vikram and his family visit?"

"A-i . . ." I, too, wondered why they'd visited. Seven years later, here I was, not arranged into an alliance. Single.

"I'm sorry to change topics. What does your father do?"

I shuddered, unsure whether from Dr. Silverstone's buzzer or by the repeat mention of Papa.

My feet tightened around the floral carpet, my mind revolting at the thought of leaving. But the color returned to my shrink's face. Smiling widely, she shut the notebook. "We meet again in a week. Perhaps we can continue this topic then?"

My wicked joy came to an untimely end. Always too short. Clumsily, I gathered my laptop bag, cell phone, and car keys under her kind stare.

"Bye." I trudged over to the door, the bag sliding down my arms with the doctor right behind me.

Outside, the night was young as a cool breeze blew through my hair, her shadow stationed in the doorway, her hand holding the knob.

As San Francisco's chilly wind barreled through, I tucked my chin into my neck and cowered into myself. Sometimes, I wished to be invisible and stay in her office, sprawl on her couch where people spilled their secrets, and I only twaddled. Unlike the paintings on her wall, showing people with toothful grins, I wouldn't hide my frown.

I stopped and turned. She had shut the door, and the office windows were dark and empty.

Two

ANNOYED that another therapy session slipped away without progress, Rhonda fidgeted one too many times, but her misery had other free givers as well. The mother inside her was tired and distracted. She'd spent the entire session counting the clock ticks, keeping herself in her chair, whole and not screaming, so harrowing were her troubles. When the alarm buzzed, a load lifted off, and she jumped to her feet like a child at school dismissal. As soon as Sia's frame blended with the night, she shut the door and grabbed her keys from the adjacent hook.

For years, her job had been effortless like a liver, a functioning organ you didn't realize existed inside your body, satisfying like your grandmother's homemade cookies, or in her case, her husband's, and anything but a chore that paid your bills, but one day you forgot how to perform. That's how Sia made her feel. The slim, long-legged athlete with downcast eyes, asked more questions than gave answers, and dropped disjointed topics that tested her, and her joy became a job that paid the bills, that now felt like working and struggling and failing.

Nothing progressed their conversations from casual to constructive, dissecting why Sia was drunk when she first visited her. After that, why had she not been intoxicated again? Something happened on that summer day. Sia wasn't married. No boyfriend, so no breakup. No divorce.

She scoured local crimes, too, around her first visit. Many crimes popped up, none that led her to her patient. Her background contained no foster homes. She even called her police friend, but she found no file under Sia's name. Born and lived in Fremont, an average citizen without Twitter or Facebook, Sia's past or present was absent like snow in Miami. It's as if she didn't exist. Her family sounded like a respectable Indian family, and while her Bay Area friends grew up with her, she knew no one from India, but she treated a patient from Iran once. However, that lady bore bruises from an abusive husband.

Today, Rhonda's gaze had fastened on Sia's age. Twenty-five years. How could Sia not talk about any friends or enemies or a boyfriend? Her emotional IQ remained teenage-like. She raked up her twenty-fifth year from her memories when she'd married her high school sweetheart, and they had been actively trying to get pregnant—grown-up pursuits.

When Sia mentioned blue eyes and blond hair, a shallow topic on the surface, Rhonda had searched through her notes to connect it to the previous discussions. But the boy Brian appeared between them without warning. Brian wasn't a friend or an ex, but just a crush. Why was he important? Did Brian hurt her? If she could get the last name—maybe he had a file at the police. She had noted to consult the identity crisis book.

She slid into her jacket when a hand brushed on her shoulders.

Cringing, she said, "I meant to sneak out but can never fool you, can I?"

Jacob was apple cheeked. "Where are you going this late at night, honey?"

"Church. Please let me. It's the only place my mind is at peace."

"Rhonda, will you let it go, please? Drop it."

"I'm going."

"I'm coming with you, not leaving you alone today." He reached for his jacket before Rhonda clutched his hand and yanked it down.

"I need to do this on my own." She swung around and left through the front door before he could respond.

Ten years ago, she used to hunger for company, a friendly chat to lighten her load. But lately, no words comforted her, not even her husband's. She only relied on silence and her own mind as crutches. And a name repeated inside her mind: Grace, Grace, Grace.

The thud of her footsteps helped anchor her focus as a cold, tingly ache rose along her throat and glittered through her eyes. People wanted to become astronauts, doctors, nurses, teachers, but not Rhonda. She had only dreamed of becoming a mother. When the doctors informed her that she and her first husband Ray couldn't bear children, she hid her sorrow at church and behind her career as a therapist, but she didn't resign or falter. For years, poking and prodding at the clinics didn't help. Pleading with the medical community didn't help. Only her prayers delivered her a miracle after ten years when she gave birth to a daughter named Grace.

So today, too, she leaned on her faith.

In fifteen minutes, she reached the stone-walled building where only yesterday she had spent hours attending mass with her son. She slipped into a pew toward the back and steepled her hands. For half an hour, she prayed and thanked God for not losing her faith even though her life had rounded a full circle. Today, the police removed her last living child from her embrace. Locking him behind bars, they left her barren of her only pursuit. This day wouldn't have happened if Grace were alive. If.

Before exiting, she slipped into the confession box and kneeled.

"Hello," a voice whispered across the meshed window.

"*Oh!* I thought no one would be here this late."

"God's house is open at all times. How have you sinned?"

Sniffling, her lower lip quivered. "I-I've been a bad mother." She dashed out of the building without waiting for a response.

Outside, she paced the sidewalk, her mind oscillating between her late daughter and Sia.

After the dire warning that her daughter wouldn't live past one week at the NICU, Grace defied the doctors by stretching her time on Earth to fifteen years.

But birth problems didn't kill Grace; the world did. Today, she would be thirty, only marginally older than Sia.

She lowered and held her knees. Praying didn't diminish her discomfort, and she hungered to seize control of her life instead of relying on religion alone.

Too old to wait for a prayer to be answered and too restless to return home tonight, robbed of her dreams, she had to do something—anything.

Else, the dark walls of her home would swallow her whole, pitting her into the hollows of a sleepless night. So she lingered there, a moist, gentle breeze whistling, a lemony floral aroma blowing past her.

She hadn't helped her children, but there was one person she could. Sia. Eight months had been wasted.

An idea jolted her, and she yanked her phone out of her pocket, her fingers fidgeting. Why did she have epiphanies right after the opportunity had left? But Sia couldn't have gotten too far since the end of the session.

She mumbled, "Screw the rules. I'm calling."

And for the first time, she dialed Sia's number.

Maybe if she could talk to Sia at a park or a lake over a coffee for no charge, somewhere other than her office, Sia would relax and share her troubles. And she, too, could—

Ring followed by a click and a hello. A female voice answered. Rhonda itched her chin. "Hello. Can I talk to Sia, please?

"Who?"

"Sia—Siana Singh."

A group of teenagers clumped out of a side street across from Rhonda.

"Siana has left for her tournament in London. Who is this?"

Holding her neck, Rhonda breathed heavily. "Yes, hi. This is Dr. Silverstone."

"Doctor? For what?"

The teenagers chortled, one rolling on the sidewalk. Rhonda rolled her eyes at them.

Cornered, her throat constricted. "I'm sorry I thought I dialed her cell phone."

A disturbance like an exchange of hands followed before a commanding male voice said, "Yes, ma'am, you did dial her cell, which she left at home. How do you know Sia?"

Rhonda pressed the end button and tucked the phone away. She hadn't considered talking to Sia's family and, in return, be interrogated. Perhaps her idea of casually meeting was wrong from the beginning, bending the rules and her professionalism. But when she ambled toward home, involuntarily, a smile grew on her face, thinking about Sia enjoying London. That would lighten her up.

The Beautiful Black-Haired Brown

"If you can dream – and not make dreams your master;
If you can think – and not make thoughts your aim;
If you can meet with triumph and disaster;
And treat those two imposters just the same."

RUDYARD KIPLING, IF

Three

LONDON. JUNE 2, 2016

WHEN I WAS a little girl, all I wanted in life was to be lucky. But I couldn't define what luck meant, even as I grew older.

But today as I collected my luggage from the conveyor belt at the London Gatwick airport, I felt it in my gut. I had qualified for the IAAF World Championship but also tore my knee ligaments. Nature worked against me, not for me: the master of bad luck.

Lonely, I limped alongside US athletes to the train station in the south terminal. When they smiled at mundane airport business or stopped at souvenir shops to buy giant Toblerone chocolate bars, I glanced at my watch. They entered the Thameslink train as though they had waltzed into the Titanic.

Like freed inmates, they gaped outside from the train at London glowing. When the tall, twisted skyscrapers loomed, one shouted, "Look, there's the Sky Garden."

"The Parliament building over the Thames River." Another clapped.

"Look back! The London Eye."

But I only beheld a dull haze. To feel like a real athlete, not a scared little person who lied weekly to her therapist, I came to win in London.

So my mind blocked all the sights and sounds, my connections with the outside world. Heck, I even stopped sensing the dull pain that shot up my thigh with each step.

When the train emerged from the underground, north of the river, the clock struck ten o'clock, and a waft of salty, buttery popcorn overcame me. My belly gurgled, and I shut my attention to its aroma, focusing only on my prayers, begging God to heal my knee so I could win my race today. Become lucky!

A fellow athlete interrupted me, advertising her performance at the 2012 London Olympics. When our station arrived, I sighed with relief and disembarked first. Besides the salty fries, I now craved physical solitude.

Warmth and chilliness had blended into a pleasant harmony in the breeze that slammed my face. It reminded me of my evening walks with Papa. We would grab the air in our fists and say, "there, we are holding our dreams in our palms now." I had challenged him that it was impossible to hold air in your hand. He had agreed. But dreams, he said, you could. I extended my bare, empty hands that refused to clump into a fist. Barren.

The camp buzzed like bees as I zigzagged past the multitudes of athletes. True, myriads of dreams suspended in the air. In the land of "a nobody" like me, everybody wanted to be somebody: a medal-winning, sponsor-winning champion. In their nervous laughs, twinkling, fluttering eyes, quivering stretches, dripping with sheer abundance of hungry and naked desire, I cringed with disgust. Why were we, humans, so needy? Why was I so needy?

Through my mind's gloom, I grabbed a white sheet at the registration desk when someone pulled it away from my weak grasp.

"No, no need to sign. Just give me your last name," he said.

Tall. Head full of thick, midnight hair. Umber cheeks with dimples. And body carved with muscles inside a hoodie jacket.

"Your last name, please."

Clear your throat, said a voice inside my head. I cleared my throat. "Singh."

"It's a common last name." He bent, scribbling on a sheet of paper. "What's your first name?"

"Siana." Not where I came from was Singh a common last name.

"Indian?" He rose to be at my eye level.

A whistle blew. Distant claps pattered through the atmosphere. Tapping his pen on the table, he cocked an eye at me. "Do you have a country?"

I unzipped my windbreaker, the big block letters USA now visible on my shirt. My face had reached the registration desk before my soul. And where was my outside voice?

He extended a welcome packet. "The United States. Why didn't you just say so?"

Past a hint of gray in his thin beard and full lips, his teeth sparkled. Quickly, I slung the bag on my shoulders, aware of my noticing concrete elements of my surroundings. His name tag read Aryan Khan.

"Are you from Pakistan?" I asked.

"I get that a lot. No, I'm not from Pakistan, Ms. Singh. I belong to California—the US. Same as you."

Surprised, I half-smiled and marched away when he yelled. "But yes, I'm an Indian in my heart, originally from Bombay, Siana Singh."

I halted in my tracks and turned to where he shuffled papers on the desk, beaming. While Aryan Khan was a Muslim name, I hadn't worried if I offended him by tying his identity with India's mortal enemy Pakistan. I swung around and trudged along to the women's locker room, sinking deeper into my inner world. The memory of the American flag in our front yard, fluttering and whooshing, came alive. So did Papa's smile.

Inside the buzzing locker room, I found an unused one at the back. After shoving in the packet, I leaned against the locker, a rhythmic drumming inside my chest. I curled my fingers into a fist, but they wouldn't stop shaking. Why had I grown so nervous? Praying, I lugged myself outside behind a train of athletes.

Where the stadium seats met the racetrack, a man dressed as a clown smiled wide and danced around. He asked runners headed to the grounds: "Who are you running for?"

"Jamaica," one said.

"China." The athlete in front of me beamed.

When he peered into my eyes, my heartbeat thundered, and I said, *"My father."*

Four

TWO COMPETITIONS today, one long jump, a one-hundred-meter race, but only one was in session. Two of us: both brown in midnight-blue uniforms, stretching and staring at each other, only one was intimidated, me. Twenty long minutes, threatening an experience of twenty years, separated me from my qualifying race, the one not in session.

Shorter than me but better built, rows of thick braids carved the other girl's head. She began marching toward me before I dropped my arms. Something about her swagger, her confidence, browbeat me.

With a grin, she extended her hand and spoke in a thick accent. "Hi. What state do you represent? I did not notice you earlier at the orientation."

Her handshake was firm.

"I missed—" A loud whistle tore through the air. "We haven't met before."

"Yes. I'm Mina from West Bengal. You stood sad and alone, made me think you can join us." Her eyelids dropped. "Your kind name?"

"My name is Siana Singh, and I'm from the United States."

"Yes, I saw." She pointed at my shirt. "I should have guessed, as you have a foreign accent. Listen, I go now. Buh-bye!"

My mouth widened while she rejoined the Indian athletes.

When she said something to her peers, ten feet from me, they erupted into a burst of mocking, roaring laughter. Occasionally, one of them casted a glance at me. I stretched my arm and twisted my torso to the side. I didn't blame Mina for her confusion. My muddy hair and caramel-coffee face didn't belong to India, and deep borders separated our similar shades of blue uniforms. It had taken me twenty-four years to admit that color divided lives and hearts. So did uniforms.

I shrugged her off and focused on my routine and my beating heart.

Aryan Khan, the registrant from the front desk, now circulated the field shaking hands and conversing with players. Too old to be an athlete, he probably coached. I straightened and jogged in my position. While my footfalls drummed a beat, I scanned the crowd clusters and profiled them—the Chinese, the Japanese, the British, and seated at the far corner, some Americans. The one who bragged about the 2012 Olympics waved.

A bell boomed through the air, and quivering, I drifted along to the track.

What if Papa could be here? He had waited for this day. If he were here, he would be the loudest cheerleader, grinning, whistling. His words reverberated through my soul: *"Meet my daughter, Siana. She's an athlete. Just like me."* But those words drenched in pride were years old.

My cheek twitched in anguish as I descended to the start position.

People, not all athletes, including Aryan congregated around us. I had studied the runners, who were mere shadows now. Except for Mina. She was new. Diverting her eyes away from me, she swiveled her neck back and forth. It clicked. Intimidated, I glanced away at once.

Papa's voice returned into my ears, a more recent voice: *"What happened to you, Siana? You used to run better."*

I *had* to win this one.

A whistle tooted and slashing forward with our bodies like knives piercing through the track, we leaped. My knee convulsed in pain, but my legs listened to my heart's directions and raced.

I started at the front. A figure passed me.

Then another, and my life's scars opened. Papa *knew* I was no good when he was murdered.

Before the race concluded, I managed to overtake an athlete to secure my spot in the race, the third spot, the barely survived spot, but I-am-so-happy-Sia spot. Roars thundered around us as we congratulated one another. But not I and Mina. Somehow, without an occurrence, something divisive had occurred between us. Mina swiveled at me upon her first finish as though she had feared me foolishly.

A smile hid deep inside my bosom though. After years of missteps, a third-place finish was a victory, only if Papa could take this memory with him instead.

After I reached the sidelines, a stinging pain pulled me down to my knees, and my eyes shut under my cupped palms. Moments later, when I faced up, a form firmed into a face, and deep, unflinching eyes stared down at me. Aryan Khan.

"Are you okay?" He extended his hand, and with his help, I rose.

Aryan led me off the racetrack. "Did you get hurt?"

"Yes."

"What does your doctor say?"

We paused. I released his arm and dusted myself before I limped over to a vacant seat, my bottom falling onto it. My life was made up of tides. A low wave fast followed the high, ensuring the timely end of my happiness.

"Who is your coach?" Aryan loomed over me like a shadow.

"My coach had an episode."

He laughed even though I wasn't aiming for funny. Away from him and his interrogations, away from the crowded seats, away from the crippling ache around my knee, the athletes chattered, bells pealed, commentators buzzed. Away from me. Away from my pain. But I was one race closer. So entrenched was I in the world away from me that Aryan's voice close to me boomed.

"What races do you have left today?"

Why did he care? "The two-hundred-meter race."

"A longer one. Are you going to run?"

A chuckle erupted from my core. "I'm here to run."

"You should skip it."

"What? I just qualified into the hundred-meter semifinals. What are you saying?"

"Skip it." He jumped into the seat next to me.

"God, who do you think you are!"

He put his hand on his chest. *"Oh,* sorry, you know nothing about me. My name is Aryan Khan, and I, too, was a runner in India, but I never made it." He pointed to my knee. "Injury killed my athletic career."

He scratched the back of his neck. "I moved to the US ten years ago, and I'm a lawyer—"

"Lawyer?"

"Yes. But in my free time, I coach athletes, so they don't make my mistakes. Do you see the boy over there?" He pointed toward the middle of the stadium. A frail guy stretched his legs. "He is my first victim. Now you know everything about me." He beamed.

"Are you a lawyer in the Silicon Valley?"

"Yes, and a coach." His eyebrows danced.

"Still, it doesn't explain—listen, I came here to run a—"

Aryan leaned forward. "You've injured your knee and need to rest it. At least, you should get it inspected. Besides, lots of coaches and sports personalities are present. Why ruin your reputation ahead of the Olympics?" He pointed his index and middle finger toward his eyes. "Focus on the real prize."

Fury propelled me out of my seat. "Aryan, thanks for your concern, but I'll run." When he opened his mouth, I said with a raised hand: "There's nothing you can do."

A pain spasm floated outward from my chest, and my fingers tingled on my journey away from Aryan, who was still seated where I'd left him.

Loneliness debilitated me.

He wasn't the only one who thought I had lost and should quit.

An hour later, like a pressure cooker's whistle loudens, the crowd's buzz had magnified to the point of release. The joy of running, a distant memory, firmed its hold on me, and I shed every bit of the sorry truth I endured in my life—I wasn't good enough; I hurt people; I, I, I, the culprit.

With my heart and soul, I ran. I passed a runner, then another, and another until I led the race.

As I widened my gap, the crowd's pitch grew, and my shoulders eased, unburdened by the imminent outcome. Necessity drove me forward. Eyeing the finish line, only a dozen feet away, a smile bounced on my lips. Claps thundered an orchestra. Roars drummed a melody.

Boom. A sharp shooting pain tore through my knee to my feet. The sting overwhelmed me.

When I fell on my knee, the crowd's roar transformed into a loud *ahh.* I struggled and rose. Effortlessly, the athletes overtook me, finishing the battle I'd almost won.

Ending me in the tournament and martyring my soul, defeat used my knee as an accomplice and spread her tentacles around me. Only yesterday, I had the dream—Papa's sole conviction—of winning and overcoming my odds and changing the course of my life. *Oh,* yesterday, return to me.

A paramedic helped me off the racetrack as someone in a white coat, a briefcase in hand, ran toward us. A layer of shame dripped off my cheeks. When I'd qualified for the tournament, I'd cried as much as I wept now. A full circle. With what face was I to return home? The same one I brought to London—the unfulfilled one.

On the sidelines, the man in the white coat told me he was an orthopedic doctor before he lifted my knee, and I brought my face to my hands. I sought the ointment of darkness beneath my palms that diminished the ache sharper than the knee, the unforgiving stabs of sorrow, radiating across my bosom.

A pair of firm hands clutched my shoulders, but I didn't lift my head. Nothing mattered now. The hands that gripped me now patted my upper back.

"This is not the end of the world," he whispered.

Ceasing to sob, I raised my moist face to peer into the kind, chocolaty eyes of Aryan. My salty tears mixed with the snots flowing down my nose, and I let them. At least, my neck was dry.

"But it is," I whispered.

The doctor bent my leg and pressed on its sides, and I cringed.

"It feels like the end, but it is not. They can nurse your knee back to health." He turned to the doctor. "Right?"

"We need an x-ray. Tear related injuries can cause ligaments to swell—that mandates no running for a week or two, at least. Then you ease into it with medication."

"Can it be more serious than a ligament tear?" Aryan crossed his arms.

"We need the x-ray to rule out a fracture."

Aryan interrogated the doctor like a lawyer, their words dimming in my mind each second that passed. Though not sobbing anymore, I imagined the skid marks on my face of sunscreen washing away with tears as I stared at nothing. Failure was strangely liberating because I had nothing left to lose or fear.

A new race was starting while they harnessed my kneecap in support bandages. Could healing the knee nurse the heart?

Aryan brought me crutches. "This will speed up your recovery ahead of the Olympic trials."

After I thanked him, I pulled myself up onto the crutches. I, a wounded warrior, lacked the will to fight. So placing one foot in front of the other, I drifted to where the defeated collected themselves or where they cleaned themselves—the locker rooms.

Aryan glided alongside me, talking into his phone in Hindi.

As soon as we reached the locker rooms, he asked, "Want to grab a bite to eat?"

Clinging to the cold steel crutch, I counted my breaths, deliberating on Aryan's offer, disallowing my desperation to snap out in the form of an eager yes.

Five

AN ENGLISH DINER. LATER THE SAME DAY

AT A CAFÉ in north London, a block away from the stadium, I listened to Aryan.

"There are only two kinds of people here," Aryan said.

The setting sun cast a mango glow on his dark hair, streaked ash gray at the base. He must have used a dye.

In the middle of the terrace, a baby coconut tree rustled melodiously, lock step with his hair strands.

Glad he didn't mention my latest failure, I smiled. "What two kinds of people?"

"The ones drinking." He pointed to a corner with a group of young adults, their eyelids heavy, their bodies slanted before one tumbled to the ground, laughing. Aryan chuckled, too. "And those who watch others get wasted. Siana—"

"Please call me Sia. And at a bar, all come to get drunk."

A server carried a ruby red martini past us.

"Sia, are you here to drink?" He half-smiled.

"No." I ogled the martini that drifted from the server's plate to the table, a flash of satisfaction dripping from the lady's eyes. My mouth watered, too.

When Aryan followed my eyes, I glanced away from the drink.

A faint smile plastered on his face before he lounged back into his chair. "I'm not here to drink either. Most customers here are athletes from the tournament, correct? Players follow a strict diet and limit liquor." He narrowed his glittering eyes. "If they splurge, it gets out of hand. I've seen plenty of athletes rebound from abstinence and succumb to addiction. It's all right if you want one drink. It'll not kill you."

Nervousness sputtered out of me in a clumsy chuckle, and my arms crossed around me in a tight hug. "No, Aryan. I haven't touched a drop of alcohol in . . ." I counted inside my head when I'd first met Dr. Silverstone, her frame hazy, my body hitting her green velvet couch, and darkness.

Plus/minus a few hours, I hadn't consumed beer in eight months and twenty-five days. But Aryan didn't need to know. I gulped my chilled water and nibbled on a fry. Was he always this professorial?

"In?" His gaze was so steady it made me want to hide.

"In months, Aryan, now drop it." My water glass poorly hid my face—it wasn't made of steel.

"Good. Is USATF providing you with a coach and pipeline to the Olympics?"

"I handled it myself and then got injured."

"What happened to your coach?" He scratched his beard.

My stomach knotted. The ease of the evening departed. The crimson sunset shed into the ash of charcoal. Despite losing at the IAAF, up until now, I had felt strangely chilled for the first time since Papa, my coach, left me. Why would I let a memory rob me of my current unexpected calm? Because I'm Sia—this is what I do. Words, places, smiles, breezes, faces—name it—everything reminded me of Papa. It tugged on me and crunched me like a ball, growing a tummy ache, even though currently, I sat upright, disallowing an eye flick to escape from my face, only letting silence ring the melody of unease.

He crossed his arms. "It's okay if you don't want to talk about it. Many relationships fail, and if you like, I can coach you."

My fingers tingly, a snicker erupted from my throat. I needed a coach, but could I trust him?

Did he believe in my abilities?

A wind gust blew a napkin from our table as Aryan grabbed the rest, and I placed my empty water cup to secure them.

"Your first order of business as my coach will be to get me to stop running," I whispered, my hair slapping my face, my shirt flapping my back.

His cheek twitched. "Hey, you heard the doctor. Consider yourself lucky it may only be a week or two's rest. Knee injuries can take months to heal. You still mingle with the community, attend the sessions and speeches, and study competitors."

Lucky??

My battle with luck was old. Owing to my tenure in the zone, I'd an unofficial Ph.D. in this subject matter. You never, never, never called people like me lucky.

"And drink?" Why did my voice shake?

"Oh no, it's not like that." He raised his hands defensively. "You were admiring the red drink, that's all. Please don't misunderstand."

They delivered our salads, and we let them sit. The kale may have been rich, but my eyes saw compost.

"I missed meals, hoarded every penny, and counted it toward savings so I could afford the flight to London—six hundred dollars to be exact." Snots returned, and I brought my sleeve to my nose, remembering the money I had to return to my uncle. "I came here to win . . . but I lost."

A wrinkle deepened on Aryan's forehead before he leaned forward. "You can't win all the races you run, and it'll not be a total loss, I promise. You get me—Aryan Khan—as your coach." He grinned. "You are an excellent runner, and I saw how well you ran despite being injured. You have what it takes, and I want to help you get past the victory line."

While the athlete Aryan coached marched toward us, I gulped a choke, unable to handle his kind words.

Oh, how I'd hungered to hear any words that believed in me. Aryan's athlete tapped his shoulder, and they fell deep into a conversation.

Thankfully, he didn't notice my tears, and I wiped them off.

Nursing the water with a straw, I zoned out their words and focused on one tiny, but important detail—even though we met in London, Aryan and I lived in the San Francisco area, and he was a lawyer. I had to probe into that more. Finally, I latched onto the anchor I needed to stop my meltdown in motion.

Michael Jackson's song "Beat It" played on the radio, and I jerked my head to its beats, my sorrow melting away. Coaches didn't moon over athletes like me. Only in the dreams I inherited from Papa, who never tired of parading his race medals from Punjab, did my invisible, unrealized future exist.

When the athlete walked away, Aryan faced me while I folded and rested my hands on the table. "So, you are a lawyer."

"Yes, I said that, and I'm also a coach." He, too, folded his hands.

"What kind of lawyer are you?" I tilted my head. *Say criminal cases.*

"I work as a prosecutor for the District Attorney." He mimicked my head tilt.

"So, mainly criminal cases?"

"Lots of them. Why?" He placed his fist under his chin.

"Does that mean you have an insight into the police reports filed in your area?"

"That's a mischaracterization of the DA's office. We are a team of prosecutors. Why?"

The server refilled my water while our salads remained untouched.

"Just curious. What cases are you fighting right now?"

"Your questions should be about sports and coaching. Do you need legal help?" He picked up his fork and played with the kale in his salad, his vision glued on me.

"Maybe. You never know."

"Clever." His eyebrows bounced.

Another chuckle erupted from deep within my core. Aryan Khan, my coach!

For now, I busied myself with my dinner, realizing it to be too soon to lay out my life story in front of the person I needed more of outside of the racetrack.

The Therapist and the Patient

"A couple hundred languages, infinite letters,
yet some emotions are left unsaid."

MISBAH KHAN, BLANKS & BLUES

Six

SAN FRANCISCO. JUNE 6, 2016

HER BACK stiff from sitting in one position, same as every day, and her feet achy—they were new—Rhonda bolted toward her home as the thunder growled. A sticky, slimy slew of regret clung to her. At the grocery store, she had mistaken a couple, a biscuit-colored athletic girl, and a turbaned man, for Sia and her father. Had she realized her mistake in time, she wouldn't have hugged the girl, who wouldn't have screamed in return, and the man wouldn't have threatened her with a call to the security, and she wouldn't have had to exit with her groceries, unfinished. She didn't need this experience.

When she reached home, the front door creaked in its eternal welcome song, and a wave of relief passed through her. She slid out of her wet rain shoes and shuffled inside to the kitchen island where Jacob stood, chopping tomatoes.

"Hi. I'm glad t-t—" On the island, a court stamp glinted on a white envelope's ripped fluttering flap.

Her hands gave way, the grocery bags falling to the floor, the apples rolling out.

Jacob scampered to her before Rhonda thrust him away, flinging the envelope at him.

"They came, they robbed, they punished, now what does the government want? Our lives?"

His lips twisted in a reverse smile. "What did you expect? It's the court date."

She yanked her phone out, her fingers trembling. "I'm calling my boy. My baby."

Gently plucking the phone from her weak grasp, Jacob placed it on the island. "We both know he's unreachable. Let it go, Rhonda. I'm worried about you."

Words were useless props. Only silence thundered in the moments that followed. Eventually, they lifted the groceries from the floor, just not each other. Gone was the time that used to be a mix of good and not-so-good. Now soaring in pain and competing in wretchedness, her days remained a constant low. The tail end of her life, a time people spent enjoying retirement and reflecting on a satisfying past, was the absolute worst time to lose her only pursuit, the first dream: one of being a good mother. The cruel verdict of defeat washed away her lifetime of accomplishments.

Jacob stabilized the last apple on the island. "Where are the eggs?"

"Sorry, I left early and did not complete the list."

"Why?"

"Enter the drama queen, Rhonda! Why? My mind. This." She pointed at the envelope. "My patient. I'm struggling with her. All of it is weighing me down, Jacob." She slumped into a chair.

"One problem at a time, okay? I know what will cheer you up."

He marched to the pantry and brought her a glass and her favorite red wine.

In that moment, she realized Jacob hadn't forgotten the core principles of self-care, the little pleasures, the small happy places from where he lived his life. Only if she could be more like him—less of a worrier, more of a warrior—no, less of a warrior, more of a nonchalant.

While Jacob poured her a glass, Rhonda spotted Sia's file on the table, the one she'd been studying. She slid the file closer as Jacob moved back to the tomatoes on the island. In one quick swoop, she guzzled the wine.

The thunder rumbled, and a honk tore through the street. Rhonda stared at the fluttering palm tree outside her window, herself swaying in her seat. If she gave up like Jacob, if she did nothing and allowed the court to convict John for life or slap him with the death penalty, she would never be able to forgive herself for the lack of trying. She pressed on Sia's file, crumpling an edge. Her inability to focus forced her to stop accepting new patients and refer several existing ones to other therapists. Sia was one of the last whom she clung to in the hope of success, of helping Sia and proving to herself that there was one thing she was still good at: her job.

A distinct aroma suspended in the air. She sniffed. *Oh,* the sweet smell of chocolate chip dough, the only refreshing part of her present. "Baking cookies?"

Jacob nodded and refilled Rhonda's glass.

"Thank you, darling." She stroked his arm.

As he trudged back to his cutting board, she stared at her notes without reading the words. Sia would arrive any minute, and she couldn't afford to get drunk, but a little merlot would help in comprehending statements about blond hair and blue eyes.

She scratched her cheek, devising a plan. Maybe she could explore more on Vikram. She rose.

Seven

AUGUST 15, 2009

I STOOD still at my cousin Nikki's wedding.

A week ago, my parents had asked me to wear a traditional emerald silk *shalwar kameez*, embellished with carrot embroidery, the one reserved for special occasions, and meet Vikram, who was bound to be here today. Though they hadn't mentioned marriage, it was an educated guess. Did the families wish we get to know one another? Date? Western arranged marriage?

So, here I stood next to Papa, Mamma, and my older brother, Sandeep.

Unlike my family, Nikki's parents, who were doctors, flaunted their wealth and held the star-studded wedding by the whistling Pacific waves.

Old aunties to young toddlers wore bright, sparkly clothes like mannequins freed from an Indian boutique's glass chambers. But unlike the skinny, malnourished ones from the stores, the guests were normal-sized.

Silicon Valley's entire Punjabi community descended on the wedding, and gossip hung in the whiskey-rich air. The men sat in one corner, drunk—not my dad.

He was drunk only with dreams, dreams he had for me. Papa's laughter crackled. "Meet my girl, Siana. She is an athlete—just like me."

"Hi." I blushed.

Sandeep leaned in with his hand. "And I'm Siana's brother—an average engineer, the odd one out. In fact, my parents have forgotten my name. Call me Sunny."

When I elbowed him, he chuckled, fitting to the humorous, protective, and always-smiling part he played in my life. Not hearing a joke from his mouth for a whole evening was impossible.

He whispered in my ear, "You better get your act together on the racetrack. Entire Punjab is waiting for you to run for the next Olympics. One loss and *dishoom*."

As Papa continued to fixate on me, some smiled, some weren't so polite.

"Athlete? What is that?" a fat aunty jeered, jerking her hands around. Wrapped in a zinc yellow saree, her ill-fitted blouse threatened to release her breasts. "My Sonu is an engineer, and Binty is a doctor. What is an athlete?"

Mamma's face mantled with embarrassment as she patted Papa's arm.

"Runner." Papa leaned in.

"Eh?" Her lips twisted.

Sandeep giggled into my ear before he marched away. Only he could laugh at something as appalling as this.

"She will run for Team USA. I'm sure of it."

When the voluptuous mom of Sonu and Binty drew Mamma to the side and leaned into her ear, so did I.

She whispered, "Tell Mr. Singh to make her a doctor or a lawyer and earn money. You cannot keep working at the Fremont Target store. How disgraceful!"

I glared at her and then at Papa, who boasted about my races to another guest. A misfit, an undiscovered minority, Papa, and his simplicity contrasted our measured and calculated world. Huddling in the far corner, Sandeep roared and high-fived his friends to what I imagined to be a football game playing on a phone. At least, his fun-loving personality won him friends.

When Papa pointed to me, I excused myself and slipped away, hiding my flushed face. I'd had enough.

The *bhangra* music ripped through my ears, and a silly laugh snuck its way outside my lips as old ladies twisted their bellies to the dance numbers.

The Punjabi kids at the wedding were sprouting doctors or engineers. And for misfits like me, the icy embrace of a solitary chair, my throne, provided a sanctuary. Just then, I spotted the curly, raven hair and shiny cyan suit of Vikram, who waved before marching to me.

"You have ignored me on Facebook," he said.

"Sorry?"

"Either you are sorry, or you are not. There is no sorry with a 'question mark.' "

Compelled to look him in the eye, I rose. "Listen, Vikram, I think you are cool, but I'm not interested in you in that way."

"Wait a minute . . ." He chuckled, flashing his hands over his head. "Did you think I was interested in you?"

"I thought our parents—"

"Who cares about them?" Like a police officer flashing her badge, he swung out his wallet, except a beautiful girl's picture beamed in place of the ID. "This is my girlfriend. We have been dating for almost a year now."

Although relieved that the "Vikram problem" didn't exist, my cheeks burned in a sudden rush of embarrassment, and I bit my tongue, sitting down, wishing I hadn't turned down a boy who didn't care for my love. It saddened a part of me that Vikram was uninterested in me, too, proving I remained unwanted in the arrangement of love and Brian.

"Are you with someone, too?" he asked.

A jolt of a lie climbed up my throat. "Of course. Brian."

That was the first time I realized I would never face the typical Indian American issues like being forced into an arranged alliance or navigating bossy in-laws. The real problem's name was Siana Singh better known as Sia. And no one could stop me.

Eight

THE TALKING ROOM. JUNE 6, 2016. PRESENT DAY

WHEN the faucet ran in the adjoining bathroom, I returned from where my head was—with Vikram—to where I was, sitting next to my crutches in the Talking Room. The IAAF was over, and so was London. Through the plane ride, I had waited for my cherished hour with the doctor as though more than one week had separated us. Years did separate us in therapy, my mind never in the present, always at a place imprisoned inside me.

The door screeched open, and Dr. Silverstone lumbered to her seat, a whiff of alcohol growing a sneeze in me. From miles away, I recognized that familiar inviting scent of misery. I sneezed. Session by session, she declined steadily, and I braced for an imminent retirement announcement.

The rhythmic clinks of the clock, the thrumming from the thunder, the pages crinkling from Dr. Silverstone's notebook, all of it filled my awareness. And suddenly, the raindrops pounded the roof, and the wind rattled the windows. Drought-ridden San Francisco welcomed rain, not the wet tips of my track pants or my damp hair. The air-conditioner hummed, goosebumps enlarging on my naked arms.

"The crutches, Sia. Are you okay?"

"I had the crutches coming for a while." I laughed so loud that the doctor jittered. "Sorry. Bad joke."

She chuckled, too. "I'm noticing signs of humor in you. That's a positive change."

My mouth flung open. Was I healing, and why hadn't I discovered my progress? But that's why I came to her. In her strange way, she uplifted me and showed me her upbeat observations.

"You want to talk about Vikram?"

"No. Nothing happened with Vikram."

"Okay. How was London?" She pointed at the crutches.

"It was a disaster."

Batting the eyelids didn't clear the smokiness of my blurry vision or keep a tear from carving down my cheek. That washed the ruse! And the newfound humor. The only comfort in my world was her tender hand stroking mine.

"Next time, it'll be better. Tell me, Sia. When did you realize you wanted to be an athlete?"

Only kindness beamed in her watery ocean-green eyes as her question drew me to a long time ago. "I never realized. But . . ." She freed an ancient memory from my locked interior.

"But?"

I closed my eyelids. The basketballs' dribbles. The whistles. The sweat-laden air.

"My father, he knew," I whispered. "I remember that day so well. He acted like a child at Disneyland when my gym teacher informed him that I could run. I'd never seen him laugh nonstop, bouncing from room to room. That's how the dreams of the 2012 Olympics started."

"That's nice. Let's talk about that some more. So it was your father, not you, who wanted you to be an athlete?"

My present thrust itself around me like a cocoon: Dr. Silverstone's voice. The pitter-patter of rain. The synthetic material of my track pants against my cold hands.

"I didn't say that—I always loved to run. But from that day, I ran for Papa. You know what he said to me in the parking lot?"

She smiled. "What?"

I thickened my voice to mimic Papa. "Your father's a college dropout who brought two hundred dollars to America—and a wife!" I hadn't laughed that day, and I wondered if I had frowned. But today, his words sounded different, sweet, funny, even cute. I laughed with him eight years later. Always late, Sia.

She grinned, too. "And how did you feel that day?"

"When my father and my teacher chatted?"

She nodded.

"Let's say, when we rode back home, we saw different dreams. In my father's eyes, I became an athlete like he used to be."

"And your dreams?"

In my dreams, I became a movie star, wearing designer gowns, shiny shoes, and diamond jewelry, worth thousands of dollars. An Oscar, yes. And loved by Brian.

"My dreams were lame teenage traps. Not meaningful."

"No dreams are lame. So you didn't want to be an athlete?"

"It's not like that. I love to run. But I still don't know what I want to be. I wish I could consult a manual."

"You want to win, don't you?"

"Yes," I whispered. "More than the air I breathe, more than my mother's freshly cooked food, more than my life."

Glowed on her face a familiar smile and an unfamiliar harmony. Perhaps it was the alcohol.

Or maybe, just maybe, this was our moment, tension-free, bias-free.

"When you are running your races, who are you running for?"

Energy burst from inside, and under her careful watch, I rose, wandering to the wall mirror by the paintings. I stared into my watery eyes, seeing the clown at the London stadium who had asked athletes the same question. Some of us weren't so lucky to secure a place in any country. We were the orphans of the world's political map.

Remembering Papa's words, I said, "I run for that place where all dreams come true. America." When I swung around, her pencil had slipped from her finger.

Her hand lay flat in her lap, her face mantled, her mouth agape.

As she returned from her trance, she cleared her throat. "Those are powerful words. Running for America is such a patriotic affair indeed."

I trudged back to the couch when she said, "Your father must be proud of you."

My body stopped in motion, sinking onto the couch. I felt sad that Papa had to die for me to embrace his dream, for me to love him how a daughter should, or for me to seek his pride.

Diverting my attention to the wall, I stopped. I couldn't look at the paintings again.

"Nice artwork you have here." Had I praised it before?

"Siana, what happened after your father realized your talent?"

She asked about the months that followed, but my mind had plunged into that one day.

As images rolled inside, words formed on my lips. "When we entered our home that day, as usual, the curry spices filled the entire house. I had barely slipped out of my sneakers when my father brought down the house, ushering my mother and brother to join. That night we celebrated, and my father offered everyone whiskey. Not me. I was too young, he said."

"Well, that's good. Your father sheltered you. What happened then?"

"My father quit moonlighting to coach me the next day."

I was surprised by my response because it wasn't until this moment when I uttered these words that I realized this—his sacrifices bothered me beyond the realm of awareness. Giving up his security guard post had delayed repairs to our car that groaned like a train's engine. I had hogged everything in the athletic pursuits, and upon my shoulders was the broken dishwasher that occupied space in our home and didn't wash to the current day, the leak in the garage that had spread mold until Sandeep found his first job out of college.

These broken things marred me but never caught Papa's attention. He was convinced we had embarked on the most significant mission of my life, if not all our lives. He said that not he but *Waheguru,* God himself, set my destiny when I was born. An athlete I would be.

Dr. Silverstone's voice brought me back.

"This was in high school. What does your father say now? Does he have the same passion?"

Not an atom moved in my body. "My father never changes. He remains constant."

"That must make your father predictable. Tell me," she leaned forward, "how did he take your injury and the result at the IAAF?"

My throat swelled up, and I pursed my lips. "He is okay. As I said, he never changes—a constant cheerleader."

"That's so good. Can we talk about the tournament now?"

"Okay."

She ran her hand through her hair. "How are you before your races? Are you calm? Do you have a ceremony you perform? Do you pray? Go to church—sorry, go to your place of worship?"

"*Gurudwara*. I'm not religious." I looked at her misspelled word, Gurudawara, in her notebook. "No, I don't have a ceremony." Unless "leave me alone" was a ceremony. I prayed a lot, though, a trait Mamma drilled into me. But where was the doctor going with this?

"How were the athletes? Did you make friends?"

Funny, she'd noticed I had mentioned no friends. Friends were the luxury of others. Even at the tournament, my aloofness had served me well. The athletes from India had snickered at me, mocking the USA allegiance on my shirt and arguably in my heart.

"Why do you ask?" I said.

"Just like that."

"I don't make friends easy, doctor. People make me uncomfortable."

"People?" Her head twitched as she lifted a brow in approval. My sorrow was her gain.

"Yes, people." I sighed. "Every one of us hungers to fill a category, a checkmark on a form. Why?"

The rain had ceased, and an eerie tune of clock tick tocks had begun.

She leaned back and crossed her arms. "I guess people feel secure when they know where they belong."

"What about those who are uncertain where they belong?"

"Are you unsure of where you belong?"

My knee erupted suddenly, and I gripped it. "I hate borders and divisions. Take the tournament, for instance." I pointed to the windows. "On one side of the field stood the Indian players I resembled, and yet didn't belong with, and the US players looked different from me. It was hard."

"Why?" Her forehead wrinkled, and she scribbled with haste.

"All the Indians kept pegging me as one of them until they realized their mistake. I marched over to the US side, and I saw . . ."

"Hmm." Her wrinkles deepened.

The timer buzzed, and she scrambled to hit the Off button. "You saw?"

Words hid from me, and no matter how much I urged them, they refused to come out at command.

Dr. Silverstone leaned forward with mouth agape, the most curious I had ever seen her. "We can continue to talk, Sia. It's not a fixed end time."

It was the first time she had wanted to extend our session and my first when I hungered to escape.

"It's okay." I rose and grabbed my light jacket, laptop bag, cell phone, car keys, and my newest addition, the crutches.

She followed me, shuffling to the door. As always, her stare burned my back before she diminished to a murky shadow in her doorway. The thunder rumbled, matching my cynical mind. I was in the pit seeing unreal images—angry, disgruntled, and spiteful.

The blond, blue eyes I once adored now glared with unfettered, hateful eyes, crossed arms, and angry frowns as though I stole their most cherished possession. So what if this was untrue? My nightmares repeated the image, showing me the gap between them and my reality.

My keys fell to the floor. When I kneeled to pick them, a man yelled, "Move it!"

Nine

RHONDA'S HOME. JUNE 12, 2016

TWO HOURS after Rhonda had stormed out on her husband, she jiggled the keys in the front door and found Jacob sitting where she had left him. In front of him lay two plates full of salad—kale, baby tomatoes, salmon, strawberries, and walnuts—exactly how Rhonda liked it. She stopped and sighed. "Sorry, dear, I ate."

He rose, his face reddening. "What? We were eating together. You are still mad about our fight."

She held her head. "No, Jacob, but they served lunch and refused to let me leave without eating. I had no choice."

"Who?"

She looked around the room from the mountain of papers on their messy dining table to the muted news playing on TV—anywhere but at him. Her guilt grew because muted TV meant he had cooked more than a salad. She suspended her purse on the hook by the door and approached Jacob. "Something smells good. Did you bake?"

"Who, Rhonda?"

"Calm down. It's amazing how crimson your face gets with a little stress." She touched his cheek.

"Not funny." He removed her hand.

"Okay, okay! I went to 16th Street to see a Sikh temple. A *Gurudwara.*"

"A what? Why?"

"I thought . . . I can help my patient better if I understand her completely, where she worships, where—"

Jacob pointed at her. "So, I was right that you're continuing to ignore us, our life, and following a singularly focused life, revolving around your p—"

"No!" She stepped toward him before he swiveled and slipped farther away.

"No? Or let me guess. Your actions have nothing to do with your patient. Rather, it's tied to John." He slumped onto the couch.

She gasped. "Don't be ridiculous, Jacob. It's about my patient, and what about the research you have been doing all these months o-on different religions, immigrants."

A siren blasted. Both stared outside. And at once, police lights flashed on the TV screen. SHOOTING IN STANFORD flashed underneath.

"Great, another shooting." Rhonda hurried to the windows and peered at the street.

When she turned, a bearded man's picture flashed on TV with the rolling caption: "The Dead Suspect Pledged Allegiance to ISIS."

Rhonda covered her mouth, and her eyes watered.

"Lone wolf again," Jacob said.

Like her in her life. She glided over to him on the couch. "I'm sorry about lunch."

"I could forget about lunch, our fight, and my longing for you, but you can't interfere with the legal proceedings. Period."

Her watery eyes spilled, and her face twitched before she tugged her long skirt's rough edge. "How is this interfering?"

"I-I have told you before to refer 'your patient' to another therapist. You don't understand her background. They—"

"Please! I need you right now, just a little lost, finding my way out of this mess, okay?"

"I know, dear. But—"

"Just hold me."

Jacob held her firmly that day, but she realized then her marriage was on the line on the other side of her troubles. She had a son in jail fighting for his life. But she had more to lose.

Ten

FREMONT, CALIFORNIA. JUNE 14, 2016

A NEW CHAPTER of my life began on Sunday, the twelfth of June. In my regimented life of practicing alone and seeing Dr. Silverstone on Mondays, a new player entered: Aryan Khan. My knee had healed. So day three of training together was starting.

I said, "Aryan, I need to talk to you about something very important."

"About our practice sessions?" He marched swiftly to the racetrack.

"No. Nothing to do with running."

He halted and set down his bag. "Then it can wait."—he raised his hand—"Get to your squats, Sia. Now!"

Let me get this out before his insanity hits the world. He brightened my days by being there when I needed his support like the air I breathed. Without him, the loss at the IAAF World Championship would have diminished me to a speck of a being. *So, thank you, Aryan.*

But Aryan was insane.

On the second day, he had croaked, "Easy on the manners! Enough of 'sorry,' 'thank you,' 'please.' *Eh* . . . I need to see anger."

So today as fog shrouded the surroundings, I grunted in between my sideways squats—seeking no pleasure, groaning only to please him and convince him I embodied anger instead of wounds. Twenty squats later, I gathered my saliva and spat on the ground. A first. The world's rudest act. The opposite of polite manners. I observed his face for signs of pleasure.

But he screamed, "Stop! I saw what you did. Are you mocking me?"

"God, no." A slight quiver of a smile snuck out of me.

"Come, take a seat. Don't forget I'm twenty years your senior."

I sat on the bench while he brought a chair for himself, jamming it right in front of me.

"You are the girl who has never made her bed, isn't it?"

"Excuse me?"

"Have you ever done your laundry?"

I crossed my arms. "Of course! What has this got to do with my running?"

"You have seen no life, child." His eyes wide, his elbows rested on his knees as he leaned forward.

"I have seen plenty! More than you can imagine. And I'm not a child."

He flung his hands high. "Then stop behaving like one. Who makes your bed in the morning? Your mother?"

"Aryan, please."

Cupping his hands together, he whispered, "If you are angry, hurl things at me, swear, if you will. Cut this 'Aryan, please' crap. Do you hear me?" When he rose, his frustration left his mouth and haunted his body as he trolled like taking a "Drunk Test" while being high.

But I commended Aryan for finding the cocoon I lived my life from; the cocoon Dr. Silverstone couldn't crack with her pointed questions that Aryan attempted to burst with jabs.

He spoke as though he performed at a stage and addressed the auditorium instead of me.

"Meet me. I'm an Indian American: meek and polite; docile and pleasing. Please come to defeat me in a race."—Buckling—"I'll bend over, thank youuuu."

My cheeks burned, and involuntarily, I chuckled before swallowing the grin, his eyes too menacing for a joke,

"Tell me about your biggest accomplishment to date?"

I knew how to make cheese and butter from milk. No, not that kind of accomplishment. How about I could drink two bottles of beer and walk a straight line? My throat became heavy, my body sinking into the hard bench.

"I have none." I wanted to say *yet.* But dreams only threatened to arrive, never really arriving. My insides knotted, and warm wetness trickled down my face. A searing pain spread from my core down to my legs.

"Oh, there come the tears again. Sia, you cry all the time—when you fail, when your feelings get hurt, and now—"

"When people put me down." Swiping at my cheeks, I rose and stormed away toward the women's locker rooms.

Inside, I ran straight into a locker's sharp edge, poking a gash on my lower jaw. Drops of blood oozed and fell into my extended hand. I splashed water, drew out two paper towels, and pressed them to my chin. My breaths uneven, my thoughts spiraling, I had frozen in front of the mirror. An attitude wasn't a bright-colored pill you took for breakfast each morning. And anger didn't always manifest as an open rant. Sometimes, it lay hidden under layers, unable to claw its way out. I was Papa's daughter, sure enough, and he taught me humility and politeness that stung Aryan. Aryan was asking for a lot. He was asking me to shed Papa's daughter, shed Papa, shed his words—my gaze fell on my ripped sneakers that resembled the ones Papa wore—shed his broken shoes.

I ground my teeth as heat flushed through my body. Recognizing the first sign of rage, I marched outside to show Aryan my boldness.

He sat on his chair, where I had left him.

"What happened to your jaw?" he asked.

"You!"

"Me?" A smile played on his face.

"You can't change who I am."

"And who are you? Who is Siana Singh? The girl who insists we call her Sia? It's my job to build you."

He rose, gently banging his chest. "What is hiding inside your core, Sia? Peel the onion."

Drawing closer by two steps, his breaths warmed my face. Three athletes ran on the racetrack in the otherwise empty stadium.

"Tell me, what will you lose if you fail at the Olympics?" He softened his tone. "I'm waiting for you to tell me that your jaw hurts, or with the Olympics gone, your dreams will break. Say it."

"My jaw hurts. At the Olympics, my dreams will break."

"*Ah,* Sia, no, they won't break, but you must change a few things. Twenty-five years of age is old for an athlete." He whispered firmly. "You are competing with teenagers, for God's sake."

He waited. But I didn't know if our conversation, rather the interrogation, was over.

"Silent Sia, I can't hold a monologue forever. Tell me, what did you major in college?" He folded his arms.

"I never went to college."

A flicker flashed past his face, an unmoving gap between his lips. Did he disbelieve that I, an Indian, never attended college?

I could tell him about my grandfather, who without a father, educated his siblings and himself. Would that fill my voids? Or Papa's? Because he, too, dropped out of school to come to America. He carried the guilt of breaking his father's heart by choosing to be different. And I bore mine.

"It's a long story," I whispered, repelled by the sight of my old, dirty shoes. I better get a new pair—the first step toward shedding Papa.

The sky transformed from pelican to obsidian, a moist lemony draft in the air.

When I stepped away, he grasped my arm, and my heart raced, expecting insults while fighting his grip. The breeze whistled, blending with his steady breaths.

"Aryan?"

Through Aryan's eyes, Papa questioned me how I could think I was "cooler" than him when I was him.

"You are hurting me, Aryan. Let go."

He didn't. I had to look away, being unable to answer Papa's questions.

All my life, I'd considered myself different from my parents, especially from Papa. All my life. How had I suddenly become identical to him? *Never studied at a college; Timid; Dreamy. Broken shoes.*

Aryan's voice shattered my thoughts. "Did daddy not give you money for college?" he said, twisting his face.

Rage blustered out of me, and I screamed, plunging onto Aryan, my cheek digging into his chest, his heart racing against my ear. Repeatedly, I jabbed him.

Our lips brushed against each other, even though the contact wasn't part of the planned fight, woman-to-man, and neither was the spark. The last punch landed him on his back.

Leaving him slumped on the ground, I marched away, my belly tingling. The funny part was I'd forgotten everything except for his naughty smile, his firm muscles, and his soft lips. Trouble.

The next day, I arrived at the stadium early, waiting for him at the audience seats, my foot tapping against the concrete. When I saw him, I rose with a jolt as I had to talk to him urgently. The stud Aryan waltzed in with hands locked together with a girl in a miniskirt and low, V-shaped, pink shirt, poorly hiding her huge and fake breasts. She carried a poodle in a handbag. They canoodled one another like auditioning for a low budget pornographic movie.

When he noticed me staring, he drew away and clapped his hands. "Okay, Sia, let's get this started. Off to the racetrack. You should be practicing there already instead of sitting on the sidelines. Don't waste a second."

The girl took a seat, as if readying herself to watch a show.

"Aryan—"

"Nope. No time."

I ran to the racetrack.

He didn't scold me today. Rather, he only taught me to not think fondly about him ever. Fine by me.

Eleven

THE TALKING ROOM. JUNE 20, 2016

WHY is it so hard to articulate fondness yet so easy to express frustration? It had been eight months since I tried to talk to Dr. Silverstone about Papa. It had been eight months since I had been failing. One more failure today, and she would hear about Papa from others, not me, and believe in my frustration, not my fondness. I couldn't afford that because I wanted her as I had once wanted Papa.

The clock ticked a tired tune, ten minutes past eight at night, and I grabbed my leg, keeping it from bouncing.

"Did you hurt your knee again?" Dr. Silverstone asked.

"No. After a tough day on the racetrack, all muscles, sort of, give up and shake in tremors. I'm used to the pain by now." It *also* shakes when I'm nervous.

"That's tough." She scribbled in her notebook, noting my every action—me tucking a strand of loose hair behind my ear, bringing my hands together, and clasping them in my lap.

I spoke steadily. "I despised my father for being a simpleton. He wasn't cool like the other dads."

"What do you mean?"

Diablo winds howled outside the window.

"Just one example, my father would carry big, heavy grocery bags while walking instead of driving from a store a mile and a half away."

Dr. Rhonda Silverstone fidgeted in her seat, her eyes fluttering. "Nothing is wrong with doing grocery on foot. I do it all the time."

"You live in a city with sidewalks. We live in the suburbs." I could point out other differences, but now wasn't the time or the place.

She tightened her hold on her notebook. "What's your father's name?"

A sigh on the inside traveled across my chest. "Why do you ask?"

"Sorry, just curious. So, you were saying your father does walks to the grocery store, and . . ."

"Yes, and patches of sidewalks were missing." Whistling winds picked up speed outside, and the windows clinked. "Cars would honk at him, and he would timidly respond with a sorry—no, with three sorrys knitted together: 'sorry, sorry, sorry.' "

She crossed her legs. "You want your father to be less modest?"

"Yes, I did. Also, it worsened his arthritis, but my father refused to listen to any advice about his health. He never saw a doctor for any ailment—small or large."

"Hmm."

An ache rose in my throat. "His disregard for himself contrasted with his love for this country. He admired the opportunities America gave him, despite wearing the same set of pants he bought from Wal-Mart *for twenty years.*"

"He's frugal." She switched her crossed leg.

"He wore pants ripped and stitched back together."

"Hmm. Wore?" Dr. Silverstone stared at her notes with a widened stare.

With any other patient, she had made a breakthrough today. Not with me. I was the problem child for her and Papa.

She swallowed. "What happened to your father?"

A smile drenched in sadness enveloped my lips while I scanned the wall filled with canvases.

My fingernails poked into my palms. "He was murdered."

"*Oh! Ahem.* I'm sorry. When?"

"You know when and by who."

For the first time, her face flushed coral while she ascended from her chair, her eyes dry and widened. She flung her notebook across the room.

I gasped, shocked at her display of emotion.

"Your father is Tejpal Singh." Her voice came out steady despite her tantrum. She lunged at her phone and glared at me. "Get out of my office."

I rose. "It's not what you think."

"I don't care." She chuckled a tune different from her innocent, car-buzz laugh. "You crossed the boundary that exists between a doctor and a patient. We are all humans with lives around careers. Leave now. Get out."

"Doctor—"

She trotted to the door and flung it open, punching numbers at her phone.

With my jacket hanging limply in my hands, I canvased the room I would never see again. Why had I thought we could talk about Papa without a fight? Her son separated me from her, me from Papa. Through my tears, I imagined myself in the canvas under the ocean wave with the rising sun—or was it setting? The faces inside the Thanksgiving dinner painting, their hearty and uneaten dinner, giggled, but did their smiles hide a secret? And the doctor. I nodded at Dr. Silverstone as though that would suffice as a goodbye. It wasn't like I would never see her again. Yet my feet fought my torso as I dragged myself out of the room that had sheltered me and my uncomfortable thoughts.

As soon as I exited, I shuddered when she slammed the door shut, as if not her home, the outside contained a criminal; not her son, I had killed my father. I turned and stared at the hollowness where Dr. Silverstone's shadow once used to stand.

Lumbering away from her home, I trudged around in circles until I realized I had slipped right past my car. Another traitor tear departed my eyes. My legs buckling, I collapsed on my knees, head in hands.

The purpose called Dr. Silverstone ended before I was ready to let her go. Without that purpose, my life shed its meaning. My mind wrestled with me. It revolted at the thought of me driving to Papa's house where he didn't live. Slumped, rocking with my head in my hands, I sat, unwilling to rise. *Oh,* I missed Dr. Silverstone like she was my mother. But why would she understand me when my family didn't.

I don't talk about my home because I cringe admitting to what we had become in the last nine months after Papa's murder. Most homes bubbled with energy, laughter, love, and some fights. We used to be like that, a mixture of happy and sad. But lately, we had diminished to a conglomeration of still images: Mamma's silence, Sandeep's frown, and Tayaji's judging eyes. Tayaji, Papa's older brother, didn't live with us. But since last August, he had assumed the role of a caretaker. He showed up unannounced.

In my eyes, he was a house guest who had outstayed his welcome.

Resigned, I drove away. When I reached my beige stucco home that blended with the rest, the American flag twirled to the breeze, sounding like marching boots on the ground.

I wiggled the keys in the front door at the ripe hour of ten o'clock of the night, fully intending to tiptoe to my cramped loft inside the dark, silent home. Wrong.

In the living room, sat everybody: Mamma wearing her white scarf, Sandeep with a face elongating with each passing day, and Tayaji. *Why Tayaji again?*

I brought my jittery hands together and greeted them. *"Sat Sri Akal."*

"Siana, come. Sit here." Tayaji patted the chair next to him. "I heard you pursued charges."

I released my bag, and it plopped to the floor.

Realizing the worst wasn't over, I scuttled to Tayaji. The fight had just begun.

Staring at the fragile milky walls of my stucco home, I sat. Why were they ivory and empty? No mirrors. No canvases. But why no photos? The walls had rotten like stale milk, rotten cheese.

"Siana?" Tayaji's voice thundered.

"The police determined enough basis to indict them with the crime. I didn't file the charges. The DA's office did." My voice was pregnant with fatigue.

Sandeep breathed loudly like an angry predator a minute before attack. My once cheerful brother had been wiped away.

Tayaji shifted in his seat. "So what? Go to the court tomorrow, and work with the DA to drop the charges. We are simple people who wish to stay out of the legal matters."

"It's not me charging the murderer. You should go tackle the DA, not me." I glanced at Mamma, praying on her rosary as she did daily ever since Papa died. Sandeep bounced his foot, resting on his knee.

Tayaji jabbed at my arm. "Sandeep has told me you have circulated the police stations and the court in your pursuits. Your efforts have sparked focus on it."

"Not my efforts, Tayaji. They sided with pursuing for justice because a person can't shoot another and be exonerated." My eyes watered, remembering the stories I grew up with about the persecution the Sikhs fled from in India. My fingers teetered, playing with one another. I whispered, "What happened to Papa can happen to others, and we need to watch this case to fruition. We, too, need to fight for justice. We live in the twenty-first century. Don't you want to avenge my father's—no, your brother's murderer?"

Mamma shouted, "Siana, watch your tone with your uncle."

Sandeep glared at me, too, before he charged to his room and slammed his bedroom door shut.

"A blind legal system will guarantee what happened to Tejpal doesn't happen to others?" Tayaji lifted a single brow. "Don't be foolish to complicate our life. After everything we have endured, we can't afford more trouble. And you need to prepare for the Olympics. Stay away from the court at all costs. Let them do this without us."

"We can't give up like—"

Sandeep blasted out of his room. "Who pays for your rent?"

"Excuse me?"

He loomed over my head. "Not excused. You lack the money for home or college, and how can you ignore your goals and indulge in this nonsense instead?"

Sandeep used to be the happy one in the family.

"My college or my rent is none of your business." I clenched my teeth. "This is my father's house as much as your father's house. Who is paying for your lodging?"

"Siana, please, no fighting." Tayaji rose, and I sank deeper into my seat.

"It is my business, Siana." Sandeep pressed his head forward. "We are all mourning Papa's loss that you refuse to close. Do something with your life. God damn it!"

"Sandeep, please do not swear."

"I'm doing a lot with my life in case you haven't noticed. I'm an international athlete—"

His hands flew to his sides. "You lost, Siana."

Why did he have to go there with me?

"Sandeep!" Mamma shouted.

A countdown began inside me. One. Two. Three. Four. On five, I said, "I lost, but I'm not giving up and am preparing for the Olympics. You should keep that in mind when you put me down."

Sandeep clenched my chair. "Preparing for the Olympics? No, you are circulating the courts instead of focusing on running. And do I remind you after how many sacrifices you are where you are?"

Tayaji grabbed his shoulder. "Stop, Sandeep. Go to your room. Let me talk to Siana in peace. Go! You are not helping."

"The state is covering the cost of the trial. It's a public prosecution."

"Siana, it's not about the money. It's about the hassle and the broken legal system," Tayaji said.

Mamma set her rosary down and nodded her head vehemently. She always agreed with Tayaji, even in Papa's presence, even when Papa differed.

Sandeep's giant shadow danced over my head, his nostrils flaring, his eyes unflinching.

"Papa would have been happy about the case, and he would have served as a witness, forget watching it from the gallery. Just how he fought for us in his living years."

"*Oh, Siana.*" Tayaji took a seat next to Mamma, his hand resting too close to hers on the couch. "Think about your mother. How will she bear you being in the court daily? What if they want personal details presented in the court? We can't do that. Remove yourself."

I wondered what they would do if the prosecutors legally summoned them as a witness. No Siana could help them then.

Sandeep rested against the wall behind them, a flimsy coffee table separating me from them. "Did you hear what happened to Vikram?" Sandeep had calmed down.

"No, what?" Mamma tilted around.

"They sued him for fighting back."

"What?" I asked.

"Some classmates tried to bully him. Claims suggest an exchange of racial slurs, etc. He fought back."

"That's strange that he would get sued for defending himself."

"Exactly, my point. This is a losing battle, sis. The court could reverse point the finger at us."

"What have we to worry about?"

"What is a slur?" Mamma asked, but Sandeep only shook his head in response.

Tayaji's eyes lit up. "See, Siana, this is dangerous. It can backfire. Stay out of the court, please. We are outsiders to this nation, and that is a fact you cannot change."

As they chimed in immaculate concord, nodding at each other, I pulled out my phone and stared at Aryan's missed call, sighing. He was returning my call.

An hour chugged along, and I grew frustrated listening to stories: the troubles of fellow Punjabi, the peace-loving immigrants, fooled to accept a new nation as their own, only to realize their facial segregation lines of color weren't washable. They would always look like an outsider: different.

I just sat there, remembering Dr. Rhonda Silverstone scribbling in her notebook, judging me like my family.

The Price for Being

*"I've been fighting to be who I am all my life.
What's the point of being who I am, if I can't have the person who was
worth all the fighting for?"*

STEPHANIE LENNOX, I DON'T REMEMBER YOU

Twelve

RHONDA took care of every minute detail of her life, studying, researching, pondering over, but because of her fascination of Jacob's stoic resignation, in some state of complacency, so it wasn't until she got down to the act of flinging out the contents of her living room almirah that she began to glimpse seething in that cauldron of insurance policies, auto, home, life, a gun license, and buried way inside, John's legal file, in it, the smoky, ominous presence of a single word—appearing just once—which quite baffled and confounded and frightened her, appearing as it did in this otherwise persuasively practical text under an endless train of legal jargon, the potential witnesses, the fine print eyes habitually glanced over, this clever imposter who voiced with breezy mockery the sly propaganda in her own office, under her roof. Or was it two words, after all?

Siana Singh. The one-word equivalent being betrayal. Betrayal from Sia, from her husband who buried John's file behind all the other nonsense that didn't insure them against attorney costs bankrupting them now, from herself for studying the wrong file all these months. She'd never walked a patient out of her office before. No matter what—not even when her patient was drunk and threatened her.

Nobody had imperiled her child before under months of a facade.

She didn't yell, sob, or call for Jacob, who had checked out long ago. He lay in bed, his eyelids droopy, she knew.

Instead, she dialed a number.

Thirteen

AT THE BASE of the bed, I lay smeared in the bag-of-clothes position. Three days and four nights. That's how long it had been since I saw Aryan.

Dutifully daily, he messaged me he was stuck in a court case. Daily, I returned home without practicing.

To train alone with my mind was the same as seeking therapy from a psychopath. So alone, I hugged the loft floor. With Sandeep and Mamma at work, machines seized over our home: The AC whistled a Dracula tune; Loud enough to shake the walls, my one-dollar alarm clock ticked on my nightstand's chipping paint. The fridge brayed. Then the siren blazed off, except the front doorbell had rung—just once, culminating my date with the household sounds. I swiped at my cheeks and marched to the door.

In a muddy suit, a tall man held an envelope. "Siana Singh?"

"Yes." I blinked, the sun spraying straight at my eyes.

"Can I see some ID?"

"Is everything all right, sir?"

"ID, please."

I reached for my coat pocket, hanging by the door, and drew out my driver's license before extending it toward him.

He didn't take it, merely glanced at it and my face, and passed me the envelope. "You have been served."

Panic over-brimmed into utter chaos. The night's darkness matched my tortured soul. And drought-ridden San Francisco bathed in perpetual rain, a storm after a storm, with the tourist trolleys half-empty, the roads wet like my face, weeping, and ranting. I glared at the Talking Room in front of her house, where I had spilled my life story in pieces. My fists curled.

I contemplated the knock. Knock, I did.

Footsteps approached, and the door flung open. Eyes widened, and Dr. Silverstone slammed it shut.

"I'm staying right here, Doctor," I shouted through the closed door.

"And I'm calling 9-1-1!"

"Go ahead. I'm staying put here. You had no right to go to the police. I spilled my most hideous secrets, and *you* betrayed me." I rested my hand against the chilly door. "But you owe me one opportunity to clarify your accusations." I poked the door with my index finger. *Please.*

Inside, footsteps shuffled fast, revealing her fear. Why was she afraid of *me?*

She croaked, "Sia, I'm warning you for the last time, go away, or I talk."

"I need to speak to you for five minutes. You may have misunderstood me." I pulled away from the door.

"You are disgruntled, and I can't trust you because you lied to me. Go away." She shouted so loudly shivers traveled through my body.

With wet khaki tips, I cowered into myself and imagined her on the phone with an emergency operator. I reached into my pocket for the temporary restraining order she had me served with, sliding my finger against it repeatedly. To the threatening growl of the thunder, I shouted. "I always had crushes on boys who looked like Brad Pitt, my ultimate crush . . ." I held my head, swaying sideways.

"You know, the blond, blue-eyed—the cool guys—a contrast to . . ." I kicked her door. "Until one of those studs murdered my father. You KNOW who. He shot him in cold blood. Your son! Your flesh and blood. So screw me if I loved them until I hated them."

No longer screaming to reach the interior, with hushed, defeated whispers, I fell onto my knees, pulling on my hair. "I hate them, but I despise myself more because it was *me* who killed my father." I sniffled.

When the sirens approached, my anxiety attack had peaked. They lifted me from the ground and dragged me to the police car, my hands over my head, my legs limp and boneless. Dr. Silverstone peered from behind the drapes meekly. When our eyes met, she shut the drapes abruptly.

Hours later, head bent, I sat low in Aryan's car. Throughout the ride to the police station, the streetlights filtering through the tint of its window, the metallic odor of cold, steel mesh barrier slathering on my throat, I had pondered over one thought: Was I dreaming? I was living the pieces of life that belonged to nightmares. For someone like me who originated from where I had, who averted the police even when we needed their help, being inside the police walls with criminals was nothing short of trauma. Luckily, Aryan answered his call, quelling my worry that my family would find out about this, too. I had hungered for Aryan's undivided attention but not like this.

Sitting in his car in silence next to his deadpan face, my hands grew numb, considering what he was thinking and not uttering. Only the squeaky wipers and the buzzing engine sounded out my troubles.

The rain drummed on the windscreen; the droplets expanding before the wipers cleaned them. I preferred the washed-out view from the clear one.

"Aryan, I've tried to talk to you for over a week. But—"

He turned sharply, curling his hand into a fist, and extending his thumb. "First, a restraining order." Straightening his index finger, he croaked louder. "Now, the jail run-in—Sia, are you not considering the Olympics? I left you alone for three days—in total. And look where I bailed you out of!" He exhaled hard and handed me some papers. "You are no Michael Phelps, just a struggling athlete who can't afford this."

A tear stung my cried-out cheek as I turned the papers over. "What is this?"

"Your bail and the notice to stay away from Dr. Silverstone and her family—the one they had served you." He pointed toward the paper. "This means you can't go knocking on her door. Do you understand?"

My head lowered, my hands pressing down on the forms. "I have kept myself out of your personal affairs—"

"Yes, I have noticed."

"Have you?" Aryan sharply turned the car, and the wheels screeched. "Who is this person? And what did you do to her?"

The wipers swished, my cold fingers tingling. "My shrink."

"Who?" He took another rash turn.

"My therapist. Please slow down, Aryan." I clutched my head.

To my surprise, he slowed the car. "Why would a therapist get a restraining order against her patient? Did you attack her?" He stared at me.

"Not physically. It's complicated—a long story about sensitive topics between us."

He slammed the breaks at a red light, and my head leaped forward before I gripped the dashboard.

"Why do you need a shrink?" Tapping his steering wheel, he turned to me. "Sia, listen to me. You freaking write in a journal or talk to a friend or family. But you don't just trust anyone with sensitive feelings. You still have to answer my question. Why would she need a restraining order?" His phone beeped, and he silenced it.

The light flipped to green, and he hit the gas pedal. His mind was occupied elsewhere. I had drawn him away from something more important, but I needed to talk to him tonight.

Tomorrow would be too late.

The wipers continued to creak, and the thunder gurgled softly while my nails dug holes into my palms. My face burned and broke into tiny spasms.

"Why do you have a restraining order from her?" he repeated.

"Her son shot my father."

Aryan pulled to the side of the road. The rain had stopped, leaving a moist muddiness in the air.

"What?" Aryan's voice had softened.

Before I could answer, his phone buzzed again. I peeked. Safia. Every time, a different woman called. The stud Aryan.

"*Eh.* I've to take this." He stepped out of the car talking into his phone, his tone professorial, imparting advice serially. I imagined the exchange so intently that I jumped when he opened the car door suddenly.

Before I could plead him, he swerved the car around.

A drunk man stared at the ice in his glass. A couple giggled into each other's ears around the bar as Aryan and I occupied an open table and ordered our drinks—water and iced tea.

His eyes didn't blink once. "Your shrink's son shot your father? Did he owe him money?"

My hands flew to my head. "No. He didn't know one thing about Papa. He just shot him walking down the street."

"And your father . . . dead?"

"Yes, Aryan."

He shifted in his seat, looking all around, a tiny shiver dancing around his lip, and his Adam's apple moving. "When?"

"August 9, 2015."

"What is your father's name?"

"Tejpal Singh."

He yanked out his phone, and its glow illuminated his face. A pensive song played as he gleaned through his cell.

"Shooting case against John Flynn, a minor?"

"Yes." My hands quaked on the table.

He cupped his mouth. *"Oh,* shoot, Sia! Did you choose me as your coach because you needed my help in the court?"

"N—"

"Because you could have simply asked. I fight for minorities all the time."

I pressed on his hands on the table, surprised at myself. "Aryan, my father was the coach I lost. I need you by the racetrack. But so does my father. Yes, it's true you being a prosecutor in the district was a big draw. I knew nothing about the law and needed to consult someone I could trust."

"I've stayed out of this case despite it being right up my alley of fighting for fellow Indians. Only if I had known."

"Are you angry at me?"

He scrunched his forehead and tilted his head, a strange kindness dripping from his eyes. "No, Sia, not at all. *Ah* . . . you lost a father, a coach. I'm so sorry."

Fat tears graced my eyes, the weight I hid in my embrace spilling, my heart lightening.

"I'm so sorry for being harsh on you, too. If I'd known the grief you carried inside you—"

"It's okay."

Hand in hand, the couple who whispered into each other's ears left together, giggling.

He clasped my hands. "We will fight. Don't worry about it. We got this one."

Exhausted, I eyed his shoulder, a longing gripping my heart.

After three long weeks, I discussed Papa with Aryan. It would be years to rest my head on his firm shoulder. For now, I warmed in the heat of his hands, thankful he didn't pull away. Before he left me home, I begged him to take over the case and fight it, realizing it would remove him from the stadium. I couldn't run myself by entrusting strangers with law degrees to decide Papa's fate. The day John murdered Papa, hate crime had tattooed onto my heart, and my friends, American friends, had become strangers with one shot. Only Aryan could help me.

Tomorrow, I would see Dr. Silverstone at the court.

An impenetrable, unbridgeable aisle in the gallery would separate us, the same way her coffee table parted us, the same way I stared at her canvases, searching for myself but finding no similarities. A mere aisle, a color tone would divide us. Right and wrong were black and white. Although the courtroom would muddle the truth, I had Aryan's strength and support. With it, I was whole.

See you in court, Dr. Silverstone. *See you soon!*

Fourteen

RHONDA'S BEDROOM. JUNE 23, 2016

RHONDA shot up in bed soaked in sweat, gasping, and flailing her arms around.

Jacob swung up and rubbed his eyes. "It's okay, honey. It was just a nightmare."

She shoved him away. Tossing her feet off the bed, she rushed to the open window and suspended her head outside. The moist, gentle breeze tousled her hair. "I can't breathe!"

The lemony light carved a square in the dark exteriors of midnight where not a soul, not a chirp of a bird existed to dispel her chaos.

When his hand pressed down on her shoulder, Rhonda swiped at her cheeks and veered around. "She wasn't supposed to live."

Jacob stepped back, his mouth hanging low. "Who?"

"Grace! She wasn't supposed to survive childbirth. W-we . . . Ray and I were to be childless." She passed Jacob and reached under the bed and flung out a heavily used scrapbook, shards of paper sticking out from its corners. As she yanked out her hospital bracelets off a flap, Jacob slumped onto the bed.

"Ten years!" she whispered.

"Since they murdered her," Jacob said.

"No! Ray and I struggled to get pregnant for ten years. And Jacob it's been fifteen years since Grace was killed." She carefully snuck the hospital tags back into their pocket while Jacob rose and paced the room.

When he reached the far corner, he swerved around. "Darling, I know all this."

She leafed through more pages and mumbled, "Crazy woman keeps repeating her life story. Why, *oh,* why?"

"Get to the point, Rhonda."

"That's the point. I fought. Grace persevered." Tubes that had dug into her as a newborn came to mind. "She clawed her way into this world. But why? What was the point?"

She tapped her picture. "Grace kept the family together."

"She did, my dear. Did you have a nightmare about her?"

"No! I dreamed about you and John."

"What?"

Rhonda jabbed her finger at him "You were patronizing me in my dream, too, telling me how my lovely dream is a nightmare. How is seeing John's tiny toes and fingers, Grace kissing them a nightmare?" She shoved the book inside the bed. "Then I saw John covering me with a blanket in the living room when I would fall asleep while mourning Grace. This is reality, Jacob, coming to me from behind shut eyes. My life is not a nightmare."

"You're right. I'm sorry. I'll not call them that."

The creases on her forehead loosened as she rose to her feet. "*Ah,* don't be sorry. You don't deserve my meltdowns nightly. My dream always starts pretty and real. I see John kissing strangers, giving his favorite toy away with a blink of an eye. That beautiful boy. But my lovely dream always ends in a disaster." Her lips quivered.

"He always comes home with the devil, the cobra tattooed on his arms. The wrong man for a charity. And do you know what I saw today?"

"What?"

"Siana. She was shoving John into a river, drowning him." She clenched her teeth and pointed at the door.

"She sat across from me for months, judging me, mocking me. There's no humanity left here. We-we must defeat her. No other option. We must!"

He drew her into an embrace. "We will."

The cool breeze whistled, and a group of people hustled out of a side alley, their laughter tearing through her sobs. *Ah,* the city sounds.

"I should have connected the dots."

"Don't be hard on yourself for having a hunch. It must be why she consumed you. People are complicated, honey, not so simple like you."

Rhonda tore from his embrace. "If Grace were alive, John would have been happy. We would be okay. All I want is to protect what's left of our lives—John. Am I wrong?"

"Not at all." He helped her get inside the covers and tucked her in tightly, planting a kiss on her forehead.

She drew in the covers. "John was messed up after 9/11. He's still trying to avenge his sister's death, even though he grew hate in his heart. He needs help, not more scars."

"Yes, honey. It's late. Tomorrow is a big day. Get some sleep."

"What will happen tomorrow?" Her eyes widened instead of shutting.

"We *fight* tomorrow for our boy."

"And?"

"We will win."

"Do you promise? Guarantee me, Jacob."

He tugged on her hand. "Yes, I promise on my life, my darling. We'll win this sucker. Siana Singh is going down."

Fifteen

JUNE 24, 2016

I HALTED in the living room. Way past his morning departure for work, dangling at the end of his seat, rocking rhythmically, frowning, as though waiting for the signal for war, armed with only the weapon of rage, he sat. Sandeep.

"Good morning," I barked.

His siren had blazed, and his battle had begun. He marched to me and crossed his arms. "Where are you going?"

He used to sneak candy to me at recess time, my brother. His jokes would fill our home with laughter. And when I landed myself in trouble, he would cover for my mistakes, hiding them from my parents. I passed around him.

"Where the hell are you going?" His breath remained on my neck.

"Where I go is none of your business."

"Ya? Well, listen up. Papa is my business." He pointed to his head. "This turban on my head—it's my burden. We asked you to stay away from the court. Where the—" He mouthed unutterable jargon. "Where are you going now?"

Mamma charged out of her room, adjusting her headscarf. "What is going on here?"

"Ma, she is spreading dirt over our name."

I rolled my eyes. "Ya, right! Being the only one fighting for your father is not called spreading dirt; it's called I got your coward ass, bro."

While struggling to get my feet into my shoes, Mamma's gentle touch stopped me, and I pinched shut my eyes.

Her pat on my shoulder was therapeutic, and her soft voice sounded out a melody that could cure the saddest of hearts. "I know you are hurting. We are all hurting. Come with me to the *Gurudwara*."

My tears muddled my vision. "If we pray for us to win the court case."

Sandeep dashed to the front door, locked it, and blocked it with his frame, standing akimbo.

"You can't keep me here."

"I'll see."

"Siana, *Puttar*, is this what you want?" She cupped my cheek, wiping a tear descending on my cheek. "Running around the court when you should prepare for your Olympic trials instead?"

"I don't have a choice." I released her hand and grabbed my keys from the table, swiping at my face. Wouldn't it be easier to lie instead that I wasn't going to the court? But that's me: Sia.

With a quick gulp of the chilly air, I raced toward the garage exit. Sandeep bounded behind me, but he could never outrun me, not as a kid with soft, chubby cheeks, and not now, as an angry big brother in a beard and a turban.

Slamming the door shut on him, I hit the garage opener, glided, and slid from under it. Outside, my heart quaked so hard I feared it would fall out as I sat inside my car parked along the street. When Sandeep's frame emerged, I hit the accelerator and zoomed away.

I wiped tears gushing down my face, remembering Papa.

One day with his arm around me and head suspended, Papa had sat next to me outside our beige stucco home on the raised wood siding, the sandy lilies swaying behind us.

"They think I'm misguiding you by encouraging you to be an athlete," he had said.

"Who?"

"Everyone—your mother, your tayaji, Sandeep—"

"Sandeep?"

"Yes, they think sports are inappropriate for girls."

Currently, a sneer emerged from my lips. "Of course, Sandeep would say that. He is my opposition." I said out loud to Papa, eight years later, driving away from my brother, my mortal enemy. Papa left, and now I was alone. While my family came around to support my athletic goals, they hadn't yet for fighting for justice, and I was a fighter.

Sixteen

THROUGH the glass double doors, a blank, faded look on his face, the kind when you are present yet not there, Aryan stared at me. I rose, sadness pounding and plodding me while he fixed his sleek black tie over his immaculate black suit and entered the courtroom lobby. A new avatar of Aryan. Would he turn me down in the morning after deliberation? In the daylight, would he change into my coach—the angry coach—upset with my shortcomings?

"Shall we?" He extended his arm, and I slinked mine into his and smiled.

A load evaporated as we marched inside, arm in arm.

He had settled with the original lawyer, and now I sat behind the lead prosecutor on Papa's case, my pillar Aryan Khan. My chin rose high. But when I peeked across the aisle, I cringed. Next to a bald man, presumably his lawyer, he sat: John Flynn—the boy who hated Papa, shot him, and now hid his blue eyes under his downcast eyelids. It had tormented me considering Papa's final moments. Did he put up a fight? Did he see John fire at him?

Following a long screech, whisked into the courtroom, Dr. Rhonda Silverstone.

Not a trace of emotion or acknowledgment that I existed filtered through her face. She rubbed John's arm as she and her husband sat a row behind.

Once the therapist I had visited to hate but ended up liking, she now was only a mother seated across a void of ten feet.

Behind her, a man, well-built and well-tattooed, squinted his eyes at me. That was the last time our eyes locked.

Because you don't do certain things unless you are ready to pay the price: stare at the sun and hurt your eyes, insert your finger into a running table fan and scrape it, inhale drugs, and hurt your father. Prices I had paid over the years taught me to not dwell on the disdain in stranger's eyes.

Aryan talked with an attorney, his hand on a paper calendar on his desk.

At the loft, where I slept, I, too, hung a calendar with heavily crossed-out dates. For ten months, relief and anxiety escaped me while darkening the past day, waiting for today. But when Aryan rose, buttoning his coat, a heavy coat of sorrow enveloped me.

Aryan said, "We are here today because the defendant, John Flynn, murdered Tejpal Singh. On August 9, 2015, a Sunday, Mr. Tejpal Singh was walking down the street with his groceries when the defendant approached Mr. Singh, said 'Get out of my country, Osama'—I repeat: 'Get out of my country, Osama.' " He knocked on the table with his index finger repeatedly.

Its drumroll felt like an unwanted visitor at the door you didn't wish to let inside your home.

Aryan's voice startled me. "Then he shot him twice, killing him on the scene. Mr. Singh was an honest, law-abiding citizen who didn't have to die. And this case, ladies and gentlemen, is not the only one. Hate incidents against Sikhs have grown yearly since 9/11 in events of mistaken identities." Aryan drew an equal in the air. "Turbaned man equals terrorist. Mistaken Identity, your Honor, but nonetheless, a murder."

While he finished his opening, I prayed to protect a helpless dream inside my heart that Papa would return home from his night shift.

I had unfinished business with him, more complicated than my need for a proper goodbye. Before I grew into the person I was today—someone who could look her brother in the eye and stick to a resolution—he left me.

Aryan's spoken words were crushing to the lies I'd believed in and shared inside the Talking Room. I knew he'd left. We had cremated him at the Purple Moon funeral home. I was there: his fingers swollen, face embalmed with methanol, his body reeking of body-preserving chemicals—nothing lifelike about the memory. Sadness blanched Mamma's face, and multiple ladies had to hold her to a seated position. Without support, she couldn't sit, walk, or stand. But fighting to penalize his murderer echoed a truth I was numb to—Papa was never returning.

The defense spent double the time establishing John's straight-A grades, his name on the honor roll, and his scholarships. What's worse, they alleged reverse racism that baffled me the most. What's the reverse? Racism is racism. Ask me—the biggest racist of all time.

When the court called a man named Divesh Patel, a short, frail man took the stand. He wore pleated brown pants and a white-and-blue collared shirt with well-oiled hair, as though a seventies' Bollywood hero had freed from the cinema screen and arrived here for an audition. But it was the wrong era. Aryan kept an eye on me, even though I sat behind him. He leaned back and asked me repeatedly if I was okay. I nodded each time. But how could I be okay? For so many months, escapism had been my coping mechanism. Like a child eyeing a favorite candy from a goodie bag, I couldn't select memories such as Vikram or Brian. Unlike the Talking Room, here, I was raw and naked.

When Mr. Patel finished his pledge, Aryan spoke seated. "Mr. Patel, did you know Mr. Tejpal Singh?"

Dressed like a hero, Mr. Patel talked like a lamb. Small shivers rippled from his clothes, his lips, and his hands. He told the court Papa visited his gas station every Sunday while carrying groceries. Every Sunday. But this one, in particular, he didn't arrive at his usual time, which was around noon, varying only by fifteen minutes. Papa was a modern-day mobile clockwork. Punctuality defined his character and drove us crazy. No one here, but I knew my role in Papa's death. He was at the wrong place at the wrong time because of me. And though he was shot in the chest, Papa didn't die of a gunshot. He died of a broken heart.

Mr. Patel told us that on this Sunday, around two o'clock, a commotion had erupted outside, and he had peeked from the window. John Flynn had said, "Get out of my country, Osama" to Papa, and as Mr. Patel rushed outside, John shot Papa twice, not once. Blood streamed from under him, lying face down, motionless. Mr. Patel pointed at John. "The boy over there stood with a gun in his hand—it has changed our street. The business has suffered. Now, we are at the spot where a hate crime took place: cursed place."

I sat upright.

"Objection, your Honor," Mr. Reynolds barked.

"Please wipe the last two sentences from the record. Mr. Patel, stick to answering the question." The judge said.

Why? Why would they wipe such significant lines from the history of Papa's life? Questions fired inside my mind. Why did Mr. Patel cry? If they had become friends, would that help Papa's court case? When I glanced at Flynn, he didn't blink an eye. He was neither regretful nor happy, neither shocked nor complacent, so unaffected as though neither his life was at stake nor could he walk free.

After Aryan finished, Mr. Reynolds spent an excruciating hour examining facts that appeared mundane on the surface. He asked how well Mr. Patel kept his shop—if it was air-conditioned, if the cash register squeaked, if he had too many customers, and if his ears operated well at his age.

"Can you make out similar-sounding words: say, Osama or Obama?"

Aryan turned to look me in the eye, thinking the same thought: How could Mr. Reynolds sound stupid and cunning in one sentence?

Mr. Patel stood by his word.

A disgusting smile plastered on Mr. Reynolds before he gathered into his seat. His stomach moved from the barely audible laughter slipping from his lips while he whispered comments into his buddy's ears.

After lunch, Aryan said, "Things are moving fast."

"Is that good?"

"We will see. I wish you had involved me sooner."

"Sorry."

Aryan frowned and spread the papers on the table while the defense called Dr. Rhonda Silverstone.

As she staggered along to the stand in her full length, flowy, floral dress, I erased my slouch and tapped on Aryan's back.

"This can't be good. Did we summon her?"

To my surprise, he widened his eyes, and his face turned red. "The person I wouldn't put on the stand is you. You didn't know who she was when you set up therapy, right?"

Seventeen

RHONDA'S FOOTSTEPS clattered against the old wooden floor, and the chair faintly squeaked when she took her oath. The fresh paint in the room worsened the metallic tang in her mouth that coffee or peppermint gum hadn't erased.

Before her lawyer approached her, she peeled off her scarf.

Mr. Reynolds, who their private attorney had referred, spent a sizable amount of time focused on her counseling career of forty years.

At sixty, she and Jacob had saved enough to live a luxurious retirement: country-trotting on historic routes, touring America's old towns, and tasting local ice cream flavors. But this trial burnt through their cash, and the retirement plan became a fantasy. Though she continued to practice, it now became a necessity versus only for the love of it.

She didn't tell this to the court.

Thankful to have her voice heard before they shut John behind bars, she answered the questions carefully and humbly. Her son had shot and killed a human being. But oblivious to the world, he lacked a murderer's mind.

He lugged guilt on his frail shoulders. To rescue his life from the concrete prison walls, where he would rub shoulders with rapists, terrorists, serial killers, and mafia gangs, she came to the court to fulfill her maternal duty.

When Mr. Reynolds asked if she recognized Sia, she had looked at her for the first time—a buttoned white shirt and formal black pants on her model-like slim figure—Sia projected an image different from the tights and sports apparel she used to wear to therapy. A hunger lurked in her eyes that irked Rhonda, testing her resolve for revenge.

Without getting into the details of their conversations, even shallow topics of blue eyes and blond hair, she told the court Sia sought her only after her father's death yet pretending her father was alive. Sia had dropped her head at that moment, but her knee acted normal, bouncing as if a vibrator was affixed underneath—typical. When asked about the restraining order and her USATF call, Sia's head had risen, and their lawyer had swung around to face Sia, too.

Guilt pricked Rhonda because the question exposed her fears. She declared that their conversations led her to question Sia's mental capacity to run for the country and that she couldn't divulge the details due to the doctor-patient privilege. The USATF staff had directed her to call the local police, but the police had already issued the restraining order. When she learned that Sia's trials were still pending, that she wasn't a part of Team USA as the doctor had thought, she had relaxed, convinced that Sia would fail to qualify for the Olympics regardless of her level of patriotism.

Rhonda didn't reveal to the court that she questioned Sia's integrity because the person who couldn't keep her knee still, who deliberately lied to her therapist, who had trouble making eye contact through the longest, thickest tuft of black eyelashes Rhonda had ever seen was unfit to run in an international tournament. She didn't tell anyone about the conversation where Sia felt divided between the US and the Indian athletes at the IAAF tournament in London as proof of disloyalty.

Lest they judged her to be a racist. She wasn't. Fear didn't equate to racism. And she was the first to admit to the court that they had learned to fear not by seeing the World Trade Center tumble to the ground but knowing the first plane that hit the tower carried her most prized possession, one she had fought her entire life for, her daughter.

They had instilled fear in their hearts—even John's. She told the court that no malice existed in John's heart. They only feared outside forces threatened their safety and freedom.

By the time the prosecutor rose to question her, her throat had dried, and she had balled up the scarf in her hand, her spirit begging to escape the room's enclosed, muggy air.

He asked, "Dr. Silverstone, tell me more about your daughter?"

And Mr. Reynolds barked, "Objection."

"You have devoted your entire line of questioning toward the victim's daughter, Mr. Reynolds—"

"She's the daughter of the deceased who spent an obscene amount of time lying to the doctor." Mr. Reynolds fired back.

Mr. Khan continued, "We are talking about backgrounds here. Is it impossible that Dr. Silverstone wrongly judged Sia based on her history?"

Rhonda's hands grew stiff in her lap.

"This is making me furious." The judge rested her head in her palm. "Mr. Khan, are you merely making a point, or is there substance in your question?"

"It's relevant, your Honor. I need to clarify what the defense insinuated a while ago in this courtroom about reverse racism, even though the doctor hasn't once said Sia discussed race in her session."

Now acid bubbles rose to her throat, and she gulped. Luckily, the judge adjourned the court to continue with Grace's topic on Monday. But Rhonda didn't like how the judge looked at John. Bias glittered through her eyes. She studied humans for a profession and recognized prejudice well. And now it threatened to hurt her son.

Eighteen

EVERY TIME Dr. Silverstone looked at me, warmth tickled my tummy, and I hungered to embrace her in a hug. When they discussed race, some in the jury glared at me. The rustling of the American flag Papa had placed in our front yard pounded my ears. A varnish of pride coated his face the first day he had brought that home. But the flag or his sentiment wasn't enough to prove his love and affection for the USA. We would be proving our allegiance forever.

Dr. Silverstone spent the next five minutes explaining how noble her son was, how he couldn't hate, how he couldn't be evil even though John had murdered my innocent father, how he had suffered enough even though the court hadn't decided his fate yet. But it wasn't how hard the doctor tried to affirm her son's kindness, his charity work, his simplicity that appalled me. It was the question that followed about whether I had referred to hate in our sessions. I had thought about hate—if she felt that emotion for my late father or me.

As soon as the judge adjourned the court, Aryan wrapped his papers with fury. Dr. Silverstone snuck a hug with John before they escorted him away. As they exited, my eyes glued on Aryan's hands stuffing his bag.

"Want to work more on the case tonight?" I asked.

"No, I've homework I need to do on my own."

My shoulders sagged as my heart knotted while I swung my backpack across my shoulders. The prospect of going home and engulfing in Sandeep's wrath stiffened me. I eyed Aryan's briefcase while following him out, wishing to hide in it and go where he went. For now, we entered the elevator.

Moments later, my gaze fell on the front of the elevator, and I elbowed Aryan.

"What?" he whispered.

I signaled by pointing my eyes at Dr. Silverstone. Without her husband, she stood in the front while we descended to the courthouse lobby. Aryan and I lined against the back wall. Came to mind the Talking Room: the conversations, the plants, the canvases on her wall, the nutty, chocolaty aroma of cookies. But the memory was laced with hurt that she felt I was mentally unfit to run for Team USA. Or was I not American enough?

A few floors down, the couple who shielded us from each other exited. When Dr. Silverstone turned to let them out, she saw us. Her face grew blush, and her entire frame shivered while the doors shut. Beads of sweat formed on her cheek, her back glued toward our faces. My heart raced, too, my fingers curling into a ball.

Ghastly silence accompanied us out, where her husband waited for her. She rushed to him.

And Aryan's back also shrank as he marched outside, but my feet became heavy, and I halted, jiggling my car keys in my pocket. I swung around.

Dr. Silverstone and her husband held hands, waddling toward another door. They had each other. Good for them. Aryan had gone already, leaving me without my core.

I placed one leg in front of another and exited.

When I entered my car, I unwillingly drove it home.

The clock struck nine when I pulled into my driveway. The blinds were open, and Sandeep paced the room.

Mamma sat on a chair with her rosary, but one glance at Sandeep's face was enough.

I reversed from the driveway, wiping a hurricane of tears.

It was the first of many nights in my car.

The next morning, a Saturday, my car's windows had fogged, and the pumpkin sun graced the horizon while my body ached. I reached for my water bottle. It was empty. I had parked at a cross section from where I could see my home and hide behind a sedan. Fifteen minutes later, our garage door grunted and lifted while Sandeep reversed out of the driveway. No Saturday could begin without him volunteering at the *Gurudwara.* Thank goodness.

After he paused at the stop sign near to me, I ducked down. Seconds thundered, but his car didn't move. When I reared my head up, he was adjusting his turban, brushing loose strands of his beard, and staring into the overhead mirror. He lifted the visor only to yank it back down, repeating his actions until a car drove up and honked. I shuddered, too. His car's tires skidded, and dust clouds grew under them as he sped away.

A heaviness crawled inside me. He never was into looks before. Lately, however, he worked on himself longer. Too young to support a dependent sister, he projected a brave front to others. But each morning, he tied his turban and left home, aiming to be inconspicuous, so no one noticed his turban or the well-combed beard. What happened to his father could happen to him. Fear, however minuscule, beat inside his heart, and he coped with this reality by adjusting to the world. He fought with me only because he worried about me. More than he realized, I understood him.

Swallowing a painful lump in my throat, I drove up and parallel parked. I emerged so fast out of my car that my back's stiffness blindsided me. Wrenched in pain, I slumped on my knees while the American flag sprayed around Papa's spirit. Brushed against my hair, a gentle breeze, blowing a flavor of cardamom *chai,* informing me Mamma was awake. I rose and limped to the front door.

Inside, I removed my shoes, picked them up, and tiptoed toward the loft.

"Siana!"

The shoes dropped to the floor, and I ossified.

The rosary dangling from her fingers, Mamma marched out of her bedroom, her floral teacup empty but unwashed on the dining table.

"I waited for you all night. Where were you?"

"M—"

She lugged me to the couch, shoving me onto it as though it was a cop car's backseat or a confession box's chair—both harbored sinners.

Without releasing me, she sat and whispered, "You cannot trust a boy who will make you secretly sleep with him at night out of wedlock. Have you been a bad girl?"

Involuntarily, I chuckled, covering my mouth with my hands.

"You find this funny." Her eyes widened.

I gulped the giggle and shook my head, my toe peering from a gaping hole in my sock. Although this conversation carried a dash of comedy to sprinkle on my serious life, my sock's rip reminded me how deep my scars ran. The night was dark and wretched. First, I'd dozed off at a gas station until a loud thud had woken me. The gas station's attendant had called for help. A cop's giant shadow loomed over me and forced me to roll down the window and face a warning ticket for parking illegally for hours, serving as proof of zero excitement in my life.

"Siana!" Mamma jolted me.

Certain truths were unutterable, and if spoken, would bleed into a thesis, nothing short: "reasons for seeing the inside of a jail," "reasons for being restrained away from people," or "reasons for leaving a bed and sleeping in a car." And none of these were worthy studies.

"Mamma, I came home when you were asleep and then went out to run in the morning."

"A person who is speaking the truth doesn't remove their shoes at the door and tiptoe hush, hush, or stare at the ground while talking."

I slid my fingers into my pocket and rubbed the warm warning ticket. I had barely pulled it out when I shoved the creased paper deeper.

"You are right. I'm sorry, and I'll never see him again." My head suspended so low my chin touched my chest.

She didn't need to know my heart was homeless like my body, and I would rather she believe I was in the loving embrace of a boy.

"See, I knew it. You promise it'll never happen again?"

That would depend entirely on Sandeep.

She jerked me again. "Siana, where do you go? If your father was a—"

"It'll never happen again, Mamma, I promise."

She opened her mouth several times to say something but gave up. Did she worry someone had dumped me because I didn't fight her on it? She knew I was a fighter.

As a smile emerged from my lips, she led me into the kitchen and stationed me on a chair, rolling dough and stuffing it with potatoes before frying it on a flat pan. When its salty scent reached my nostrils, a wait ticked in my belly as my mouth drooled. Most days, I ate a bagel with cream cheese in the morning and a glass of milk in the evening—the essentials. As soon as she slid the *paratha* onto my plate, I broke a steamy piece that crunched and melted in my mouth. *Oh,* the savory, sleep-inducing flux of butter! I devoured it like a beggar until no crumb remained. She kept making, and I ate until I burped and chugged a giant glass of warm milk. The guilt of being a burden on Sandeep, only a year older, who blamed me for all his problems, toyed with my mind and kept me from consuming groceries paid by his credit card. But, man, did it feel nice to eat Mamma's cooked food.

Ten minutes later, I fought a bout of sleep while brushing my teeth in the bathroom and staring at my phone resting on the sink.

Aryan hadn't called.

When I turned the faucet off, a faint conversation rippled through the open door. It was too early for Sandeep to return from the *Gurudwara.*

In the living room, Mamma and Tayaji sat together on the couch, unaware of my arrival. They laughed at once, her cheeks red, her scarf laying on her lap. Chuckling, he placed his hand on her shoulder.

Little bits of Papa floated inside my head: *"Gurjit, it does not look good, married women talking to other men."* I hadn't realized the significance of his words other than thinking Papa was insecure.

She removed his hand from her shoulder. Good. But then she stroked it, and I turned around.

"Siana?"

My fingers balled into a fist. "Y-yes."

"We were waiting for you. Come."

My feet dragged with my body, my heart a sack of stones. I found the two inches of gap between them and lowered before Mamma scooched. The middle was the place to be to keep them apart.

"How's the running coming along?" Tayaji said.

"Good."

"How's the preparation f—"

"All good."

"Siana? You seem rushed."

"Yes, I need to run."

Tayaji's head vibrated. "Yes, yes. You must work hard."

"Yes. Are you staying?"

He glanced at Mamma, then at me. "Yes. No, I was about to leave." Rising heavily, he pulled out his wallet from the back pocket. He extended bills to me as I rose to his eye level.

"What is this?"

"For your expenditures, *Puttar.*"

Fresh ink wafted from the glittering, sashaying bills—Benjamin Franklin's face shimmering.

Papa's voice rang: *"Take your money, Veerji. I'm man enough to provide for my wife and children. So what if I am not an engineer?"*

"I don't need your money." Only in our culture, did we baby adults. Twenty-five-year-old adults.

Mamma rose. "Siana, be respectful. It's okay. *Veerji,* we will ask if we need anything."

He shoved his shiny bills into the wallet before Mamma waved him goodbye at the door.

Me? I grew icicles standing there, confounded by her unfounded reverence of Tayaji that hurt Papa. To avoid the community gossip, she had even sided with Tayaji to get me married. But Papa didn't bother about what people thought. He said I had dreams, not a husband to follow.

I watched Mamma shake her head and disappear into her room.

Nineteen

MONDAY EVENING

MAMMA said only children roller-skated. But while my body had aged, my mind was raw like unbaked banana bread dough. And so was my weight. When I tied the shoelaces and glided outside, she must have wondered why a runner like me needed skates suddenly. I weighed under a mountain of words—the sounds and sights I couldn't erase at will and wished to separate my feet from the ground. Today, I arrived home early from the court: early enough to watch the start of sunset, early enough to listen to birds chirping and flying, early enough to see the squirrels hopping around, and early enough to avoid Sandeep, who was still at his work.

But the day had begun wrong. Quite wrong.

It started with the stink of soiled diapers, the echoes wailing across the tall courtroom's lobby, the bearded man's photo glued on TV, and then Aryan waltzing into the courtroom with words "Go Away" grizzled on his jet-black leather bag. Besides that discrepancy, Aryan had fit his part. Not a speck of dust rested on his immaculate suit, not an expression warmed his face, and not a hair was out of place. I searched for answers in his face, but he had sealed his lips in indifference.

He bickered with the defense attorney in front of the judge even before the session began. Worried that Papa had been wrong about America and its possibilities, I had sunk lower into my seat.

My roller skates railed against the road as I turned onto Johnston Street. Our neighbor Mrs. Patel, strolling on her daily evening walk, yelled a hello. I raised my hand but continued, a melodious breeze propelling me forward. Dr. Silverstone's testimony had lasted three-quarters of the day. We had traded seats, and no longer on the receiving end of questions, I got to learn about her life now. Her daughter Grace was fifteen when she visited New Jersey for a chess tournament. At fifteen, I'd only cultivated bad habits and had no awareness about anything outside my world of fantasies.

I grabbed a light post to stop. Mathis Street bustled under the descending sun. Pondering over the doctor's testimony, I sat on the sidewalk and tightened my shoelaces, the cars buzzing past me.

When Aryan grilled Dr. Silverstone to clarify "what outside forces" caused 9/11 and continued to target us, she had given a roundabout answer. It wasn't until Aryan asked her starkly if she considered my father "an outside force" had I gathered why Aryan spent half an hour defining outsiders. She had shouted she wasn't a racist. I knew that. But when Dr. Silverstone brought up the recent Stanford shooting by a man alleging allegiance to ISIS, Aryan dug deeper. He pointed out that the shooter had a mahogany face. And that was it—a series of objections followed.

I resumed skating while the traffic on Mathis drowned out the skates' squeak against the sidewalk. When pressed on John's killing of my father on the street on which I sashayed on now, the doctor's response had further troubled me. Why did John's remorse and praying at the church count as pardon? Aryan asked if John had issues. Once again, the doctor had acknowledged he got angry, stating that anger didn't make him a murderer. *Dr. Silverstone, shooting and killing an unarmed person is murder. It makes him a murderer.* She had continued endlessly explaining how her son wasn't a racist, or a white supremacist, or someone who disliked the influx of immigrants, but her eyes fluttered one too many times.

After Dr. Silverstone's testimony concluded, color returned to her face as it used to when our therapy sessions would end. *Oh,* but she wasn't the most colorful witness of the day. A lady named Candace Goldberg, wearing makeup like a troubled teenager—smoky black eyes, layers of necklaces, shimmering nail paint, and a glittering magenta bow on her shoes—cussed and confirmed that John didn't say "Get out of my Country, Osama." And her home was right above the shooting, compared to the gas station that was across the street. And her ears were so sensitive bird chirps bothered her.

Escaping the courtroom today felt like I had been acquitted of a crime. Aryan went his way and I mine. And now, I pretended to fly away like I was a fleeting thought on roller skates.

The path to justice wasn't paved.

Twenty

JUNE 28, 2016

A DULLNESS suspended in the air, not a vapor, not a scent it carried. It was Wednesday, and I was sore from sporadic running sessions. I rattled the front door, but it didn't open. The same thing happened with the garage exit.

My cheeks burning, I gulped a swig of air and yelled, "Sandeep!"

Mamma thumped out of her room, adjusting the scarf. "What's wrong?"

"I can't get out."

Her scarf kept falling off her head while she jolted the doors and jimmied the knob. "Why would Sandeep lock the outside of the home?"

She cupped her cheeks while I paced the living room.

"To imprison me inside." I pulled on my hair. "How dare he!"

She plodded to a chair and slumped into it.

"Mamma, I have to run, and the court is in session. How dare he cage us?"

I marched to the dining table and unplugged my phone from the wall. "I'm calling the cops."

Mamma rose with lightning speed and clutched my shoulders.

"I'll talk to Sandeep tonight. He did wrong, but his mistake doesn't justify you turning against the entire family. And did you say you'll call the police? On your big brother, your blood?" She jolted me again. "Siana, what's wrong with you?" She trotted to her room, whispering, "Calling the police on her brother!"

I dropped my phone on the table and lumbered to the front, shimming the largest window by the door. It squeaked but didn't yield. So I yanked out a scarf from a dresser drawer and wrapped it around my hand, staring at the pane. When I stretched my covered fist back, I meant to smash it and escape, not tremble and plummet to my knees. But plans rarely worked out. Why couldn't I do this? Shattering the window would grant me freedom, but it would also add to my debt to Sandeep, imprisoning me deeper.

Resigning to my fate, I messaged Aryan and informed him of my plight. I plopped into a seat while Aryan promised to update me every hour, expressing irritation I was spending the day locked up in my home instead of running.

Counting my breaths, I stared at Mamma's bedroom. *What did she do behind her shut door?* A babbling breeze swelled outside, informing me of the weather. How sweet the outdoors became just with the aid of a lock? Another thought crossed my mind, and I rose.

I marched to the kitchen where, as I suspected, the back door opened, and I chuckled. Sandeep! How could he think he could confine me inside the home? No one could lock me in, not even Papa.

The fresh chilly air tousled my hair. As I folded my arms around myself to keep warm, my phone beeped.

Aryan: *The tearful neighbor said Mr. Singh was kind and polite.*

I circled the home to the front door. A giant metallic lock secured the manual bolt. Stunned that Sandeep had fallen back to the medieval methods, I rattled it. Solid.

The rusted lock appeared fallow in the morning sun, and the swish of traffic from Mathis street howled. I glanced at my watch: quarter to nine. Unable to tolerate the endless nonsense at the court now, I chose to skip and run instead.

Sweating, a half an hour later, another text from Aryan flashed: *Mr. Smith, the boss, said Mr. Singh was punctual with a high work ethic.*

I read it while running and didn't stop. But the text Aryan sent fifteen minutes later halted me in my tracks: *Ms. Amanda Stevens, a regular customer, said Mr. Singh was friendly and humorous.*

My hand holding the phone dropped to the side. I never got to laugh at one of Papa's jokes. In his living years, he labored, and he never relaxed or took vacations, his life one of perpetual hard work with few returns. *Oh,* how I wanted to bribe God to return him so he could live his life right.

Buried in the avalanche of sadness, I marched toward home, and when I reached Fill 'N Go, I sat down on the raised sidewalk and texted Aryan back: *What about me? When do I take a stand?*

Three ellipses appeared, disappeared, and reappeared. Waiting, I exhaled deeply.

And prove how you stalked Dr. Silverstone and tampered with the investigation?

My head rested on my phone, which beeped again. Aryan: *The court has excused Friday for your Olympic Track and Field Trials. First and the last exception as per the judge.*

I walked home briskly, my phone in my hands. When I arrived, the lock wasn't gracing the front door. I dashed inside where Mamma met me. Behind her, Sandeep cradled flowers, bumping shoulders with the uninvited guest: Tayaji.

She drew me away and shoved herself between them and me. "Siana, behave." Mamma dragged me away from them and jostled me onto the couch. "Sit nicely, and we can talk. See, he came back."

A ticking time bomb boomed inside my head, staring at Sandeep, who sought the shelter of the length of a table while extending the flowers to me. When I didn't oblige, he dropped the bouquet and sat across. I snatched the lilies and threw them at the front door while Mamma rolled her eyes. Did she call Tayaji as Sandeep's bodyguard?

Seething, I watched my opposition gather and collect their thoughts. God, why no support existed for me in this home?

"How is the preparation going for your Olympic trials?" Tayaji folded his hands.

"Terrible." I pointed at Sandeep. "He locked me in the house."

"I just found out. Sandeep, this is not proper behavior. Say sorry." He patted Sandeep's shoulders, who stared at his shoes.

"I brought her flowers, didn't I? And she escaped, all right."

"Not all right," I shouted.

"You can't behave like children anymore." Tayaji extended his index finger. "It's unsafe to put a lock outside the home. Please promise me never to use this tactic again."

His eyelids drooped, and he wrinkled his lips and whispered, "Okay."

"Siana, I'm sorry Sandeep acted this way, but it does not matter now. You are leaving for Oregon tomorrow. Do you feel ready?" He rocked his fist in the air.

Only a slit emerged from my lips, no words.

"Siana, answer." Mamma patted my back.

"I've been putting in two hours every morning."

"Tejpal would be so happy. Make him proud on Friday."

"Hanji."

"Know your competition—research them online."

"I have. My coach has been on top of it."

"Your coach? Who?"

"Aryan Khan."

"Muslim?"

"Yes."

He convulsed and scratched his beard. "Be careful, Siana. Muslims are rigid people. If Tejpal were alive, you would not have to seek outside help from a Muslim man."

Disgust breathed in and out of me. My fingers curled into a fist, and my teeth ground inside my mouth. How was I supposed to live in this world?

Fatherless?

I rose, slipped around the couch, and clenched its backside. Mamma bounced to her feet, too.

"What's happening at the court?" Tayaji asked.

I looked at Mamma's face. Why did she care so much for Tayaji and need him to drive all conversations with me? But I said nothing to her, my stare traveling from her to Sandeep's pained eyes. The a/c vent on the ground blew air, the flower petals of the tossed bouquet fluttering.

Perhaps they worried I would fail again and miss the last chance to secure a spot in Team USA if they continued to oppose me.

"Siana?" My mother shouted.

"The court is okay," I whispered, not letting go of the couch's back.

When I turned to leave, Tayaji leaned forward. "Where are you going? Sit and have lunch with us." *Oh,* he had invited *himself* to dine with us.

"It's okay. I'll eat later." I lumbered toward the loft.

Sandeep's voice stopped me midway. "Siana does not break bread with us."

The formality in his tone stung. He wasn't the brother he used to be: he went from wiping boogers on his sleeves to getting his clothes dry cleaned weekly, from cracking jokes to these formal taunts, from happy to heavy. He was new.

"What am I hearing, Siana?" Tayaji crossed his arms.

I joined Sandeep's grin. "Breaking bread? Seriously? Those are your words, Sandeep. And Tayaji, I eat at home sometimes when Sandeep is not here."

"She eats with me. That's right." Mamma lifted her chin.

Having no energy to fight or argue, I left. Sandeep assumed I dined at a deli and didn't notice my pants loosening around me. I didn't eat to compete but to survive. When I crashed on my bed, I was drowning in my depression, and a ring stiffened the air.

It was Aryan: *Are you able to escape your prison?*

I brought a pillow over my head. My phone beeped again. He commanded me to meet him for dinner.

It started as a faint beard that only grew thicker with time. His hair remained fit for shampoo commercials featuring "the secret to a head full of hair in the middle age."

"What would you like to eat?" Aryan glanced above his menu.

"Anything."

"You look as if you are dying. We have discussed this so many times before—the factor separating two contestants is muscle. It's what distinguishes American athletes from the world: their physical strength."

He signaled to the waiter and ordered two trays of grilled chicken.

"Are you following the diet regimen I gave you?"

I shook my head.

He pounded the table. "Why are you putting yourself at a disadvantage? Do you want to lose?"

"Hmm."

"Sia, are you listening?" His index finger stretched.

"Yes, sir."

He chuckled, deepening his dimples. "You sir'd me, which is okay." He glanced at his folded hand, his thumb tapping the knuckles, his face pale. "I need to talk to you."

I rose in my seat. "Me, too. How was it today at the court?"

"It was all right. Not bad. Circumstantial evidence is mounting that Flynn fired the shot in self-defense." He spread out his fingers. "Out of the five eyewitnesses, four testified against Mr. Patel, who was my strongest witness. Proving the motive of hate is hard, but I'm working through that. We can win it. What I wan—"

"What can we do?" My knee burst into a fit.

"I have contacted the media to report on the case, but racial lines have split the public into two sides. So, it can backfire, and besides, Sia, I want you to focus on your goals. With the trials starting, this is too big of a distraction. That's what I want to talk to you today."

"It's life, and you'll be there with me in Oregon for the trials."

"Just till Sunday. You are on your own for most of the last rounds."

"I'll be fine." I gulped down my water.

"Sia, your race times have dropped from excellent to struggling. Have you overlooked it? We need to add more practices. Skip court tomorrow."

A bag of mulch, my heart, words stumbled out of my mouth. "It's bad enough I'm the only one, pursuing justice for Papa's murder. My family doesn't care. Why? Because they have lived their lives in fear of discrimination, segregation, and suffering more than their fair share. They are content with the ordinary." I blew into a tissue. "So, I'm the only one here, and I can't . . . just disappear, Aryan."

"Do you have a cold?"

His phone rang, and he signaled he had to take it, scurrying away with it while the waiter set our food on the table.

Unwillingly, I served myself and chewed on a leg piece. When the acid reflux hit me, I coughed, gulping it down with a giant glass of water. Some days the food rejected me. Aryan was right that in the sea of my frustrations, I had forgotten my health, and my running had suffered. I let Papa down again.

Aryan waltzed back and seated himself.

"One of your girlfriends?"

He stopped his recline back for a moment. Smiling faintly, he said, "No, my wife."

"What?" I forgot to breathe.

"Don't be so shocked, Sia. I'm forty-six. I have a wife and children."

"Where are they? How many kids?"

He let out more of his dimpled laugh, placing a cloth napkin in his lap. "Four. My wife—ex-wife—Safia and the children live with my parents in Bombay."

"Your ex?"

"Yes!"

"Why do they live with your parents if . . ."

"If we are divorced?"

"Yeah." I played with the chicken on my plate.

"She divorced me. So did my parents."

"What? Why?"

He picked up his fork, looking beyond me. "Why who divorced who?"

"Everything."

"Well, my wife and I separated because we didn't like the same home."

"What?"

"She hated America, and I disliked India. Within her first month here, she returned to India with the children and denied this country a chance." He sliced a piece of chicken. "Ten years have passed."

"And your parents?"

A paleness deepened on his face, his eyes the color of wet mud. "They chose her. Isn't it obvious? Drop it, Sia."

I ate for a minute, but my mind wasn't in my plate. It was with him. "What did she hate about America?"

"*Ah,* Sia!"

"Tell me, please."

"She found society here mechanical, shallow—business-like, too independent. TOO FREE. And I found society there too hypocritical. Why are we talking about this?"

"How can your parents divorce you?"

He chewed and talked. "Close your mouth, Sia. It's a big world out there, and shit happens."

"Are you okay with it?"

"Of course." He pointed at my plate. "Eat."

"And what about your girlfriends here?" I drummed my fingers on the table.

"What girlfriends?"

"The girls you bring to the practice, the—"

"They are just girls. They mean nothing, and as I said, we are not together, Safia and I."

I glanced at the families who dined around us as our server whisked over to us. Aryan declined when asked if we needed anything else. When I picked my silverware, Aryan had finished. He was a fast eater indeed.

I rotated my fork in the air. "Do you miss your children? Their birthdays?"

He glanced down and whispered, "Sia, I don't want to talk about this."

I pictured Papa at my plays, my concerts, and my races, glued on the sidelines. A slouch deepened on my back.

He continued, "I know not the milestones that exist. It's as if I have no children, but you will not understand." He brought his hands together. "My life isn't important, and this meeting is about you. Eat, Sia! The whole plate is unfinished."

"I can't finish—"

"Try."

I ate in silence and asked him no more questions about his strange life. The stud Aryan had been married once. Yet he lived his life freely—or to quote his wife, too freely. Since when was freedom a liability?

After ten minutes of silence, he slammed his empty glass on the table. "If your father were here, what would he tell you two days before your trials?"

I swallowed. Papa would be more nervous than me. A grin expanded on my lips. "He would repeat his favorite slogan."

He smiled. "What slogan?"

House of Milk and Cheese

"Nothing exists;
All is a dream. God—man—the world—
The sun, the moon, the wilderness of stars—a dream, all a dream;
They have no existence.
Nothing exists save the empty space—and you!"

MARK TWAIN, THE MYSTERIOUS STRANGER

Twenty-One

THE SUPERMARKET IN THE CITY. DECEMBER 1996

THE CART'S WHEELS' rattling and whistling grew with each second. So did the tickles in my belly. My hair bounced, and I crackled. "Stop, stop, I'm ticklish."

Papa obeyed and slowed down, huffing. His eyes enlarged. "Look around you. What do you see?"

I was only five.

My feet dangled under my seat on the cart, and goosebumps enlarged on my arms from being near the freezer. Eying the milk cartons, I squinted before expanding my hands. "I see a house of milk and cheese."

His laughter sputtered. "Yes, my dreamer. A grocery store can be a house of milk and cheese." He tickled me with his fingers as I chuckled, closing into my body.

"America is the Land of Dreams. Here, anything is possible."

After Papa lugged me and the cart over to the apples, he felt each piece before tossing them into a bag while I played with Dhanno, my Barbie doll.

As I lifted her leg for a cartwheel, its leg popped out, and a fat tear rolled out of my eyes. Whimpering, I glanced above at Papa, who had receded farther on to the potatoes.

I shoved the leg into its socket, but the plastic had snapped completely. Weeping into my folded arms, I flung Dhanno to the floor.

Papa's footfalls thudded before his hands stroked my hair. When I reared my wet face, he was lifting Dhanno.

"She is dead." I pursed my lips.

"We can seal it with scotch tape and hot glue at home. Dhanno will be fine." He thrust her into my hands, securing the broken leg in his pocket.

"Like that?"

"Like what?"

I pointed at the rip on his pants that Mamma had stitched the night before. "Like your old pants?"

When he said yes, it only bolstered my crying. "I don't want old Dhanno or ripped pants. This is a grocery store, not a house of milk and cheese. We don't live in a Land of Dreams. You are wrong. It's the land of broken dolls."

His smile vanished before he dropped the potatoes into the cart and flung me out.

I tugged on his cheeks. "Where are we going?"

When he reached outside, bright sunlight hurt my eyes, and I covered my face with legless Dhanno. Not at our usual grocery store near our home, we were in the city center where Papa had business. A sprint of a block brought us to the end of the land, clouds floating over the red bridge. Papa pointed at it. "There. What do you see?"

I shrugged my shoulders. "A bridge."

"It's your dreams." He snatched a lump of air. "Never let them go. So what if your doll broke? Do you stop dreaming? No. We left India in search of a better life." He hurled me onto his shoulder, marching nearer to the bridge. His voice came out soft and sweet. "Siana, I never went to college. Neither did your mother. But we always have food on our table, a roof over our heads, and love inside our home. Bounties of this country."

Papa's words felt like a jigsaw puzzle as a shiny black car whisked past us. He pointed to it. "Who do you think is driving that car?"

"I don't know."

He traversed downhill toward the traffic jam at the bridge's entrance. "It could be a CEO of a bank or its peon. Both drive cars. Equality. The dignity of labor. These are gifts from America. If you can work hard for it, you can achieve it."

I frowned at Dhanno, but I didn't interrupt Papa. I, sort of, guessed he was telling me that where we were was better than the other country he came from—India. I stared into Dhanno's eyes. She was gone. Unfixable! As the wind frisked my hair, I wrapped my arm around his neck, my chin resting over his turban, and Dhanno scrambling between my fingers. Papa's voice wobbled, but he spoke without slowing down, the tunnel of breeze tooting in my ear. "When you grow up, you will do what I couldn't. You will realize this great nation's true potential. You will!"

Twenty-Two

THE AIRPORT. JUNE 30, 2016

TWENTY YEARS after the Dhanno accident and Papa's lecture, I brought along the broken doll Dhanno as a souvenir to remind me of Papa, his convictions for America, and his pursuit of happiness. Leaning against the conveyor belt, I stood in the security line at the San Francisco airport. When an officer approached me, I glanced at her funny, wondering what business she had. She was TSA and belonged.

"Special screening," she barked.

I followed her, eyeing Aryan's back, who collected bags on the other side.

Away from him and the public and into a threateningly quiet room, I lumbered.

Inside an office, she and I settled around a desk, and I handed her my driver's license. She stared at it and my face.

"Is everything all right?" I leaned in, folding my hands.

The sharp-featured, petite African American lady typed on her computer. "Hmm, your name is on the no-fly list, and I have to run extra checks."

The room's lights hurt my eyes. I'd just returned from London less than two months ago.

I scratched my head. "So, does this mean I can't make the flight?"

"Maybe."

A scream sounded inside me, and my leg threw a jittery fit. I was the broken doll Dhanno now. The desired response was "Don't be ridiculous." I had violated no law to merit this.

While I ached to tell her where I was headed, who I was, even if a nobody, she asked me no questions and talked into a phone, glancing my way, now and then.

"Are you okay?"

I was about to yell no when she raised her hand, said something into the phone, hung up, and marched out of the room. Edging close to my flight's departure time, seconds melted into minutes.

Did Aryan wait for me?

I trudged over to the door and knocked. The eerily empty hallway at seven o'clock of the evening could easily pass off for midnight. "Hello? Help . . . help!"

Down the barren hallway with beige walls, she emerged from another room and dashed toward me, her hand on her holster, and the steel handcuff half-fallen from her pocket. "What's wrong? Ms. Singh, go to your seat. Why are you shouting out here?"

I shifted from foot to foot, neither providing the support my body needed. "How long will it be? I can't miss my flight."

When I passed her from the side, she gripped my shoulder tightly. "I'm waiting for the clearance to come through. Please calm down."

She rested her other hand on her gun, and two male officers scuttled in our direction.

"Why am I restricted in this room like a criminal? I am a regular person—ordinary." My eyes moistened.

"I told you, you need to wait for your clearance. It is a routine check. Do you have a problem?"

Heck, yes, I had a problem. My face burned. Was it red? Drenched in sweat, my shirt clung to my back, and I loosened the top button.

The male officers talked to her, but their voices felt as though coming from underwater.

Time wouldn't stop, and neither would my trials nor my flight. Did they know they verified people with hopes, dreams, and grief? And how did I shrink to the size of a name on a list?

Some words wobbled in the air, but I wasn't listening.

When my eyes opened, I popped up. Strips of cadmium yellow streamed in the inkiness of night while the vehicle cut through the sooty road. As though severely jet lagged, my brain spun inside my skull.

"Good morning, princess." Aryan's voice shattered my rude awakening.

A saffron glow glinting on his hair, his eyes fastened on the road, and his hands on the steering wheel.

"What's going on?"

"What's going on?" He extended his finger as he typically did while reading out the bulleted list in his mind. "I didn't realize I harbored a terrorist. You can't fly legally anymore. Your blackouts are continuing. You missed your flight, and so did I."

He glanced at me with his chin up, and I couldn't tell if he was impressed or upset.

"I heard you put up a fight. It's a good thing you aren't behind bars. So, here we are, in my car, driving to our destination instead."

Shaking his head, he turned into a side street followed by a gas station. "I claimed you like lost baggage, Sia. You must get your blackouts and your priorities checked before you mess with the TSA."

Stationed in front of a pump, he reached behind his seat, and handed me a box. "Eat."

The cold, transparent plastic box contained a salad loaded with proteins.

My head throbbing, I pulled my body upright. "What time is it?"

"Nine o'clock. We just left the San Francisco airport."

A peculiar awareness of my immediate surroundings gripped me: his SUV's perpetual new-car scent, the heated leather seats, and the traffic's steady buzz. And his steady attentive stare. My presence only rubbed itself on my face when I was this disturbed. At that moment, solitude and pain knotted inside my chest.

"I feel sick. What is happening?" I said.

A distant horn blazed while his car keys clinked from him playing with them. "God is testing you."

I banged my head back on the seat. "I'm utterly unprepared for any tests."

"Sia, what happens in the court is outside of your control. You only master your performance and give it your best. This is it for you. I disbelieve in second chances." He grabbed my hand. "You run tomorrow to redeem your father, and the racetrack is your battlefield, not the courtroom, not the TSA. Your enemies are the athletes running against you. All you need to do is to make the time. Give your life tomorrow, Sia."

Melodious Aryan. My only companion, perhaps my best friend Aryan. My heart leaped out of my body and landed on my hand. Or so it felt.

"I need to fill the car." He slipped outside and shut the door.

When I dug into the juicy, crunchy kale, a motorcycle clattered into the gas station, alarming me. I glanced past it at the convenience store, and my eyes widened. Papa had worked at this gas station. One of their employees served as a character witness for him. Not ready to face the images life was throwing at me, I glanced away quickly. I saw Papa everywhere, but here, his disappointment in me was ambient. When the pump started, his hands in his pocket, Aryan marched inside the brightly lit store.

A police car pulled up next to my window.

Shockingly, I ducked down. Dreams were old, but fear was new, now feeling unsafe in Papa's America. The memory of the airport returned: they had confiscated my phone. Did I wrestle with the TSA agent?

I reached for my purse at my feet and yanked out a Ziplock bag, holding my phone like evidence. My hands flew to my head. Will the government now discover my dark thoughts of killing myself?

When Aryan returned from the convenience store, my heart thumped until we left the gas station. Soon, the city lights started to dwindle into the night.

"What happened at the airport is wrong," I whispered, my throat heavy, threatening to collapse.

"Fight for another day."

"Why?"

"Because today, you are fighting to restore yourself. Someone rightly said that the best revenge is living well. Show the world your core, Sia. It's the only way to redeem who you are, what your father stood for, and why he labored for you. Show them. They didn't know the abilities and grit of the person they cross-checked. Damn it! Win the Gold and become famous."

I took my lips under my teeth, choking with tears, but luckily the darkness concealed them while I dug my fork into the salad.

Papa's words rang. *"For you, my puttar, the sky is the limit. You will realize this country's full potential. You will do the things I was unable to do. You will see."*

Bruised but alive.

Twenty-Three

EUGENE, OREGON. JULY 1, 2016

THE RUBBERY, fresh paint aroma of the racetrack dominated the air at the Hayward Field. The long jumps dispersed clouds of dry sand.

And I marched to the start line for my first race with Aryan patting my back but saying nothing. When Aryan got nervous, he spoke less, lines formed on his forehead, and the stubble darkened on his face. He looked more attractive.

Buried under the stakes that weren't about qualifying for the Olympics alone but also about regaining my self-respect, I swallowed.

Aryan marched to the sidelines and crossed his arms while I jogged in place, trying to fool my heart into forgetting the memory of the altercation with the TSA. Through waves of heat across my head, I wondered if the United States rejected me as a citizen, as a person.

Coaches yelled; they cheered. Not Aryan. He didn't lift a finger, and his arms remained crossed, only strands of his hair danced. I heard words but none coming from the field. Listening to the voices inside my head, I swiveled my neck and kneeled.

Redeem yourself.

Give it your life.

The racetrack is your battleground, not the courtroom.

Gunshot. Boom. We bolted.

Land of Dreams.

The breeze slapped my moist, teary face, and I pumped air in my clasped mouth. That day I fought to secure my place in the United States of America, not just in the tournament.

Your daughter has talent, Mr. Singh. Papa's face erupting into a smile, the happiest kind.

Sandeep's voice rang. "Papa, please don't raise your hopes on Siana."

A rope slammed across my chest, and I fell on my knees, holding my head.

Coming in first provided a temporary ointment to my bleeding wounds while Aryan's brawny hands yanked me upright and into a tight hug. "You did it!"

Having secured a spot in the hundred-meter semifinal race, I wished the TSA lady was here to see they couldn't diminish me. They failed.

It was a strange Sunday night. The birds were quiet, and a cool draft whooshed in harmonious concord. Having broken a record in my first race, the athletes feared running against me even though I came in second in the semifinal race. In his hotel room, Aryan rolled his clothes into his suitcase while I stood on the balcony, my phone to my ear. I'd just told Mamma I was in the hundred-meter final, and she was sobbing. "Your father would be so proud! I prayed all weekend long for you. *Waheguru* listened, and you will make it, *Puttar.*"

When someone murmured in the background, I asked, "What is happening at home?"

"Same old, *Beta.* The Sainis rejected Sandeep's marriage proposal, and we may have to go to India to find him a bride."

The background noise grew.

"Tayaji is here. Talk to him. He wants to speak to you."

"Mamma, I got to go." I slammed the call end button.

"Is everything okay?" Aryan asked through the open balcony door.

I nodded and stationed there for fifteen minutes to calm my disdain for the man in front of whom Papa couldn't measure up. Two brothers, one rich at heart, one in the wallet, two lives, but only one got to live, the older one. The story of Tayaji and Papa was what was wrong with this unfair world. Room for one. One more anxiety toyed with me of Aryan, my pillar, my backbone, leaving on the last flight tonight. I turned. He stuffed another shirt so focused he could be writing a thesis. What excuse could make him stay? But I needed him at the court, too.

That suitcase he filled with clothes, I wished to hide in, always, every day. How did his family learn to live without his steady support?

I lumbered to a chair by the round coffee table. "Do you talk to your children?"

He raised his head above the suitcase, shook his head, and continued with his business. Not a sliver of emotion escaped his face while I scratched my neck, silencing the barrage of questions for Aryan.

Suddenly, he froze, a catatonic stare resting on his face before he dropped the pants into the bag. When he marched and sat across from me, pointing his palms up on the table, I didn't know what to do. So I rested my hands over his extended palms.

"Are you nervous?" He clasped my hands.

"Yes," I whispered.

"Promise me."

"What?" I straightened.

"Run for your father."

The notepad's sheets crinkled as a bubbly breeze flung them around.

"Sia, all you need to think about is your father, period, and I'll take care of business in San Francisco. Nothing is wrong with embracing your parents' dreams."

He tugged on my hands. "Do you realize what it means for a first-generation Indian to be so close to being in the Olympics? Your father was the first person to believe in you long before me. You must eat like a champion and build on the momentum. Do you understand? Make it into the Olympics on Tuesday, Siana. I'm sorry that I'll not be here, but I'm leaving my words with you."

I needed the whole of him. He didn't know how weak my insides were, and I pressed down on my vibrating leg and nodded. My throat crunched in fear, shoving back tears. What if I *lose* the final race, Aryan?

Leaving behind his touch, he rose, and I folded my hand on top of the other to keep Aryan with me forever, locked in my hands' embrace.

But the rest of him left for San Francisco soon. And for the first time in days, I filled the void with slow simmering worry about Dr. Silverstone and John.

Twenty-Four

CALIFORNIA COURT OF ALAMEDA. JULY 5, 2016

WHILE on the stand, John's melodious voice sounded a soothing song as Rhonda closed her eyes. She had skipped church the past weekend—a first. After spending the entire Saturday educating herself about California laws, on Sunday, she and her husband spent several carefree moments in the city: treading the streets of San Francisco, eating a crab cooked live under their eyes at the Fisherman's Wharf, and trekking across the Golden Gate Bridge. Only one image bothered her later—a small group of protesters had gathered in their street that morning. She worried about that endlessly, and Jacob didn't seem to care as usual.

Mr. Reynolds's voice tore through her subconscious. And Rhonda's focus returned to the clicks of the courtroom, the cautionary murmurs of the spectators, and the formal suits of her neighbors.

John was wearing his favorite suit, too, the one she had bought for his college graduation. College graduation? But John might never get to experience graduation—she shuddered.

"What do you do when you are free?" Mr. Reynolds asked from his seat.

"At the juvenile jail—"

"Sorry, Mr. Flynn. I meant your hobbies as a free member of society, not at the jail."

John replied he didn't like to brag about charity. Yes, he didn't. Her boy had been painting the library and performing chores to bring meaning back to his life.

When Mr. Reynolds asked him how he found time to do the extra community work, John coughed into his fist. "Mr. Reynolds, I had to take a break from school after last year, and I hope to finish my education now regardless of what the court decides. I'm preparing for the SAT exams and being homeschooled—or 'jailschooled', if you will."

"Why were you not going to school before the warrant?"

"Life has been hard for us after this incident." He clasped and unclasped his quivering hands. "No one wanted me in their school."

Rhonda wanted to scream and storm out of there. Suddenly, she craved a confession box, the missed Sunday mass ballooning into a bad omen. But her chair trapped her while Jacob caressed her stiff hands.

"I'm sorry to hear about the impact this event has had on your life, and thank you for spending your time positively. What I don't get is why didn't your family provide bail and free you?"

John peered around the courtroom, but not at Rhonda. "I brought shame to my family. My parents are counselors, and they call this a natural consequence of my mistake of killing Mr. Tejpal Singh."

"Do you always carry a gun?"

"No. I started carrying a gun when a bunch of gang members threatened my family."

"Gang members?"

"Yes, Hispanic gang members were tailgating my old man for driving too slowly, and we fought. I learned evil lived in this world and carried the gun."

That gun he stole from Jacob didn't protect. But she and her husband were divided even on gun control.

"But you are underage to get a license."

"Yes, it's my father's gun that I carried for protection."

"Did you tell Mr. Singh to get out of your country?"

Rhonda leaned in and grabbed her knees. They were going to lock him up for tens of years, maybe for his lifetime. She knew it. Despite being under eighteen, despite their appeals, he wasn't tried as a juvenile. The judge still looked strangely at him. Why did the legal system not forgive and allow sinners to heal as church did? That judge wasn't God. Rhonda was losing her mind to insanity.

John chuckled, his teeth the color of dying sun, his cheeks hollow like moon craters, his clothes loose like the truth, and his ribs carving his shirt like a corpse.

"I did not tell Mr. Singh to get out of any country."

"Did you approach Mr. Singh?"

"Absolutely not."

"Why did you shoot Mr. Singh?"

I jogged, but it didn't ease my anxiety. Unable to shuffle out of the awareness that John was talking on the stand right about now, unable to sleep a full night, unable to be present, I was confused, muddled, perplexed, anything but what I should have been at the start of my final run, the trials' most significant contest. Aryan thought I could willfully switch off my mind. *Think about the Olympics.* But neither did I operate that way, nor any magic ointment existed for my open wounds. Whistles rang in the air, and I took guttural breaths, worried that Aryan hadn't called during the breaks, and the day was ending.

We filled our positions and kneeled. My tears ejected early.

The shot fired, and we sprang forward.

Rhonda stroked her chest as John spoke about Siana's father.

"When I passed him, he tugged on my shoulder and started yelling, patronizing me for showing disrespect. I may have accidentally bumped into him while crossing him, I think. He took it badly."

"How did you respond?" Mr. Reynolds crossed his arms.

"I put my hands in the air." He lifted his hands in the air. "I didn't want a fight, but he went on and on, talking into my face, and I got scared."

Rhonda shifted in the chair and placed one foot on top of another.

"And?"

"I told him several times I have a gun, and I'll shoot, but he only got more agitated. He said something like, 'I am not scared of you, punk—' "

"He said punk?"

"Yes, or something similar. When he touched my shoulder, I fired."

Rhonda rocked back and forth. *Maybe, Siana's father didn't speak English.*

Mr. Reynolds tapped his foot. "Did you run?"

I ran. Aryan had explained to me the advantage of running and coming from behind, but I was desperate to win and started at the front.

A runner overtook me. I panicked and scuttled, but another figure crossed me—both athletes only slightly ahead of me.

In a race, you only needed to be marginally better.

When the third one tried, I clenched my teeth and compressed my face until it burned, holding my breath. I fought with every fiber of my being, eying the finish line mere steps away. My slipping to the fourth position spelled death for me in the Olympics.

God, no, God, this can't be IAAF all over again. No!

Rhonda recited her prayers as John said, "Run? No, sir. I refused to move because I had wronged. When the police arrived, I told them exactly what had happened. They handcuffed me, and I voluntarily left with them."

Mr. Reynolds extended two fingers. "Why did you fire two times?"

"I-It was by mistake because I was scared. My arms were shaky, and the bullets just fired."

"No more questions, your Honor."

The race ended, and I huffed, holding my stomach, staring at the dark board, no results in sight. Ten seconds later, it lit. I had tied at the third spot with the New York athlete.

I grabbed my water bottle just as the referees approached us, explaining the rules to tiebreak, but their words had lost meaning even though they spoke in English.

Staring past them into nothingness, my heart pounded, and I yanked open the lid of my bottle, scarfing down the water.

Rhonda didn't blink while the prosecutor questioned John, standing right next to him. "Mr. Singh got angry at you just because you bumped into him?"

"Yes."

Mr. Khan walked straight into the railings separating him from John. "Like this?"

How absurd, thought Rhonda. She prayed for this hour to get over. The sun had set. Why not this day?

He stepped away. "The times when most people say, excuse me, and walk around, he was enraged?"

"Yes."

Mr. Khan marched to his seat. "Why were you so scared of Mr. Singh?"

John shrugged. "He was aggressive."

"Did he have a weapon he threatened you with?"

Rhonda quavered. The scared person carried the weapon, always.

"Maybe. I had no way to tell and felt threatened. So, yeah, the way he was talking was frightening."

"What way is that?"

"I don't know how to describe it."

A time that felt ancient when she used to worry about Sia when she had visited a Sikh temple to understand Sia better thrust itself into the present. At the Sikh temple, men wearing swords had huddled together. They had kindly ushered her in and alleviated her fears, unlike how Sia's father had treated John. But then she remembered her grocery visit when she had hugged the wrong girl, whose father did threaten her.

She crossed her legs.

"It's all right. You were afraid of Mr. Singh—"

"Because of his actions only, sir."

"Mr. Flynn, have you ever had encounters with the law before? Drunken driving? Domestic abuse?"

Rhonda sighed.

"Yes—once before. I got into a fight with my friends on a basketball court."

"Just once?" The lawyer dangled his pen between his fingers.

"Yes."

"Did you instigate that fight, too, Mr. Flynn?"

The prosecutor spent a great deal of time establishing John's school fights to be significant enough to be considered a pattern that he was always battling. Would they punish him for all past faults?

Rhonda eyed Sia's empty chair.

Where was she?

I faced the coach and the New York athlete. "Yes," I said without an awareness of what "the yes" entailed.

Someone handed the coach a quarter, and I asked for heads. He flung the coin high into the belly of the crimson sky before it landed on the ground.

Heads!

Buckling, I fell on my knees, my head secured in my hands. *Don't forget you have talent, Siana. You don't deserve to be ringing groceries when you can soar on the racetrack or wear gold at your wedding when you can win it at the Olympics.* Papa. Papa. Papa. Every second of every day, I lived for him, undoing the last several years, even though Papa had permanently departed. I was in Team USA.

Papa, I made it, Papa. I did it.

I stared at the sky as though looking into his eyes. Players patted my back, and the girl from New York, who had lost, cried on her coach's shoulder. Swiping at my cheeks, I rose. Aryan hadn't called once, and I instantly dialed his number, unsure of what I was more eager to do: give him my news or discover what had happened at the court. I checked the time: six o'clock. When I reached the locker rooms and rested against the wall, the phone continued to ring ominously. Even scarier was the silence.

Rhonda leaned forward as her eyes fastened on the prosecutor's lit phone before he flipped it.

He asked, "How bad were the injuries of others involved in the school fight?"

"A guy had a broken nose and nerves pinched on the hand." John lingered on each syllable.

Rhonda crossed her arms.

The slick-looking lawyer spent the next ten minutes firming up how John's punishment was more severe than his peers. She worried if he tried to add years to John's sentence. She had planned for all scenarios of the verdict on how John could reclaim his life.

After John covered his community service as required by that fight, the prosecutor said something that pricked her skin.

"Because Mr. Flynn from the record, you were the perpetrator. You have a history of outbursts—"

"But this time, *he* started it."

"Who?" Mr. Khan stopped rocking, and his eyes lit.

"What's his name—the . . ."

Rhonda clutched her hands together, whispering, "Tejpal Singh."

But no one could hear her, nor could she telepathically make John say it.

"He has a name, Mr. Flynn. Do you not know his name?"

John nodded and chuckled as Rhonda's cheeks burned. His chuckle bothered her. Maybe he was nervous.

"Who started it?" The lawyer's pitch had risen, a strange smirk mixed into his face.

"Mr. Singh, who else?" John's face mantled with blush before he flung his hands.

"Why did you have trouble saying Mr. Tejpal Singh's name?"

"I forgot, sir. I had no trouble."

They asked no more questions, and the judge adjourned the court. When Mr. Khan brought his lit phone out of his pocket and dashed out of court, Rhonda worried about their next plans. She, too, rose and followed John as far as she could while the guards escorted him away.

I sat at the edge of the bed, phone to my ear. Twenty rings and three-quarters of the night later, Aryan answered his phone.

"Hi, what time is it?" His voice came muffled.

"3:30 a.m. and to avoid a call at this hour, you reply to me at a reasonable hour."

"I deserve it. Congratulations, Sia. I'm so proud of you. Y—"

"No, no, no." I paced the room with my hand on my head.

His heavy sleep-laden voice angered me. Did he look up my results, learn I qualified for Team USA, and sleep? The Aryan I knew would open a bottle of champagne and party.

"Okay, fine. It's not a big deal I made it into Team USA b—"

"It is, Sia! I—"

"How was the court? Did they conclude?"

Deep breathing followed. "It was good. And no conclusion in sight yet. Sia, you did it."

"Aryan, what happened at the court today?" I hissed.

"The bulk of the case is over." A yawn was audible. "Flynn testified, and nothing unexpected happened." He stated cold facts like a doctor who had seen too many deaths, and one more altered nothing.

I ended the call and held my hands, keeping them from hurling around objects. If Aryan were here, I would happily unleash my wrath. *Oh,* Coach Aryan would be pleased.

When the phone rang, I shut it off and slammed it on the bed, darting outside where the crickets chirped so loud, I longed for a pair of noise-blocking headphones. The fog floated like silk sheets around me as my thoughts bubbled inside. I wanted to interview the cheerful people in the world and learn from their secrets. Today, I'd fulfilled Papa's pursuits. But fear, anxiety, and loneliness were my soul's only tangible pieces. Why?

For the rest of the week, I spoke zero words to Aryan. And just like that, Monday arrived when I had to return home. So I sat on a bus, staring at the Pacific Ocean's crashing waves, returning home a winner and a part of Team USA. A smile lingered on my lips as the bus pulled into the San Francisco station.

Happy but eager to be at the court to see the end, I hauled down my overhead bag and followed the slow-moving heads out of the bus.

When my feet touched the ground, I halted, and people swerved around me. Aryan stood tall in his suit and black sunglasses with golden rims. He wasn't expected to be here. Motionless, only his hair swayed in the breeze while people continued to glide around us.

This meeting was a celebration, a jubilation. We'd won, and our efforts had yielded the desired result. And here we were, two statues, unwilling to bridge the distance of ten feet. My entire frame shuddered, head to toe. Two teenagers laughed and chased one another like they were toddlers as our gazes glued on each other.

His being at the Greyhound station at nine o'clock with a dark complexion could only mean one thing. The final verdict had been announced. Papa had lost.

My feet fought my body and covered the ten steps forward before I melted into a sob storm on his shoulder. And he let me for the first time, not reprimanding me for my tears. Holding me with one hand, patting my back with the other, he kept saying, "I'm sorry. I'm sorry. I let you down."

His being sorry only emboldened my crying. The arrogant, stubborn man who was never apologetic—he was sorry. I hated that he was sorry.

Twenty-Five

RHONDA'S HOME. SAME DAY

RHONDA graced a smile on her face as an insane worry escaped her heart. God had answered her prayers, allowing John to begin his healing. While his life wouldn't be normal today, with each day, he would inch toward it. They returned home whole, marking the end of their steep attorney fees.

She marched to the fridge and brought a drink to John, who was slipping out of his shoes.

He declined.

"It's your favorite fruit punch." She frowned.

"I'm not thirsty, Mother."

She placed the drink on the coffee table and drew him into an embrace, his ribs poking her, while Jacob set John's bag by the door.

"You worry too much. Don't." John tore himself from Rhonda and brushed her wet eyes. "I'll be in my room."

"Your room?" All she wanted was to watch him eat, having filled her fridge with his favorite comfort food, and here John wanted to be alone.

Jacob touched John's shoulder. "Stay."

"I'm tired, Dad, and I need to make a few phone calls."

As though he left for his prison cell, Rhonda shifted on her feet, swallowing, watching him recede away. When John reached the stairs, Rhonda hollered. "Wait, John, Scarlet called. Do you want to go on a date with her?"

John emitted a puff of air. "Scarlet and I have different views on life and politics. She is too . . ."

"Socialist?"

"Yes, yes." He raised his hand. "She wants the government in her backyard, and I wish never to see their faces. She is my ex and will remain that way. Okay?" He climbed the stairs and reached his room's doorstep when he halted, staring at the wall of pictures leading up to his room. "Photos always appear happier."

Rhonda marched to the base of the stairs. "I disagree. Those were our good days."

Jacob slumped on a chair in the living room when John's phone ring stiffened the air.

Fury enveloping her, Rhonda climbed the stairs to John so fast her breathing catapulted into a storm. She snatched the phone out of the palm of his hand. "You are making a fresh start, mister. A clean start. New friends. No more tattooed men in my home." She huffed.

John laughed at her, the phone continuing to ring. Snatching it back from Rhonda, he answered the call. "Hi, Brad. My mom was having a fit. You are *fam* now. How are you, *bruh*?" He slammed the door of his room shut.

With watery eyes, Rhonda stared at Jacob, who had come to the base of the stairs.

"Are you going to take away his phone next?" Jacob said.

An idea sparked, and she pulled out her phone from her pocket, dialing a number. "Henry? We need to arrange a get together for John."

Twenty-Six

THE FARTHER I drove from the greyhound station, the closer I got to the Talking Room. The sour chlorine thickened the air, and I followed its source to rousing roars past the Talking Room to their Commons building. Once before, too, the doctor had hosted a party there. The burnt barbeque aroma had welcomed me then, ahead of my session. And it did today. Dressed in naked celebration, they covered their bottoms with swimming trunks. Their cheers chimed through the street as I parked, and their screams shouted out their success. Half a century full of teenagers. No adults. Not even Dr. Silverstone. And one dead body—that no one could see, except for me.

I ached at places I didn't know I had inside me. Dr. Silverstone lost her daughter on 9/11. Consequently, Sikhs across the country had their lives changed. During evening strolls, behind cash registers, and in Papa's case, while walking down the street with his groceries, white supremacists attacked them. That day, Papa became a statistic adding to those killed in hate crimes. But I thought our case was different. I would win. But I lost. And I had no place I would rather be than in my car, watching them celebrate my loss.

Grinning, Flynn rose from a seat and exchanged a high-five.

When a car passed me, I lowered into my seat.

Avenging Papa's death lay directly in my hands now.

A penalty for using a gun without a license was the same as giving candy to a child hungry for a parent's love. How could an armed man claim self-defense against an unarmed person? Law defied common sense.

Hot anxiety boiled up my spine. With fury, I flung out of my car.

Our eyes met. John dropped his arms and heeded my approach. He gestured to a boy who ran in the opposite direction while his friends stopped their chatter and stared. The music blasted as the scene unfolded in slow motion. No one came near me while I plunged on John Flynn and wrapped my hands around his pale neck.

Forceful hands broke my grasp. Dr. Silverstone. She had her hair tied in a bun instead of the typical ponytail.

"Please leave before the police get here for your own sake." Her extended index finger quivered.

"I have a better idea, Mom— *Yo,* Henry, fetch my gun from my pant pockets." He pointed behind him. "*Bruh,* over there."

The Henry guy followed the command.

Heaving, I lifted my chin while my hands dangled by my side. "Will you murder me, too, how you shot my father?"

"OMG, delightfully. You are trespassing, and this ruling will also be in my favor. Easy!" He snapped his fingers.

"John!" Dr. Silverstone shouted.

"Mom, this isn't cool." He turned to me. "Go back to your fucking shit hole." He spat at me but missed.

And I slapped his face so hard it left a rosy mark on his skin. When Henry arrived with the gun, Dr. Silverstone snatched it from him before John could grab it.

I glowered at Dr. Silverstone's face.

"Siana, please leave now. You know I have a restraining order."

My eyelids fluttered. "I would like to see your son fire the shot."

John pointed his index finger to my forehead, uttering syllables I couldn't decipher. Footsteps thudded all around me. The crowd huddled in clusters.

Her eyes watery, Dr. Silverstone pressed the gun to her bosom. "I'm a click away from dialing 9-1-1."

A familiar hand cupped around my shoulder. Aryan.

"We were just leaving." Aryan pulled me away, but I fought him hard.

He had the nerve to follow me. What did he do—watch my moves before approaching the party?

"Look who is here—all the incompetent losers." John's voice shattered our struggle.

Aryan released me and pointed his index finger at John with pursed lips and crooked eyes.

If there were to be a fight, it had to be me, Aryan, not you. But he had assumed the role of my protector. Why?

When John reached for the gun, Dr. Silverstone slung it away while Aryan and I stared at each other. A second later, I lugged my burdensome body, too big to carry through life, back to my car. Behind me, they squabbled over themselves, two fights breaking. But the boy who threatened me didn't know I begged to die. I desired his shot.

Aryan hovered over me as I slipped inside my car. *No shots fired.*

"You need to think about your priorities, Sia. I'm right behind you, and no detours this time."

Before he could pull away, I held his hand. "Got it. But I need to make a pit stop at the grocery store. Not a detour."

"I'm coming with you."

"Don't you have important cases to take care of?" I lifted just one brow.

He smirked and raised his hands before leaving for his car. As I glanced at John one last time, for a moment, I saw it: his fear in the tremble in his hands, the ruddiness of his cheeks, and the shimmers in his eyes. He projected the same guilt I hid. We were conjoined in hurting the same man.

I hit the accelerator and lost Aryan's car in no time. Lest the police pulled me over, no one could reach my darkness.

When Mistakes Were Cool

*"I shall be telling this with a sigh.
Somewhere ages and ages hence:
Two roads diverged in a wood,
and I, I took the one less traveled by;
And that has made all the difference."*

ROBERT FROST, THE ROAD NOT TAKEN

Twenty-Seven

THE GROCERY STORE. SAME DAY, A LITTLE LATER

EITHER the flowers were too lovely or too droopy or the wrong color: the red roses, the color of blood; the white ones, the color of death; the yellow ones, Papa's favorite color. I picked the yellow to remind Mamma of him.

Irony guided my choice as I had to quash the chemistry between her and Tayaji with memories. The court denied Papa a fair trial. And I didn't want his memories, too, to dwindle.

At home, I had to pretend to be whole, to be happy because I had entered Team USA and would run in the 2016 Olympics, a month away.

So despite being broken beyond repair, I bought roses, prepared smiles, pondered small talks, and contemplated celebratory actions.

You would think life's cruelties had a limit?

No.

When I lifted my head over the flowers, there, he was—the person who didn't exist outside of the Talking Room, whom I'd used as a pawn to describe my racism against myself and my fascination of blue eyes and blond hair, the boy I had once loved and hung out with—Brian Bensen.

Uncontrolled images bombarded my mind: Brian holding a beer, his girlfriend canoodling him, his house roaring with music, our classmates getting wasted in his yard, my tugging my dress lower, and him asking me about Papa.

Currently, he browsed through the wine collection. Nothing had changed. Contemplating approaching him, I reared my chin. He wasn't the boy I'd once loved. He'd cleaned up: maize khaki shorts, a trendy t-shirt, groomed hair, a fuller body. And then he turned around to a black-and-red stroller. Smiling, he leaned into it. The flowers fell from my hands. A woman I didn't recognize approached him and stroked his back as he doted into the stroller. It wasn't his girlfriend from school. Unable to contain the past I had willfully forgotten, in a whirlwind of panic, I dropped to where the flowers sprawled on the ground. Afraid he would see me and say hello, I picked up the fallen roses and slid into the neighboring stationery aisle. But love notes inscribed on cards popped in front of me, and I closed my eyes.

It felt like it was yesterday when I had begged Papa. "My life is boring. I don't get to do anything fun. I really want to go to my friend's party tonight."

While Papa had stared at the floor, contemplating, I was ready to climb out of a window. Then he looked up, his eyes glittering. "Go! Go to your party and live your life."

First party. Whiskey. Each party upgraded the stake. When I had declined the offer for drugs, Brian had squinted at me. "I thought you wanted my life."

That was it. I had inhaled the magic and left my dreams—Papa's dreams—behind.

His giggle on the other side of the aisle rippled through the shelves. He was baby-talking, cooing. My hand reached for the cold steel shelf as I walked along with his voice, thankful the walls were opaque. He argued on getting only organic bananas.

She responded to Brian today, but I heard my voice from years ago. *"You know what they call a child in Punjabi?* Puttar. *What kind of word is* 'puttar?' *It's like 'put her here.' My parents don't realize my wants and desires. They are planning my life like a worksheet."*

Unable to bear more of Brian, I lifted my chin and marched to the checkout line, but no longer was I in the present, transporting to years ago. In the cashier in a bottle green uniform and hat, I saw myself when I had worn that circus-clown uniform and worked here, saving for college—what had funded the IAAF instead—that and Tayaji's loan. She checked out my roses like I had scanned beer bottles for Brian and his then-girlfriend. He had apologized for not inviting me to his party and asked me where I'd been. I had tarried on the answer, whipping up excuses instead of the truth that I had bargained for my life with Papa, vowing never to see him again. We were a middle-class family who couldn't afford the rehabilitation costs for drug addicts. I had traded dreams with Papa.

"Sia!" a voice shouted.

Currently, Brian stood right behind me. He split into a wide grin, his shiny platinum wedding band sparkling on his finger. Would he apologize *for not inviting me* to his *wedding* now like he had for his farewell party?

Before I could smile back, he embraced me into a hug and introduced me to his wife. Five years made such a difference. Five years. His checkout items were still liquor loaded: wine, whiskey, beer. But no words formed inside my throat, only a heavy, achy lump.

"How have you been?" he asked again.

The cashier handed me the flowers and the receipt. Only the following words emerged. "Good. Nice to see you, but I really have to go."

My hair bouncing, I stormed outside, leaving behind the medley of smells from his Polo cologne, his minty aftershave, and his cinnamon-laced hair gel.

Same mistakes. Brian and I made the same mistakes. But we landed in such different places.

When I shut the door to my car, I couldn't bring myself to turn it on.

Twenty times I had told Papa I was quitting. He didn't listen. Convinced only running could salvage me, he pushed me despite my threats of escaping from home once I hit eighteen.

He said if I chose not to run, he would find me at a lost home of addicted children like the young adults in Punjab, wasted in the fields of mustard, unemployed, and heavily overdosed.

I judged Papa as pessimistic and paranoid.

One day, we had state levels in Sacramento. And the night before, I had returned home hammered from Brian's party, dragging my feet, unable to walk a straight line.

Papa had jerked me out of sleep hours later at five o'clock. "Get up, young lady." He had barked.

"And I told you I'm not running," I had croaked back.

"I'm your father. And I'll drag you out of the bed if I have to."

Currently, I turned on the ignition, and the car's thumping to a roar startled me.

When I had dared Papa to force me, he had latched on my foot, yanked me off the bed, and hauled me into the living room.

I had flung my arms in the air, the previous night's hangover splitting into a violent headache. "HELP! HELP! Someone, dial 9-1-1! HELP!"

When Mamma had tried to rescue me from him, Papa's chest had heaved, and he dropped my foot. I had only eyed my phone tethered to the charging cable, eager to call 9-1-1, ready to report my authoritarian dad.

His mouth open, he had eyeballed Mamma and me. "Siana, have I taught you nothing?"

His eyes were the widest I'd ever seen. "I'm the only one supporting your athletic career. No one else wants this but me. Your substance abuse—"

"Papa, I told you I don't want to be an athlete."

"W-what do you want to be?" He stepped back.

"I want to go to college like my friends and study business."

"Like your drug addict friends?"

Currently, I drove on autopilot.

The day he dragged me out of my bed started the downfall.

That morning I had no choice but to slip into the car with Papa.

No choice.

But the coup would begin hours later at Sacramento.

That crisp winter afternoon, I had lost the first race over at Sacramento's state level tournament.

Papa patted my back. "No worries, *Puttar*. We must discuss your technique before your three evening races."

Showing me how my breathing and my posture were incorrect, asking me to even check my thoughts, he guided me.

I lost the next race, and then another.

After the last lost game of the day, Papa spoke no words.

He suspended his head and followed me to the lockers. There, he whispered, "What's wrong with you, Siana? You are just killing your chances for the trials for the 2012 Olympics."

When he glanced up, his eyes were creamy and cloudy.

"I'm bad, Papa. I did well amongst high school kids. With these professionals, I don't measure up. Can't you see?"

As I entered the women's locker room, I cringed.

A half-hour later, I reemerged in my jeans and tank top. Having not moved an inch, he stood where I had left him, staring at the floor, his hands folded as though in prayer.

He lifted his face. "Maybe you need a professional coach. It has been a while since I ran. And—"

"No, Papa, I need to go to college like everybody else."

"Siana, will you forgive me?"

My bag fell from my shoulders. "What?"

"I know I have been rough with you. But I wanted to build your character and push you to be better. My father raised me that way. He would slap me if I misbehaved. It made me strong, but I'm sorry, my *puttar*, I've hurt you instead of helping." He stroked his forehead. "If you want to quit running and go to college, we must agree on one thing."

"What is it?" I lifted the fallen bag as we strolled toward the parking lot where a flock of birds flew away, and a gentle breeze sang a symphony.

"I don't distinguish between a boy and a girl. I treat you both equally."

He cleared his throat. "Your brother went to the university first. If you were older, we would do the same for you . . . He has more time left to finish his college, at which point I will have saved enough to fund your education, too. And I have used all my savings on your tournament fees and supplies. Can you wait?"

"I could work and save, too." I was quick to respond, the guilt of blowing his savings weighing on me.

A twitch left his face as though he expected a different response, but a load lifted off me.

When we reached the car, he brushed the dust off its roof. "And if you wish to stop practicing in the meantime . . ." He pressed on the car. "That's your call. If you continue, we'll find you a better coach than me, delightfully, but take a day or two to decide, okay?" He clutched my shoulders. "Don't forget you have talent."

He nudged me. "You pick whether you want to aim for the Olympics or quit. It's your call, but I have zero tolerance for drugs and alcohol. I never touched a drop of alcohol when I was your age, and I expect no less from you. Understood?"

When I arrived home from the grocery store, I parallel parked. Papa had changed overnight after the Sacramento tournament. No longer betting that I would practice and become a national runner, that I was special, he spent more and more time away from me. We spoke no words, and guilt shrouded both of us. I never saw Brian again; I never drank; I never did drugs, and I never dreamed.

Escapism rewarded me with yawny, challenge-lacking existence, and Papa became a TV addict. I started saving my salary from the grocery store job.

Way to quash your dreams! I, Sia, a moron.

Today, irreparable from meeting Brian, I emerged from my car, my past faucet of memories gushing.

Some incidents left a mark and a bunch of "what ifs." What if I had never met Brian, never quit running, competed in the 2012 Olympics, won some sponsors, and gone to college earlier? That would alter where Papa was on August 9, 2015.

With my arms drawn around myself, I dragged over to the front door but couldn't get my hands to open it. I had to live with one burden for the rest of my life—one of squashing Papa's heart and dreams. This unerasable stain began with cocaine, beer, and disparaging Papa in Brian's basement. But I and I alone owned that guilt. In my new goal-less existence, what I hadn't realized was who I was, who I wanted to be, and where my purpose lay. I chose mediocrity over the pedestal on which Papa had placed me. And I didn't realize that until the day before his murder.

Currently, by itself, the front door flung open—Mamma. She threw her hands to her face as the scent of *samosas* wafted out, announcing the ongoing celebration.

Sandeep, who held a plate full of sweets, set it down and marched toward us. Other shadows came into focus behind Mamma—Tayaji, the neighbors, the aunties we only met at the *Gurudwara*—they clapped at once as though I finished a sonnet at the year-end recital.

Mamma hugged and kissed me as if I was a baby. Her warm tears wet my cheeks while Sandeep patted my back, swiping at his eyes. "You made it, sis. You made it into Team USA. Papa would be so proud."

They led me into the house.

"We have been waiting for you for hours. We were expecting you in the morning. What happened?" Mamma said.

"Traffic."

Darn, I had left the flowers in the car.

Sandeep was opening a bottle of whiskey. Tayaji was saying, "Now we need a big party."

Me? I smelled Brian's cologne and John's smoky breath in one instance.

They were so happy, and I had no words to excuse myself. So with my suitcase, I slipped inconspicuously to the loft.

"What's wrong with her?" Sandeep asked.

I trudged over to the loft and plucked out my clothes from the suitcase. Outside, they whispered like bees.

As Mamma entered the loft, she yanked the clothes out of my hands and assembled them into my laundry basket, one by one.

I slumped on my bed with a thud.

"You lost at the court," she said. Not requiring an answer, she organized my shoes in the bottom drawer, shoving in the last one.

She sat next to me. "I did not want to see this hurt in your eyes, Siana, but I could not protect you from chasing an impossible dream."

My voice quivered. "You thought the court case was unwinnable?"

"Yes. Justice seldom comes from institutions men have created to serve the few. In Punjab, grave damage has been happening to Sikhs right in our backyards." She patted me. "Countless unsolved court cases are still pending from the 1980s. A courtroom is a wrong place to search for fairness, Siana. All you have to do is to live your life with a happy heart because we are here for a limited time, and our purpose is to be happy."

I could never accept that.

"Siana, come with us to the *Gurudwara*. We must thank God for where you are today after all the missteps, mistakes, and blunders."

I chuckled involuntarily. But I declined. I said I was tired. Mentally. Physically. Emotionally. She gave up, and soon, the buzz from the outside dwindled and completely sucked into a vacuum when the last door slammed shut. They were praying for our bounties as I trudged to the living room, empty now, but picturing my gym teacher, his head low with Papa.

Twenty-Eight

DESPITE the new normal of no more early morning practices for years, I slept in particularly late that Saturday morning. My acceptance letter from UC Berkeley lay on the dining table, and I was ready to start the new chapter of my life: No more ringing groceries and on to becoming an educated professional.

When I loitered into the living room, the sun rays had cast long shadows. "Coffee!" screamed my soul. But midway, I had to stop and hold a chair for support. Across from Papa sat my classmate David and my high school gym teacher, Mr. Stevenson.

Papa rose. "Look who is here. Say hello."

I shook David's hand. Staring at the floor, Mr. Stevenson never rose to greet me.

As we sat, Papa said, "David, you must have won good money?"

"You mean in the 2012 Olympics, sir?" David said.

"Yes, you won the Bronze medal in the four-hundred-meter race, didn't you?"

"Yes, sir. And I won sponsors."

Mr. Stevenson coughed into his hand. "Sia, what am I hearing? Have you given up running?"

My heart snuck up to my throat. "Just professionally, sir."

Though Mamma marched into the room with tea and biscuits, which she set on the table between us, no one picked a cup.

"I had great hopes from you." Mr. Stevenson talked with his hands. "You aren't even going to college, and shockingly, you were uninspired to run for your country with the talent and grit you have. Or should I say had?"

I stared at my feet, clutching, and releasing my hands. David, too, fidgeted in his seat.

Papa's head shivered a little as he forced a smile. "Siana is going to business school."

"Mr. Singh, David is graduating with honors in Computer Science from Stanford. Sports didn't keep him from his career. Sia, you had high ambitions in high school, but clearly, I was wrong about you. What do you do if you aren't playing professionally or going to college?"

Why was he here? I stiffened, my chin dipping, my shoulders drawing into me. "I work at a local grocery store as a cashier, saving for college, and I'll start my undergrad in a week," I whispered.

A slight pause and a deep gulp later, he said, "I was unaware you had stopped running and came here hoping you and David could train together ahead of 2016."

Papa offered him a cup of tea.

"No, thank you, Mr. Singh. I have lost my appetite." He rose, and they plodded their way across the room.

When they exited, I grabbed the doorknob. "I'm sorry, sir."

"No, you're not." He slid into his car.

And I shut the door slowly.

Inside, Papa helped Mamma clean as I followed them like a duckling puttering behind her Mamma.

"We should order five dozen *laddoos*," Mamma said in the kitchen.

"More than that." Papa placed the filled cups on the counter.

"*Laddoos* for?" I asked.

"Sandeep, who else?" Mamma said.

Oh, Sandeep! Years-long search for his soulmate was culminating. From a line of girls Sandeep had talked with only on the phone, the latest one had a musical voice and fluttering laughter.

When Papa asked him if they would speak again, Sandeep's cheeks, visible from over his scant beard, glowed like cherry.

The next day—yesterday—Papa showed him her matrimonial photo taken in a professional studio. Posing in a side angle as though auditioning for a movie, she looked no less than a star. It was love at first sight, and Sandeep said yes to marrying the girl right away, with only a week of phone conversations. They called the project "Sandeep getting married." I called it "Sandeep getting laid."

"When are we meeting the girl's family, our in-laws?" Mamma crossed her arms.

"Not in-laws yet." Papa frowned. "In a week. We'll finalize the details and make the marriage official then."

I sat on the couch and grabbed a biscuit from the coffee table. Everything was falling into place. Then why was I so darn sad?

When Papa sat at the dining table, I marched to him. He scribbled in the wedding planner, either unaware of me or ignoring me.

I clenched his chair. "What are you doing?"

"Making a list of people to invite to the engagement party." He tapped the sheet with his pen.

"I'm sorry."

He raised his eyebrows at me. "What for?"

"For quitting."

"Quitting?"

"Running."

Returning to his list, his body relaxed. "It is not your fault."

"But it is." Bothered with how unbothered he was, I fidgeted one too many times.

He put his eyeglasses down and sighed. "No, Siana. It was my fault. I shouldn't have pushed you so much. But don't worry about it now. It's spilled milk."

"Is it 'spilled milk'?"

"Yes, *Puttar.*" He rose and clinched my shoulders. "Don't worry about what your teacher said. Here, you can be anything you dream of. Do you want to study business? You study business. Remember, America is the Land of Dreams."

As he marched to the kitchen, I meandered behind him. "Papa, I would like to resume my training if you will support me one more time. I may have made a mistake."

He peeled a banana. "Siana, this is no joke. You don't hop on the bandwagon one day, only to get off the next day." He fisted tight. "You must endure and persevere to be an athlete. Competition is tough. Do you remember how the state-levels ended?"

I nodded, pleading with my eyes. "Yes, but I didn't apply myself then. And I was wrong."

He bit into his banana. "Are you sure, Siana?"

I said yes then, and again each of the ten times Papa reconfirmed.

After we planned to wake at five the following morning, a ghost of my past named Brian called me in the night. He had suddenly awakened to our lack of contact. And I couldn't say no when he invited me "for old time's sake."

The next thing I remembered was grabbing a pillow and shoving it over my head to drown out Papa's voice. Moments later, he quit jolting me and left. The next few hours felt like seconds.

Right after hopping out of bed, I fumbled for Tylenol in the bathroom and lumbered to the living room where my parents sat.

"What time is it?"

"It's twelve-thirty." Papa leaned back on the couch.

Writhing in pain, I pressed on my forehead. "It's Sunday. You haven't gone to get groceries yet?"

Mamma sobbed into her scarf.

"Did you forget everything?" Papa asked.

A whiff of air escaped my lips. "I overslept, and we missed our practice this morning."

At once, I pinched my eyes and curled my fingers. This situation was so wrong. I was so wrong.

"You overslept if you awoke by six for a five o'clock practice. It's past noon, young lady."

Young lady? I'd forgotten last night as though it never existed, including my coming home from Brian's place.

He tilted his head. "Where were you last night?"

"I was at Brian's—and I told you before leaving." My heart raced, and my cheeks burned, frustrated, I owed lengthy explanations as an adult.

"Did you drink?"

I glanced around. "I may have had a beer."

His eyebrows arched as his body slid to the edge. "Just a beer? They dragged you here, unconscious." His voice quivered. "What have I done wrong to deserve this from you?"

"It was just a beer, Papa, relax!"

His eyes widened. "Relax? You think you are so cool—this 'hip' kid in town?"

My head vibrating, my index finger extending, I laughed out loud, and I don't know what came over me, but spite and venom spewed out. "No, Papa, you're the cool one with your tattered pants. When my classmates' parents visited the school, they wore nice clothes, spoke fluently and confidently. But you—you would even communicate wrong with the teachers; So please save your lecture about—" Those were the *last words* I ever said to Papa.

"That's enough, Siana!" shouted Mamma, who seldom raised her voice at me. She stroked his shoulder and spoke in Punjabi, but I understood her. She told him to forget about me, buy the groceries before the *Gurudwara* visit, and leave me alone to ruin my life. They had a wedding to plan.

Papa left; Mama left; Sandeep didn't. Not yet. And I eyed the acceptance letter on the dining table. Sighing, I clumped to the kitchen, threw instant coffee into a cup, and beat it with a spoon. I then called Brian, my ear and shoulder squeezing the phone in between.

He answered on the second ring. "What's up, babe?"

"Babe?" I set the cup down on the kitchen table.

"Sorry. Sia."

"What happened last night?"

He giggled. "Don't you remember?"

"No."

"You got wasted, man."

A fat tear fell as my lips wrinkled. "Did we do pot?"

"Is this a test?"

"Brian!"

"Yes, it's all we did, and everyone got wasted, but I brought you home somehow in one piece."

My knees buckled, and I grasped the counter to keep from falling. "I got to go." I hit the end button and threw my phone over the counter. With my cup, I scampered to the sink, drained the beat-up coffee, and washed it five times, sobbing like a child.

All teenagers had scary dreams about messing up before big exams, fearing to sleep in, and missing the test. The difference between them and me was they woke up from their horrors, but their nightmares were my reality. My poor father was a witness that I slept in on my most critical days. He had a fool for a daughter. Pulling on my hair, I marched out of the kitchen and paced the living room.

When he would return, I would fall to my knees, beg him for forgiveness, and overwrite my last-spoken, disgusting words with kinder, gentler, loving ones, just as a daughter should. While I was the worst damn daughter in the world, I would vow to grow up and not repeat my mistakes. I felt the urgency, aware of how much time I had lost—a deficit of seven years.

So I waited. Rocked. Breathed. Prayed.

Sandeep gabbled into his phone. His shut bedroom door couldn't contain his bursting laughter and hushed whispers. When people fell in love, their outside world ceased to exist. He nurtured fresh hope inside his heart.

Soon, his door flung open, and my eyelids fluttered. I turned to hide my cried-out face as he made his way to the front door.

"Hey," Sandeep said.

He put his feet into his shoes, his backpack on his shoulders.

Although we avoided sharing our business, I needed help today and could have used an older brother yelling at me for my stupidities.

I brushed my hands together, mustering my voice.

But when I opened my mouth, he had disappeared outside, just as Papa had. He, too, left.

Mamma was out with my aunt, shopping for his wedding. So what if it wasn't final yet? Mounting to our debt, his wedding ceremony, the first after fifteen years in our immediate family, would be a grand affair. But Tayaji had already promised to loan us money, and they would hire singers from India to perform at the reception. And I was starting college—admission fees paid off. Our lives were bubbling with excitement.

An hour passed while I paced the living room, head in hand. Another hour dragged. But no sign of Papa.

At three, I called his cell. He didn't answer.

Half an hour later, the doorbell boomed.

But Papa had the keys. Maybe he forgot today.

I bolted to the door, ready to embrace him in a big, bear hug.

But when I flung it open, I stared at two police officers instead.

"Is this Mr. Tejpal Singh's residence?" the taller one asked.

A sharp pain shot down my throat. Around and around twirled the officers and my house's white walls. Their voices, too, dimmed and grew muffled as though a Tsunami surrounded us, and yet, we strangely stood upright. It was the first of my blackouts.

"Are you all right, miss?" a winding voice said, and the lights turned off.

Almost a year had passed since the shooting. After Papa died, a lot changed. I never went to college and sunk deeper into my addiction. And then one day, I reared my head, popped open my laptop lid, and googled: John Flynn. Without a Facebook page of my own, I used Sandeep's account to locate his mother, the therapist. She had a fancy page for her business.

The first day I sought her out, I intended to hurt her, threaten her, curse at her, but to prepare myself, I had five cans of beer first.

The moment I sat down, I collapsed, sleep-deprived, drowning in the arms of the best nap I had had in a month. Only silence, tears, and wakeful ticktack of clocks reverberated my home. She sustained me. I sobered up and started running again and dreaming about justice, leveling with John what he snatched from me.

Propelling me out of bed each morning, the hope for justice drove me forward. I packed off the empty beer cans into a dumpster, paid off my credit card debt from beer, therapy, stadium memberships, and tournaments, including London, from my savings for college. When the funds fell short, Tayaji wielded the power of financial superiority. From that day till today, I had the hope of redemption, of revenge, of justice. Not once had I considered John walking free. And now, my purpose fled my spirit, leaving me not knowing what to do with myself. I had traveled a full circle—from forgetting that fateful day to being in it again.

Presently, I pulled out the roses from the car and headed straight to Mamma's bedroom. As I loomed over her bed, tightness spread across my chest, imagining Mamma—her rosary rotating between her fingers and her thanking God for our bounties.

Our losses outnumbered our gains, but my humble mother never forgot her blessings. Caressing her pillow and kissing it, I placed the flowers on it but didn't leave a note. She would know I was thinking of Papa.

With a letter pad and pen, I lumbered along to Sandeep's bedroom where I sat and wrote:

Dear Sandeep,
I agree with you more than is clear from my actions. Thank you for looking out for me. I ruined your life because your engagement broke when our father died, and he passed away because of me.

Sudden ache crawled through my body. Death brought grave misfortune, and no Punjabi family could risk testing bad luck by forming an alliance where a tragedy had struck. I cost Sandeep his first love. I bent and finished the note.

I agree with you more than I let on, but I love you, and you are all I have. I wish you can live your life in a turban without fear despite the scars we carry. Sorry for everything.
Sadly,
Siana.

I hid the letter under his pillow and stormed out of the house.

Away, the road slipped under my car. There was the road, and there was me. And my mind. And my burden. And my mistakes. My guilt. Nothing else. I saw nothing, felt nothing, believed nothing.

After driving for an hour past the Golden Gate Bridge, I twisted my lips and swerved sharply into the first parking of the Golden Gate Recreation Area. There, I marched around the hill until the end of the land. Scattered clouds hung low, and amber hew cast a halo over the landscape. Air ruffled my hair. I stretched my hands like a bird, my throat parching. And even though my legs revolted in a mad frenzy, I was clear on what I had to do.

"Are you all right?" a male voice asked.

My hands dropped, and heavily, I swung around. A boyish man, his eyes the color of a swimming pool, spoke into his phone.

"I'm fine."

"Step away from the edge, please, miss."

Who was he to tell me to step away? Heat rose through my spine.

"Listen, I'm on the phone with a 9-1-1 operator, and the police will arrive any minute."

I stepped away from the coast, widening my eyes, the police sirens growing. *No, not seeing the police station again, not today.* Only after I assured him, did he hang up, as I lumbered away toward the parking lot. *Next time, Sia, pick a private place instead of the land's edge littered with tourists and joggers alike.* My misery needed cold loneliness. The stranger watched me get into my car and drive away.

When I entered through the front door, Mamma jumped out of her chair. *"Oh* good, Siana, you are back."

"Why do you look surprised?" I slammed the keys on the table by the entrance, an unintended quiver mixing with my intentional smile.

"You have been . . ." She swallowed. "Never mind. I'm just glad you are here in time for dinner." She clasped my hand. "I have made your favorite kidney beans. Come, eat."

I kissed her on the cheek before she led me into the kitchen.

There, she handed me a plate, and her hands quaked as she scooped rice and kidney beans from the pans on the stove. "I also cooked cinnamon chicken for you. Athletes need a lot of proteins." Lifting her chin, she yanked out a leg piece onto my plate. "I have cut down on the spices."

I placed the plate on the counter and hugged her in a tight embrace.

Laughing, she patted my back. "What is it, *Puttar?*"

I tore away. "Do you think Papa would forgive me for what I did?"

"What are you saying?" She frowned.

"It's all right." I lifted the plate from the counter and headed outside with it.

She followed me to the dining table. "Your father never kept a grudge, Siana, and would be proud you made it into the Olympics in less than a year after all the mistakes you have made. He would be so happy."

I played with my fork and whispered, "Do you think I killed him?"

"Don't be absurd!" She smacked my shoulder and marched to her room. In an instant, she reappeared with the yellow roses, shoving them into a vase on the table, smiling. "The flowers are lovely. I should give you a gift on your win, not the other way around."

After she finished with the vase, she sat down and watched me, resting her chin on her palm, smiling affectionately.

My mother.

"Where's your food?"

"I'll eat later. They served a lot of food at the *Gurudwara.* And we kept having tea after tea after tea."

"Where is Sandeep?"

"He left from the *Gurudwara* for his work trip to Dallas."

I finished quickly. After Mamma went into her bedroom, I snuck into Sandeep's room and retrieved my letter. For now, it belonged to me.

Twenty-Nine

STANFORD SHOPPING CENTER. JULY 15, 2016

EVERY CHORE became a task: waking. Brushing teeth. Running. Even crying. To make matters worse, Aryan upped the training. We are on the last stretch of a ten-mile, summer, desert hike: he said. It may seem like it will never end, but it will: he said. He said a lot of things.

Pain and bent-out-of-shape sneakers defined my new existence. After a strenuous session on the racetrack, I studied the shoe collection on a store's outside display, thirty minutes before the mall closed. But activity in the periphery of my eye drifted my focus away.

I turned.

In a gray hoodie over fleece pants so low that his boxers peeked from underneath and ivory earplugs affixed to his ears, a boy jerked his index and middle finger rhythmically. John Flynn! Same face, different attire. His courtroom suits, the placid expression, hands folded in his lap came to mind.

Which boy did Papa see: the stoic defendant or the hip-hop artist?

Removed from the outside world, he reminded me of me when I was seventeen: aloof, withdrawn, and uninterested.

Just then, he waltzed into a clothes display, the dresses tumbling to the ground. As he yanked the headphones out of his ears, his hands trembled in a frenzy while picking the clothes, but the rack kept falling. A bulky lady offered help, and he kept declining. A shopkeeper assured him all was okay, but "I'll pay for it," he kept saying.

And I couldn't tear away, my feet bringing me nearer by ten steps.

"You broke nothing." The blond-haired shopkeeper smiled. She wore fashionably tattered jeans on her long, slender legs, and her fancy checkered shirt tucked in from the front and hung from behind.

John paused, staring into her grassy eyes as I took three more steps in his direction.

"You are beautiful." He didn't move a finger.

A chord shook inside me as the girl blushed, steadying the rack to an upright position.

"Thank you," she said.

"Can I pay for the damages?"

"There are no damages." She chuckled.

He wrested the top of the rack. "The hinge looks loose."

"It's fine, thank you." She adjusted the hinge slightly. "Easily fixable. See?"

John nodded and turned away, and I kneeled, pretending to tie my shoelace. Mouthing inaudible words to the girl, who was arranging the dresses on the rack, he spun three times. Finally, he lumbered away, shaking his head pointed at his shoes.

When he stepped on the escalators headed down, he noticed me. His body stiffened, and the tenderness he displayed around the girl morphed into a steady, stern, blink-less stare. Midway, he lifted his middle finger and stuck it in my direction.

Jitters arose as I lifted my body, my eyes glued on him.

He, too, didn't lose focus from me and fell flat when he hit the unmoving ground.

Clumsily, he rose, faced up at me, his wide eyes bloodshot, as though I had caused his fall.

Then he dashed away.

I felt my jaw lowering, my stomach hardening as I brought my watch to my eyes—twenty minutes till nine, the closing time. To let go of John's thoughts, I jerked my arms and hands as though finishing a strength exercise. As two shop workers moved the fallen rack inside, instead of entering the shoe store, I followed them. Inside, the air-conditioned breeze rubbed against my arms. I reached the back of the store to where they stationed the previously fallen rack.

"Can I help you?" someone asked. The same shopgirl, who had helped John, carried a pile of clothes.

I shook my head with a smile, sliding my hand against a black dress's net fabric. With it, I marched inside a fitting room behind the racks. The price tag said one hundred nine dollars, only allowing for a modeling session in front of the mirrors. After I slid into the beauty and turned to one side, I felt dejected at how perfectly it fit around my frame. It was a shame I couldn't buy it. I shoved my hair behind my ears when a voice became audible from outside. "Hey, you are back. I hope you aren't offering more money."

I pressed my ear against the door.

He laughed. "No, I have embarrassed myself enough. *Ah* . . . I want to buy a dress for a girl. Can you help me?"

I gasped and opened the chilly door softly and slightly. My heart began its marathon.

"Sure. What does she like?" The shopgirl swayed sideways, her hair bouncing.

"That's the thing I don't know, but maybe you can help." John's cheeks had flushed. "She is your age. What are girls like you into these days?"

"Is it for a party?" She marched to the same rack as my black dress as I receded away from the opening.

"Sure."

I leaned back into the opening, their sides toward me.

"What's her size?" She flipped through the dresses.

"Your size."

She drew out the same black one I wore. "These lace cocktail dresses are selling like hotcakes. They fit a range of body sizes."

I turned to the mirror and slanted to a side. She was right.

"Do you like it?" He asked.

I quickly returned to the opening.

"Yes."

"I'll get it."

I wondered why John came back. Was he hitting on the shopgirl or looking for me at the back of the store? The thought sent a tingling pulse across my chest, and I locked the door.

But the lock couldn't contain their voices.

"She'll love it. It's a brilliant choice. We have a discount going on today: Thirty percent off on all full-priced items."

"It's for you."

"What?" the shopgirl said loudly.

What! I closed into the door with my ear.

"You are the girl I want to get this dress for," he said.

Her voice came out soft and shaky. "I mean . . . I would love to, but I can't. It's store policy."

"You don't have to tell anyone."

Oh, John—that was desperate.

"Sorry. I can't. And besides, my boyfriend wouldn't like me accepting expensive gifts from someone else."

Good girl.

"Sure. I'm sorry to offend you."

When the footsteps thudded away, I emerged from the fitting room.

"No, you didn't offend at all. I found it sweet . . ." she was saying, but John had left.

She turned to me, pointing to the dress "Hi, do you need help? It looks lovely."

I brushed past her toward the exit. When I reached the door, the girl yelled from behind. "You can't go outside wearing store merchandise."

I stopped and looked all around, but John was nowhere. When I was about to turn, I spotted him standing in the Reebok store's doorway, staring at a sneaker in his hand. He turned the shoe around, and a second later, he drew his hand back and smashed the shoe into the store as someone shrieked.

"Ah!" I muttered.

Under the shopgirl's steady and worrisome stare, following my every move, I nipped inside. *No, I'm not stealing the dress, girl.* In the fitting room, I slipped out of it, still shaken.

In ten minutes, the mall would close.

When I came out, the girl talked into her cell phone, and I waited for her to finish.

Unhinged, she continued. "He was so cute. I lied to him about a boyfriend. I dunno what I thou—" Seeing me, she ended her call, her cheeks red. "Not getting it, *eh?* It looked lovely on you."

I smiled. "He's not a good guy."

"Sorry?" Her smile disappeared.

"Never mind." I stared low, marching to the shoe store.

I couldn't afford the visit to the mall to go empty-handed. Running was my lifeline, and I had to risk meeting John for it. He wasn't there. I had barely entered the store when my phone rang with an unknown number. *What now?* I picked it up. "Hello."

"Hi, is this Siana Singh?" A female voice spoke.

I sat on a chair inside the shop. "Speaking."

"Are you Mr. Tejpal Singh's daughter?"

"Yes." I straightened.

"You recently lost a court case against the shooter?"

I scratched my head. "Yes, yes, all me. Who is this?"

"My name is Indrani Baath. I run an NGO and host a local social program on PBS. Would you be willing to give an interview? I want to cover your case."

How will your mother endure this disgrace? Tayaji's plea rang in my ears and flashed in front of my eyes, Sandeep's angry face, Mamma's rosary beads slipping between her fingers, and her lips moving in prayer. How could I continue to oppose my family, my flesh, my blood, and my soul?

My head dropped to my free hand. "No."

"What?" Her pitch grew.

"I'm not willing to give an interview. My family has endured enough." I rose heavily.

"So, allow such hate crimes to continue? What is one more murder where hundreds have died?"

"Excuse me? Lose a loved one and suffer to realize—"

"I have. I lost my son," she whispered.

Belabored silence thundered as I paced the shop. "Listen, I'm sorry for your loss, but my family can no longer endure the publicity." I sighed. "I can't be on TV discussing my father."

The shopkeepers brought in the outside displays. Another girl drew the shutters down halfway, me being their last and only customer inside. I trudged out of the shop with my phone against my ear as heavy breathing stiffened the line.

She said, "You have my phone number now, and this is my cell phone if you change your mind." Her pitch blended into a coarse whisper. "Know this, people care. They are marching outside John Flynn's home with or without your desire for justice every Sunday."

"Okay."

"Wasn't it a Sunday?"

Descending on the escalators, I gripped the phone harder. "What?"

"He shot your father on a Sunday, right? When a bullet shattered your life?"

"Yes." My muscles compressed.

She hissed, "We will shatter all Sundays for him until he caves, even though it's a shame you are silent."

Dial tone beeped, and I stared at my phone with watery eyes. *No, woman, I haven't been silent. I just . . . I just have given it my all and have no more to offer.* My throat parched as I approached the front exit. There, my feet glued to the floor. Outside, with his hoodie over his head, hands in his pocket, and vision piercing through me, John Flynn stood. He had waited.

I swung around and marched down a hallway leading to the restrooms with a sign for security.

Inside there, I found a guard. "Hi, there is someone out there who is threatening me. I need help."

I panted.

A moment later, the security guard marched with me, and I led him to the exit. "He was here. Maybe he is farther along that way."

He followed me out where my hair bounced, jolted by a sudden breeze, as I glanced around, but he was nowhere. "Maybe he is hiding in one of the parked cars." *Or maybe he waited for a different girl.*

The officer cocked his head. "Go home, Miss. Call 9-1-1 if needed. The mall is closed, and I don't see anybody here."

My eyes fluttered, hoping he would walk me to the car, but I had outstretched my welcome. After he left, I lingered surveying my surroundings. The wind whistled a draconian tune while the cars buzzed on the nearby freeway. The petrol fumes suspended in the night sky where charcoal clouds floated under the stars.

And fear clung to my heart as I slipped into my cold car.

I wasn't afraid of being killed but of surviving the attack.

Borders

"There was a long hard time when I kept far from me the remembrance of what I had thrown away when I was quite ignorant of its worth."

CHARLES DICKENS, GREAT EXPECTATIONS

Thirty

JOHN'S ROOM. JULY 16, 2016

RHONDA felt compelled to read out loud. So she did.

> "I don't brush my teeth until my gums swell because I care for them with the same devotion with which I care for this world. Every day, I dream of running away from home without taking a penny from my mom. A wooden cabin with a leaky roof and my thoughts are all I need rather than this home where I am caged and not tolerated. My mom doesn't understand me."

Rhonda flipped John's diary shut. She'd hungered for truth, but his words were too harsh. It was past midnight, and John wasn't home. Another broken curfew.

John said she ran her home like a dictator. But dictators felt powerful until taken down. If she was a dictator, her son, the mastermind behind the coup, was taking her down. She went back to the diary. Next page.

> "I'm the worst damn son in the world!"

That's all the entire page contained. Next page.

> "Can you ever confess to a murder and be forgiven?"

Another one-liner. Bruised beyond repair, Rhonda shoved the diary into his cupboard, upset that his rough exterior hid so much guilt.

And so it was; the frogs ribbitted, lending a hollow resonance to the silence, and a black breeze slid along the corridor with the African violets, tacking down in long-memorized cross-stitch Jacob's gurgles, and with it, she descended the stairs into deeper darkness.

Her journal remained empty, now too aware that raw, unfiltered emotions required a metallic heart to read. John's life, his diary, his actions rudely enforced truths that shouldn't have been true. Parents and children should be alike. They shared the genes. Then her chest ached. She didn't share genes with John. She and Jacob, too, were miles apart. He visited the local farmer's market and read magazines to sleep. She had lost herself and couldn't even fake sleep.

She shook her head, forbidding herself to think. But suppressing the thought meant she had already consumed it whole and drained herself hollow. She sat in the dark, the night's stillness offering absolutely no comfort for her until John arrived. He didn't waltz into the home. John struggled with the lock for several minutes. Without turning on the lights, he lumbered to the fridge and drank orange juice straight from the carton. Had it not been for the fridge's light, she wouldn't have seen the fresh bloody bruise on his face. When she asked him about it, he dropped the orange juice on his shirt and now on the floor. It took them a few minutes after turning on the lights to tidy the kitchen, uttering zero words.

But the silence spoke thunderously between them:

Why are you up so late?

Why do you hang out with those boys so different from us? And those websites you spend time on are fake.

We are not discussing this again, Rhonda.

Call me: Mother. Remind me that our bond doesn't need the same blood group or DNA.

I would tell you, but I'm sure the Jews have rigged our home. They are watching.

I won't be able to save you next time, John.

Wistful glances and sighs delivered the many unsaid words while Rhonda helped clean his bruise and led him to his room. There, she waited for him while he changed before she tucked him inside the bed with a peck on the forehead.

When John was in kindergarten, he would blow kisses at her from the classroom window. Securing the memory in her heart, she watched him sleep—the same way as she used to when he was pure and innocent, unformed, untainted—before his diary existed, before he spoiled it with complex human conditions.

Still in her ochroid robe, swaying her head and mumbling gibberish, Rhonda slept on the couch. The warmth of a plush embrace calmed her shivering feet and hands, a shush spreading through her ears. A smile settled on her lips, and she opened her eyes.

By the table, he kneeled, flipping through her printouts and whispering the titles: "Missouri Mosque Vandalism. Charleston Church Shooting. The Umpqua Community College Shooting. How the Alt-Right Movement is brainwashing young rebels? 2014 Isla Vista Killings."

"John?" Eyes puffy and glassy, Rhonda rose.

"Good morning, Mom. What are these papers?" John swished the printouts.

Rhonda adjusted her ruffled hair and clasped her hands, biting her lip.

"Mother, I've asked you not to worry about me," he shouted before throwing the papers on the table. "These articles have a theme, and they're about me. I—"

"John." She reached for him, but he stepped back.

"A world separates you and me." His head quaked, but his pitch rose with each word. "I'm fighting for our rights, especially of white men that are under attack, and I don't expect you to understand being a woman."

"A woman?" She leaned forward.

"It's my job to protect you, care for—"

"I need no taking care of." Rhonda pouted and crossed her arms. Rather, she had been the one looking after him.

A caring dictator.

He gathered the papers and stacked them in a neat pile. "Sure. Be born a white man in this century and be sidelined." He bent and planted a kiss on her forehead. "It's not your fault."

When his phone rang, Rhonda peeked. It was the friend she wished he never saw again.

He silenced it and marched to the kitchen where he mixed batter with water.

She joined him. "What you making?"

"Warm breakfast. I'm afraid the orange juice is all done, but I'll buy a carton today." He smiled, spreading the pancake mix and stirring eggs.

"Of course, Son. Thank you." Smiling, she patted his back. "It smells superb. I'm sorry about the articles."

The egg mixture sizzled onto the pan. Picking broken eggshells, he tossed them into the trash before Jacob sauntered down the stairs.

"You didn't come to bed?" Jacob said to Rhonda as John silenced his phone again.

"I slept while watching TV. Sorry." She looked at her feet, wishing Jacob wouldn't start the morning with that complaint. He slid past her to the coffee machine.

Hastily, John slipped the pancakes and eggs onto two plates. "Well, it's a nice morning—not the right time to argue." He smiled wide. "Enjoy your breakfast, and I have to go."

Rhonda held his shoulder. "Where?"

"Quick business. I'll get the orange juice and be back in a jiffy, promise." He winked, gliding to the front door.

"First eat with us the breakfast you cooked."

Salty, buttery, and untouched, the eggs oozed steam.

"I have to go." Wearing a white vest and black pants, he slipped into his outside shoes and disappeared.

They were shedding their life, bit by bit. Eating together was the first ritual to end. Now, he had even quit studying for his SATs.

Two hours passed, and John didn't return.

Another two hours chugged and still no sign of John.

Jacob brought carryout from the local Chinese café. Not Rhonda, the wretched evening consumed dinner, John-less.

Soon, Jacob climbed the stairs toward their bedroom. "You are not coming again?"

"No. I'll wait for John." With the TV remote, Rhonda settled on the couch.

"Again today?" In the middle of the staircase, he stared at his feet, holding the railing.

"Yes."

"I miss my wife."

"I miss us, too." With the remote, she drew a circle in the air. "And by us, I mean all of us."

Jacob didn't question her, just hung his head, and lumbered to the bedroom.

By midnight, Rhonda was hooked on family videos, replacing one DVD after another. In every video, she hunted for clues to help John in the present, hoping that the past revealed answers to her current misery.

Rhonda had watched the first four years of videos and was on fifth when her eyes shut at three o'clock. For now, the darkness swallowed her worry, only her ears fastened on the TV's metallic voices.

An hour later, a chuckle that didn't originate from TV awoke her. John sat on the edge of the couch, laughing. On TV, he wore a rainbow birthday hat and blue cake smeared on his face. Then, he hid his dirty face into her floral dress, cleaning it, to the roars of the guests.

"Do you remember this?" Fixing her hair, she sat upright.

He shook his head. The smile wiped off his face, a brooding sorrow painting over. "Go to sleep with your husband. Don't throw your life away for me."

"Start coming home at a decent hour then. Okay?"

Bright afternoon lights carved lines across John's bedroom when Rhonda entered his room. John lay asleep.

"Wake up, dear. It's noon. Come, join us for lunch." She patted him.

Grabbing a pillow, he buried his head under it. "I'm not hungry."

"You have skipped breakfast, too. Your father is waiting. Please come with me, John."

As though a storm had barreled through, sprawled around the room clothes, cigarette butts, and crumpled paper. John was nothing short of a hurricane himself. The pain he hid inside was ambient here.

His madder, puffy eyes blinking, he reared his head out of the pillow. "Are they gone?"

"Who?"

"The people outside."

"The protesters? They are still chanting."

He threw the pillow across the room. "I will take my gun and shoot them, one by one, angry rascals."

Unwritten in his diary, unspoken, unexpressed, his frustration with the protests stunned Rhonda. Her eyes welled into an ocean, mulling over his words about shooting them. What had taken hours to shove inside, their disagreements, their different DNAs, just surfaced without notice. "John, this is not how I raised you."

"Ya, how did you raise me?" He tilted his head.

"Please come and eat with us."

"I told you I'm not hungry." John rose. And without warning, he popped, bursting into a volcano of tears, breaking into Rhonda's arms, shattering his angry persona. His entire frame shook against her body.

The last time he had embraced her like this was as a three-foot-high toddler, shivering from night terrors.

She joined his wild weeping match. "It's okay, my baby. We will fix it. I promise. It'll be okay."

Thirty-One

JULY 17, 2016

ALL WAS OKAY—for now. As I snatched the grocery list from
Mamma's hands, a peal of laughter erupted from my core. I exited
our home, feeling the paper between my fingers. Mamma had
insisted she would get to the groceries later. But this Sunday, only
one thought comforted my anxieties. Papa. She relented to my
pleas, eventually.

The thrust of the present moment ballooned: the cars whirring
past, the breeze's gentle tickle, the sun spraying everything in sight.
When Fill 'N Go came, I lifted my head, and a window jutted
open from the brick building—home of one of the witnesses. I
entered the gas station and greeted Mr. Patel.

The packet of cigarettes in his hands dropped. "Siana, what
brings you here?"

"Nothing, just here to say hi." I beamed, grabbing a chewing
gum from the candy assortment by the cash register.

Forcing a trembling smile, he rang it.

Later at the grocery store, I stuck to the list with precise
discipline, and I enjoyed my stroll, my secret vacation. It relieved
my stress, serving as a quiet retreat from people and the mundane
nonsense.

No one except my thoughts escorted me, leaving me strangely cathartic. I could see how this trip relieved Papa's stress, why he left his car behind. When I reached my front door, I felt light as my wallet. Cardamom spices dripped from the air, and I brought my watch to my face: thirty minutes after one, too early for Mamma's evening *chai* and too late for morning.

Inside, a familiar shape from my past filled the couch, a teacup in her hand. I almost dropped the grocery bags.

Mamma offloaded the bags from my hands, just not my pain. She nudged me with her elbow. "Are you going to greet your visitor?"

While Mamma lugged the groceries to the kitchen, the door closing behind her, I trudged over to Dr. Silverstone without removing my shoes.

"Hi, Sia." She smiled.

"Hi." My descent onto the chair felt like sliding down a Drop Ride at an amusement park.

She placed her full teacup on the table between us. "How are you?"

"Why are you here?" I stared at my old, loose shoes, ones I had to replace and couldn't because of her son. I bent my toes, cringing.

"I know you don't want to see me anymore, but please give me five minutes of your time."

"Does Mamma know who you are?"

"No, I didn't tell her about that or our therapy session, and I have no intention of hiding, though. I'm here as a private citizen, not your therapist."

Seconds thundered as our unflinching eyes rested on each other, the spices from her masala *chai* now bothering my nostrils.

"Please get to the point." I scanned my living room's canvasless, minimalistic walls. On the table by the front door lay Sandeep's neatly set turban, and my palms sweated. The ticking of the clock reached my ears for the first time, and I wondered why Mamma hadn't returned.

Dr. Silverstone cleared her throat. "How do I say this? I'm so sorry for your loss and can't—"

"Let me stop you right there. Honestly, an apology is inappropriate. Why are you not afraid of me anymore? I could have one hundred guns stashed in this home."

The kitchen door flung open. Mamma scratched her cheek as I slid to the edge of my seat.

Dr. Silverstone's facial color had paled.

"Siana, is everything okay?" Mamma adjusted her headscarf.

"Yes."

Her eyes darted from the doctor to me. "I'll be in my bedroom."

When Mamma staggered off to her room, Dr. Silverstone leaned back, her cheeks glistening. She whispered, "We are getting hate mail. Our neighbors are petitioning the board to expel us b-b . . ." She buried her face into a tissue.

As though my muscles suddenly flew from my body and my bones melted, my entire frame shrank into itself. Hope had long fled my soul.

Even those who had defeated me were miserable.

As I sagged into my chair, she blew her nose into a tissue. "But first, I'm so sorry for judging you. I couldn't bridge the divide. All my problems in life, be it losing my daughter, or the man John is growing into, offer no excuse, but I have contemplated a fair amount whether I was fair to you as a doctor." She leaned forward. "Can I make it up to you? Let me refer you to another doctor, please."

In other words, she was telling me I was sick, mentally unfit. Did she worry that I would run for America carrying my mind?

I curled my fingers into my palms, spotting an opportunity sitting across from me. "You don't have to refer me to another doctor, but I need meds. Can you help me?" I said.

Her head vibrating, her body elongated and stiffened. "What meds?"

"Painkillers, the narcotic ones. I'm in a lot of discomfort from my practices."

"Running can be painful. Consult your primary care physician."

"Can't you just write me a prescription?"

She crossed her legs. "Lots of painkillers exist, and I am unsure if you need the n—"

"I can't sleep at night because of the muscle pain."

"You should cut down on the severity of your practice."

"Okay. Is that all?" I said with a lot of air in every syllable.

"Can you forgive my boy?"

My jaw fell, and I rose from my seat, my shadow hanging on her teacup.

She steepled her hands. "I'm begging you for your help. Please! John was a remarkably sweet kid, but his life . . . *eh,* has been rough. The grief of losing a child can take over a family. He is an immature boy keeping the wrong company. He has lost his way."

Rising, she grabbed her purse while I marched to the front door and flung it open.

She clutched the straps of her purse and spoke so fast as though her train would leave the station. "I must help John because the court has let him go, but he is not free, Sia. I'm seeking redemption for my son and begging for your forgiveness. John is too proud to ask, but I'm witnessing his slow demise. This incident is wearing him down, and he is killing himself, drowning in a sea of alcohol. John needs help, and liberation will come with a pardon, so he can continue with his life, which halted when he fired the shot. He wronged you. He understands, but he can't undo it." She teetered, trudging over to me, an arm's length of barrier parting us.

I couldn't see her eyes or her expressions, only my ripped shoes in view. I whispered, "I'm a small person, Dr. Silverstone, who can't forgive herself, and the hands that pulled the trigger are free now to harm others."

"I know my son well. He is not a danger to society."

My chin rose. "And I'm not his parole officer."

Dr. Silverstone clutched the open door. "Make the marches stop."

Indrani Baath's powerful words rang in my ears of shattering all Sundays for John, the one he broke for me. Thankfully, Ms. Baath spared my family any attention.

I shifted on my feet. "Will your son surrender and admit he killed my father out of hate, not self-defense?"

She grew pale. "The trial's—"

"Over. So is our meeting." I pinched my eyes, shocked at the venom flowing out of me.

She had begged with words, with restraint, with her eyes, with her tears, and now, she just left. Just like that. Abruptly. Without thought, without lingering.

Why did I need more of her anyway? Worse than the sting of my rudeness, worse than the ache of a broken heart, was the sight of her sagging shoulders, her figure receding into the whiteness of sunlight.

That evening, my stomach knotted, and I bent over.

When I rose, I was huffing, and Aryan stood with arms akimbo. "You look like someone has died."

"I feel unwell." I clutched my belly, squinting under the bright afternoon sun. "Can we cancel?"

He marched away from me, clapping. "Nope. Let's go."

"Aryan, I'll faint." My hands dropped to my knees.

He spread his arms. "We have no time left to practice."

"Please, cancel only today." I pleaded with my eyes. "Have I ever missed our practices?"

He paused, scratching his beard. His chocolaty eyes pierced through mine, and I worried they would extract my sad truth.

"Okay, just one time. Dine with me." He snapped his finger.

"Sorry, Aryan. I'm busy."

Pointing at my face, he neared me. "Now, either you are unwell, or you are busy. Pick one excuse."

I tapped my foot on the ground. "I'm unwell and want to go home and lie down."

"Rest after an early dinner with me." He passed me, gesturing for me to follow him.

Gosh, stubborn Aryan.

I lumbered to the women's locker room. Ever since losing the court case, I ignored Aryan, who instilled hope where it didn't belong. Although I was utterly unprepared to face his interrogation, I had no choice and met him in the parking lot with my belongings five minutes later. He wore his expensive sunglasses, the ones lined with thin gold that now glinted in the evening sun.

Right before we reached his car, I halted and craned my neck low, peeking inside a parked car. A boy sat inside.

"Is everything all right?" Aryan asked, standing in front of his car door.

"Yes."

What use were words when they often misinformed? If I told Aryan I had mistaken the boy for John, he would laugh at me. Like my brother. Or Tayaji. My mother would give me her famous head shake. Aryan's interrogation hadn't yet started, yet I was sweating.

When he pulled out of the parking lot, I said, "Guess who showed up at my home today?"

"Who?"

"My shrink."

"Ya?"

"Yes. She had the nerve."

Aryan didn't take the bait. It wasn't until later after he drove through a back alley and we entered an Indian restaurant, illuminated by dull red light, did he ask: "What did Dr. Silverstone want from you, anyway?"

"Forgiveness."

His eyes twitched. "Interesting."

A server filled our glasses with water.

"Okay, tell me what's wrong with you and your health?"

He changed topics. What's wrong? My constant depression. Hopelessness. A sense that something God-awful would happen. The right question for me should have been: what's right with your world?

"Nothing. Just fatigue." I sipped my water, glad that Aryan ordered as usual without consulting me.

Strangely, his hands and head shook while handing the menu to the server as though having a gentle fit. "Last week must have been hard for you. The hope of justice can keep a person in mourning going and losing it must be difficult." He adjusted in his seat. "I blame myself and keep thinking if I could have worked harder, brought diverse witnesses, or asked different questions, a—"

"What's done is done. Don't torture yourself like that."

"Right. But it's not over." He flicked his finger at me, his eyes smiling. "Have you been following the news? Protestors are marching against hate crimes. Not just here. Washington D.C. Chicago. Dallas. An ugly clash broke with the police in the city. Your court case has uncovered a delicate matter, Sia, and an NGO organized the march specifically for the Sikhs who are being targeted."

A tingling sensation peaked inside my body, hearing this from his mouth. "What should we do? Should we join forces?"

"One problem at a time, okay? Olympics. Olympics. Olympics. Only that should consume you, Sia, until August, only until August."

All the adrenaline that had risen, I felt its ashes crumble. My body lowered, and I whispered, "It will be a year next month since John shot him."

His expression softened. "Sia, my dear, I have filed paperwork to take this to a higher court, and I promise you I'll fight until we get justice."

"Define justice." I let my misery spill out of my eyes.

"Okay, justice will start by locking his murderer in prison where he belongs. And teaching the world it's wrong to fear people like your father."

"A courtroom will grant me justice?" *I would walk free.*

"The first part for sure."

"None of this will get me Papa back."

"True. But keep hope. Justice also lies in spreading awareness, so no one else suffers the same tragedy as you did, and I'll call that the greater cause of our mission. Let me know how I can help outside the courtroom."

"I need no help and know what I must do."

The creamy spinach and garlic smell oozed from the food as the server laid it on the table: *Palak Paneer, Chicken Vindaloo,* and *Dal Tadka.*

I adjusted my hair while Aryan put generous portions on my plate.

"What is it you must do?" he asked.

"Food is here, so let's drop it, okay?"

"Okay."

A car whooshed, and I shot up from a bed, my eyes wide open.

"John!" I whispered coarsely.

Nothing.

My breaths hastened, not recognizing the bedroom lit by a dim mustard overhead light. Sinking into the soft, creamy sheets over a plush mattress, I drew to my neck the blanket draping my body. I scanned the room: one full-length mirror, zero items on the table in front of it, one wooden cupboard, and one man sleeping on the floor: Aryan rested his head near my feet. *Oh, only Aryan and not the villain who never left my mind since meeting him at the mall.* My heartbeat returned, and my body relaxed.

I remembered what happened.

Not having the confidence, he could leave me alone for one moment, Aryan had refused to drive me to my parked car. So what if he was right. I had no desire for him to chauffeur me every day, lest Tayaji spotted the "Muslim man." Threatening to shut off, further aggravated by arguing with Aryan, my head spun. And I lied to him about my family being in India. That's the last thing I remembered. Inky nothingness had followed, and now, I rested in his home. He indeed didn't leave alone.

I pressed on my aching head and climbed out, tiptoeing carefully, but as soon as I reached him, his eyes opened as mine shut. "Hey, I'm sorry," I whispered. My cheeks burned.

"Of course, you are sorry. How are you feeling?" His thick, silky hair hung on one side, and his long eyelashes drooped over his big, puffy, dense eyes and high cheekbones.

"Better."

"Why are you whispering, and where are you going?"

"I'm going home, Aryan." My voice sounded thicker, and it was hard not to whisper. "I hate to impose, and you have already done enough for me."

"Okay, but you shouldn't be alone."

"I'm an adult woman, and you don't have to baby me."

He rose to face me, blocking my exit. "I know you are an adult woman. B . . ." His face darkened, and lips pursed.

My tongue tangled as our gazes lowered to our lips. Aryan's face glowed as my lips reached over and melted into his. My limp fingers charged with a sudden current rose to his cheeks, then to his head, and caressed his soft hair. It was a reflex response. He pulled on my shirt, holding it in a knot on my back as I rose to tiptoes, his muscular contours brushing against me. My breathing was on a roller coaster when our bodies inched toward the bed. But he drew his lips away and tore his body from mine, holding my neck and stationing me an arm's length away.

His chest heaved as he stared at the bed. "You are right. I'll take you to your home."

The next morning, I jogged to the field, ready with a plan to handle Aryan and make him love me forever. Four miles, an ordinary distance to the stadium where I'd parked my car, wasn't enough to summon him. Fresh with the memory of his soft lips and his silky hair beneath my fingers, I ran. Beads of sweat formed on my face, and in no time, my back drenched in sweat, and my mind sagged under the burden of his memory—him pushing me away, him kissing me hard.

When I reached the stadium, I gripped my knees, mouthing my prepared speech.

Wiping my face with my arm, I rose, but Aryan was absent, threatening my words with no ears. Instead, a head full of gray hair, a face full of uniform wrinkles, came into focus.

A tall man in a white shirt and shorts extended his hands. "Siana Singh?"

Rang in my ears, Aryan's words from two days ago: "Siana, you need a professional coach now, not a failed athlete, a wannabe coach."

"Yes." Staring at the man's shiny, ashy hair, I shook his hand lightly.

"I'm Dennis Stanley. Aryan Khan spoke highly about you, and I'm looking forward to coaching you."

My eyes lowered to his classy, sparkly shoes. Unlike Aryan, who sweated alongside me, Coach Dennis must order others to run, but like Aryan, he probably didn't chitchat, sticking to the routines, a true professional that he was. Except Aryan saw through my core.

"Ms. Singh?"

I crossed my arms. "I'm not changing my coach but thank you for the kind words." Leaving him with his mouth open, I ran away, a storm howling inside me.

I jogged and did my routines alone. Unseen to the world, my anger bubbled and dripped in my sweat. I wished to quit and shout at Aryan for judging me correctly. I was me, Sia—boiling on the inside, mellow on the outside.

At 4:15 p.m., for twenty minutes, under a hot, steamy shower, I stood. Aryan had directed me on everything: diet, routine, bedtimes, meditation, and cold, quick showers. I revolted against him with a long one. Screw him.

At 4:45 p.m., I stared at my reflection on my car's window, holding my chest in which Aryan poked a hole. But I didn't drive it out today either. Instead, I hurled my gym bag inside, shut the door, and beeped with my key, locking it. Marching behind the stadium, my thighs sore, I lifted my chin high. In no time, I reached the mud-colored townhome, where three steps led to a porch with one royal red wooden front door, one swing, one chair, and two glass windows, one open.

My index finger and thumb played with each other, my feet shuffling to and away from the steps. As a fight broke inside my heart, my knees threatened to buckle. I couldn't choose between my hunger and my disdain for him, between my loneliness and my hope.

Stiffening, I swallowed and climbed the three steps past the door and the swing to the open window. A bright, banana light filled the living room and the kitchen area before Aryan emerged and marched to the fridge. His hands quivered as he yanked out bread and eggs. When my phone buzzed, I shuddered, ducking down.

It was Aryan: *How long do you plan to stand by the window?*

I stood up as he continued to cook. Who ate eggs and bread for dinner?

Turning my back to him and leaning against the window, I replied: *I don't know.*

Aryan: *What do you want?*

Me: *Figure out your mystery.*

No mystery. Go home and eat with your family. I saw your mother greet you last night when I dropped you.

Sighing, I put my phone away in the back pocket as he flipped the omelet before sliding it onto a plate.

I dragged myself to the swing and rocked to release my worries.

The sky darkened into a shade of periwinkle. The birds trilled, and the crickets stridulated. A boy glided on a skateboard.

When the water ran inside, it reminded me of Dr. Silverstone, who had washed her hands at the start of our sessions.

A few minutes later, he emerged with two jumbo garbage bags and tossed them into the bins down the three steps. Bummed that he returned to his home without acknowledging me, I rocked harder. The night swallowed the last streak of sunlight when the porch lamp turned on, and Aryan came out, carrying two cups of steamy coffee, handing one to me.

"Thank you." Warm and milky, exactly how I liked my coffee, I gulped a tiny sip, careful not to burn my tongue. Sugary! Yum. Its vapors alone injected me with a dose of energy, charging me with the courage to reel Aryan back into my life.

He sat on the adjacent chair and greeted a neighbor.

"Why do your hands shake?" The warmth of the cup spread through my fingers.

"They've shaken from a long time since I was little, but it's no big deal."

"Have you seen a doctor?"

His eyelids heavy, fatigue laced his watery eyes. "Sia, consider Coach Stanley. He is excellent and has trained a lot of outstanding athletes. I—".

"I'm angry at you because you didn't show up at the stadium today, and you forced your coach's decision on me." I set the coffee cup on the round, metal table between us. "I like someone who understands me and my history by my side."

I forced myself to look directly into his earth-colored eyes, whispering, "Are you doing this because of last night?"

His face mantling, he jumped in his seat. "What? Nothing happened last night. You got it?"

I laughed at the miserable, never-ending episode called my life. "Was it that bad?"

"Drop it, Sia. Nothing is happening between us, and nothing can develop between us, ever. We are bound professionally, and I'm closer to your father's age than yours."

"So?"

"So what?" His eyes widened.

I glanced away, my hand dropping to my lap. "I'm willing to forget about the kiss and everything . . ." My vision, too, fell to my loose shoes.

Really, could I forget? My prepared speech disintegrated behind my eyes as my aspirations downgraded to not losing Aryan's physical presence in my world. I whispered, "If you agree to coach me and stay by my side."

He popped his foot on his knee. "I'll stand by your side at the Olympics, Sia. I know your history, and I refuse to abandon you over a kiss, no matter how unwise. But please consider the training from the coach. Don't risk your future." Aryan brushed imaginary wrinkles off his jeans. "It's late. Please leave unless you need something from me."

One last time, I peered at his pale face that lacked an ounce of love. I marched away without glancing back, my coffee cold in my cup. When I was out of view, I dashed to my car, swiping at my cheeks as if with each wipe I could want him less.

Another day descended without Aryan, and restlessness settled inside me. I was broken from before. But now, I felt robbed of any residual hope.

Thirty minutes after a long steamy shower at the stadium, my legs did what my heart feared the most and brought me to his home, my fingers playing with each other, thinking of words, not too angry and not too loving, to coax Aryan to return to my life. From the bottom of the three steps, his living room appeared dark, and I suspended my head. At once, the bright banana glow illuminated the window. My mouth opened, and my feet propelled me up the three steps. Aryan wasn't in the kitchen, but distinct sighs and whimpers raised goosebumps on my arms. Steps away from the kitchen, on the living room floor, his naked back rolled on a woman with artificially red hair. I covered my mouth and turned, my knees buckling, but I grasped the porch railing to keep from falling. My eyes rained tears as I dashed away from his home—again—tasting humiliation in the foul metallic flavor in my mouth.

Thirty-Two

HOME

PAIN played a symphony inside me—rising and falling, drumming and coaxing. Toward home, I drove without stopping. It took one hard blow to realize I'd nowhere else to go. One rejection from Aryan shrank my possibilities outside of home to zero.

When I flung open the door of my home, Sandeep sat at the edge of the couch.

Seeing me, he rose. "Hi. I have been waiting for you."

I took off my sneakers, shoving my gym bag into the coat closet. "I'm not in the mood for a fight, okay?"

"Not fighting." He narrowed his eyes with a forward head tilt. "Have you been crying?"

"Where is Mamma?"

He sighed and looked at his hands as though they were dirty. "Mamma is out shopping."

When he pointed at the couch, we sat.

"By herself?"

"Yes. I need to talk to you." He drew out a photo from his pocket. A handsome turbaned boy graced a sparkling smile.

"Please, I don't have time for any arrangement of marriage, either. You know I fly to Brazil for the Olympics."

"Relax, Siana. I'm not that selfless to plan your wedding when my single life won't leave me. Unlike you, I'm content with an arranged marriage, but it doesn't agree with me so much." He tapped the picture. "This photo was of Ranbir Singh Baath, a freshman from Stanford."

The name sounded familiar.

My body relaxed even though a knot tightened in my throat. "You said 'was.' "

"Yes. Ranbir came to America a few years ago to join his grandparents in California." His eyes watering, his voice deepened. "He was studying medicine aiming to cure cancer. How do I know? He was my best friend, even though he was four years my junior. Well . . ."

Now I remembered. The two of them volunteered at the *Gurudwara* together.

"What happened to him?"

Sandeep cleared his throat and fluttered his eyelids, battling tears. "Last week, at the university, they assaulted him so severely that he passed into a coma. Two days later, he was brain dead and taken off life support. He was only twenty-two."

This day couldn't possibly get worse. I hadn't shrugged off Aryan's thoughts yet, and now this.

While Sandeep and I led disparate lives—he, a college graduate at a sedentary nine-to-five desk job, and I, a college illiterate, an active athlete, he, an ignorer of adversities, and I, a fighter—I wondered if we approached this news with the same attitude. It pained me to see his cheeks glistening with tears.

He sniffled. "He died of a hate crime. Ranbir took part in the local rallies. Are you aware of the demonstrations?"

"Yes."

"Have you marched with them?"

I sighed. "No, Aryan doesn't let me—" Screw Aryan! "because of the Olympics, and after losing the court case without the family's support, I can't keep fighting alone. So, no, I haven't marched."

"I'm sorry, Siana, my little sis. I have been unkind and indifferent to your causes when we needed to unite in this battle."

He flipped his leg on the couch. "I see things differently now. The hate crimes have become an epidemic, and I want to fight for justice and put an end to this nonsense."

I didn't see this coming. Caressing Sandeep's arms, I drew him into an embrace. Sandeep put a missing peg into my life. For the first time, we rocked and cried together how we used to when we were little, before we became teenagers and different human beings, and above everything else, before we lost our father.

The keys rattled in the front door, and we broke free as Mamma entered the living room.

"Hi, Mamma." Sandeep turned and marched to his bedroom.

"Hi." I rose, smiling, and pointing at the loft.

"Where are you going? I just got here." She spread her hands.

"Mamma, I have to prepare for a work deadline tomorrow." Sandeep turned the doorknob, smiled, and shut the door.

"And Mamma, I have a headache. Can I miss dinner?"

"Siana!" Mamma's mouth widened.

I sighed and smiled. "I'll stay."

We still were the family of few words—our hearts' unutterable bits, like the relationship between Mamma and Tayaji I never forgot or discussed, if spoken, would shatter our lives. Mamma marched to the kitchen, mouthing inaudible complaints as I followed her. Silently, we warmed *daal, sabzi,* and *roti.*

Ten minutes later, over dinner, Mamma told me about her friends fattening, who didn't exercise and only watched mushy Indian soap operas.

"But you watch the same TV shows." I shrugged.

"Yes, but I walk daily. I tell my friends I'm a runner's mother, and I can jog and break a leg."

I chuckled.

She grasped her knee. "I mean, I would get a plaster, but it would heal fast."

Crackling laughter came straight out of my stomach as my eyes watered.

After we finished eating, I helped her wash the dishes, wipe the counters, and sweep the floor as she made yogurt in the oven—the same she did every night for the twenty-five years I knew her.

A revolt was in order. After skipping practice for two days, on a Sunday, the 24th of July, Sandeep and I marched in front of Dr. Silverstone's house with hundreds of people of all colors. Only one purpose was left in my life. Aryan-less. Loveless. Helpless. But not hopeless. Not spineless. These marches sustained me. And I couldn't live in fear of facing Papa's murderer again.

We paraded statistics on banners of hate crime against Sikhs. One of those statistics was Papa.

The only guilt that troubled me was for Dr. Silverstone, who had pleaded with me to leave them alone. But she also refused to accept that John shot Papa out of hate.

Did the marches help? It gave me a temporary sense of relief, but we were just bees buzzing, a white noise people ignored. I believed, though, that prayers moved mountains, and a hundred voices marching together created waves that changed lives. Intentions generated ripples, and we were in the 'generating ripples' business.

A day when protestors gathered in front of their home was upon Rhonda. But unlike the previous Sundays, when the association board members would ring them incessantly, complaining about the people in the street, and John would sleep till two o'clock, today, the phone didn't ring, and John had showered. And he had agreed to accompany them to church—a first in a long time. She was happy. Faith would save her son as it had saved her.

On the drive to the church, Rhonda stole glances at John in his best suit. A strange loving ache, not painful, traveled through her body as she curled a loose strand of her hair. John's moods had oscillated hard. Two days after coming home with a bloody face, he laughed so much Rhonda forgot their troubles.

But the happiness was always short-lived with John. Maybe, homeschooling was puncturing his spirit. At the church, she clenched his hand, greeting everyone with her widest smile. As the sermons began, peace rained on her heart with John beside her, singing, swaying, and chanting vocal endorsements. She cried out of joy, and today, she didn't stop at the confession box, weeping for her sins or her shortcomings.

With a full but light heart, they returned, but when they turned into their street, the protesters surrounded their car. Not until Jacob hooted the honk, did they part ways, allowing them to enter their home.

John hissed, "Rascals."

Rhonda swung around, staring at him glaring out of the window. When she followed his vision, she found Sia—Siana Singh—standing in the middle of the crowd, her eyes wide, her chin high. As soon as their eyes met, Rhonda turned and covered her mouth while the garage door screeched open. It was war!

And for the first time, she realized her home wasn't hers anymore.

The home she brought Grace into, she carried her body from, where her practice started and grew, whose walls spoke to her and sheltered her lonely soul, she would have to leave to rid the protestors and the neighbors' wrath.

When the garage door thudded shut, she shuddered.

Jacob turned off the car and pounded on the steering wheel. "No wonder Sia is out there marching. You shouldn't have begged her."

John grabbed her seat's back. "What? Mother? You begged her?"

The photosensitive garage light shut, leaving them in the dark with Rhonda sobbing.

"Mother, tell me, please, that you didn't beg her." John punched the seat.

She sobbed harder.

And John flung the back door open, slamming it shut so hard the whole car vibrated. The overhead light turned on as he scurried into the home.

She stared ahead with her mouth agape. Darkness engulfed her soul, her fingers chilling with fear. She wasn't ready to leave her home, an extension of her soul. Not yet.

Thirty-Three

SAN MATEO, CALIFORNIA. LATER THE SAME DAY

A FAINT SMILE on my face, a steady pace beneath my feet, the park's rustling willow trees surrounding me, I pressed against my heart an acceptance letter with a scholarship to the University of California at Berkeley—same school, same student, different year, different admission, new major, new sports scholarship. Despite spending thousands last year, I failed to start my undergrad because of what happened to Papa. But now, almost a year later, bit by bit, I was placing the pieces of my life back together. This time around, nothing could stop me. And I walked it off at a neighborhood park.

When I reached a playground, my phone beeped. *I heard you have been missing the practices. Are you out of your mind?* Phony Aryan.

I moved it away from my eyes, unable to look at his name that reminded me of love, not his betrayal. At the playground, a few boys and girls played on the swings, and to one side, a gaggle of young teenagers laughed, holding lit cigarettes. I itched to go to them, jolt them, and say, "Are you stupid exhaling ash on little children at their playground? I used to be like you, and no cigarette will fill the void. Extinguish it and find your real fire."

I shrugged and strutted away instead.

As I turned, the sky had darkened to coal soot. A streetlight flickering, not a shadow fluttered.

A fast-moving car swished past me, and I halted, jittering from head to toe. I imagined teenagers inside like I and Brian used to be at eighteen in a hurry to waste ourselves on drugs and alcohol. The thought instigated me to end the stroll. This was supposed to be a happy walk.

I swung around and chose a set of stairs down a side alley, hoping for a shortcut.

That's when it truly started.

As if a trapped bird struggled to break free, tree leaves rustled behind me, and I froze with widened eyes. I turned and scanned the area in the darkness of eight thirty: nothing. Annoyed at my imaginary fear, I chuckled and marched purposefully, the playground minutes away.

But seconds later, another set of footfalls joined mine. The thuds grew and shrank with my pace. I halted. The footsteps, too, stopped. Clutching my chest, I lifted my chin and counted my steady breaths. No sound rang in the air except for my gasps.

I was eight when I had learned sound traveled in ripples from a physical object. I listened intently. Not a bird's chirp. Not a car on the road. Only my steady breathing and my heart thumping.

And then, a gush of footfalls broke my rhythmic sighs, spinning toward me like a big swirl of a wild desert wind. I had an urge to run, but I waited for it. As a grave shadow grew, it pushed me flat on the ground, and strong hands wrapped around my neck, strangling me.

Choking, I stared into the boney, pale face of John Flynn. His skeleton fingers—long, narrow, stony, and freakishly strong—dug into me. I squealed but shouting was useless. My hot face burned.

He spoke in a snake's whisper. "End the marches and stay away from my home, bitch. If I see you near my home again, I will KILL you!"

I nodded vehemently, and he released me, disappearing into the night's impenetrable cloak. Rising, I coughed and panted, dashing away with all my might.

The wheels screeched to a dead halt in front of Aryan's house. Thankful the living room light glowed from the window, I pounded on his doorbell repeatedly.

When he opened the door, I embraced him.

"Sia, what's wrong?" He patted my back.

"Say no words and ask me no questions. Just hold me for a moment." I shut the door behind me with my foot.

I sniffled, my tears wetting his shirt.

"What is wrong, Siana? You're scaring me. What happened?" Aryan stroked my hair.

I tore myself from him. "When I was a little girl, I used to believe in fairy tales." I extended my hands forward as though holding a box. "I thought my one-thousand-square-foot ranch, stucco home was a stone-walled castle, trapping me inside its walls. My parents were the guards with pistols of their dreams on me. And one day, a prince would come dashing and crumble my castle's thick walls, free me from my bondage, and steal me from right under Papa's nose. And I would live happily ever after." Through a film of tears, Aryan's face appeared pale, or maybe, it was pale. "Today, I know it was just a fairy tale. In this world, fables are absent, and exist no princes, only men—deeply flawed men. And people no longer trust fairy tales. I am—I was a bloody exception."

Aryan's face tinged with a deep shade of burgundy as he stood motionless, not even moving a finger as though I blamed him for my disappointments.

"The only other person who believed in fairy tales was Papa. H-he maintained against all odds that my life would be a dream: I would have the luxuries he didn't have because of America's greatness. It's a good thing he died before life squashed his beliefs. If he had lived, he would find out people like John Flynn roamed the streets, discontent, disappointed, and hateful." I shook him, holding him by his shoulders. "Why are you not saying anything?"

He lifted his eyebrows, sighing. "I'm listening, Sia, trying to understand what could have happened for your heart to open like that."

"John tried to strangle me at the park."

"What? Wait, all this is about John?" His eyes widened, a sigh of relief escaping his tight lips in the form of a smile. "This is huge. We need to report this—"

I extended my stretched palm. "Aryan, this is nothing to do with John."

He stiffened again. "Is this about me?"

My hands flew to my stomach, chuckling. "Yes, it's about you, too. It's about all the men—and boys—I have fancied." I paced his living room, steps away from where he had sex with the other woman. "I have been chasing the wrong dream. All along it was me breaking my castle from inside out, and I succeeded. When I emerged outside, I had damaged my home, and no one waited for me outside. I was completely alone."

He breathed heavy and pointed to the couch. "Do you want to sit down?"

"How come Erica is not here today?"

He stared at his slippers. "It's not steady. Sometimes, it's Erica." He glanced up at me. "Sometimes, it's someone else."

I pouted, tilting my head. "Poor Erica, too, didn't find her prince charming." I lumbered to the couch and dropped into it as he followed and took the solo chair.

"Yes, Erica is wasting her time with me, but unlike you, she isn't looking for a fairy tale." He brushed his hands through his tiny beard. "All men are not flawed. You will go to college—"

"Berkeley."

He extended out his palm.

"I got accepted into Berkeley with a scholarship."

His eyes beamed. "That's splendid news! Why are you sad? You should be celebrating."

"Because this is Siana. It's what I do." I snapped my finger.

"No, you used to be confused in the past. Today is the clearest I have heard you speak. I'm flawed but look at your father—he wasn't. He was a dedicated father and husband."

He adjusted himself on the chair. "In Berkeley, you'll meet new people. Some may be perfect for your fairy tale. Your opportunities are endless with a line of boys waiting for their princess, but it may not be him rescuing you, Siana. Society made these rules. What if the prince needs rescuing?"

"An older prince?" I raised my brows.

Wind gusts howled outside the window. Rain only threatened to drown the drought. Clouds rolled across the skies as quickly as they arrived. And the grass gilded. I blamed the Diablo winds.

His face trembled slightly while his lips parted. When his hands shivered, he clasped them together as though to keep them from shaking. "Siana, I may have coached you in sports and helped you as a lawyer, but I'm not good at giving romantic advice, and I'm not a nice human being, outside of my professional boundaries."

The apartment window rattled with the wind, and I clutched the armrests, bracing for Aryan's words—unnecessary words that could not, would not, speak of love.

He continued. "You worry me. Your peers consume themselves morning, day, and night with what they term as a 'once-in-a-lifetime' opportunity. They are watching what they eat and monitoring their thoughts. Tirelessly, they are meditating, practicing, and slashing their bodies with pain every second you are missing from your practice sessions consumed by fairy tales." He jabbed his finger at me. "And you are right that fairy tales belong in a book. In actual life, you must work hard for everything, and you don't fall for a man like me, even in your wildest dreams. I have spoken. The final ten days remain—that's all you have."

He reached into a drawer next to him and pulled out a notepad and pen. "First things first, John Flynn—where and how did he follow you?"

I told stubborn Aryan everything. And he grew angry that I started marching for justice, but Aryan couldn't control me. Neither could Papa.

In the morning, we were getting a restraining order against John. Aryan said I should pray for a second meeting after the Olympics. Until then, I was to stay away from John. I worried him.

He followed me home that night and picked me up for practice the next day. And every day after that.

From the day I broke down in front of him, he sheltered me. He no longer dismissed me, rubbing his changing girlfriends at my face. Without my professing love to him, he knew I cried for him that night after John threatened me at the park.

But Aryan's razor-sharp focus rested on the Olympics. He termed everything else a distraction—the princes, the devils, the causes, the losses, and the wins. Somehow, when Aryan sheltered, I was protected. I didn't see John Flynn again. The last Sunday, July 31, Aryan took me out of town to practice on the mountainside. He made sure I didn't attend the Shattering Sundays justice march, enticing John, but metaphorically, he carried me like a prince. He didn't want me to think of him that way, but he remained the only imperfect, flawed man who ruled my world even if he was twenty years my senior. He was my prince and my fairy tale.

Thirty-Four

THE STADIUM. AUGUST 3, 2016

THE DAY before our flight, I reached the stadium to find Aryan pacing. On a bench by the racetrack, red roses lay next to a chilled champagne bottle, dripping beads of condensation.

When he noticed me, he wrapped me in a hug. "Today is the happiest day of my life."

"What's the occasion?"

"My daughter agreed to meet me." He broke free, holding my shoulders. "I'm so happy, Sia. A load has lifted off my chest. I've lived my life—never mind—she is here now, and she is my second chance."

His dimples deepened as he surveyed the bench as though it was a decorated hall of his love.

Refreshed by Aryan's sensitive side, a smile sputtered out of my core.

He pointed at me. "Get ready, missy. You are unexcused."

Missy? "Right, don't worry about me, Aryan. I'll do the routines on my own. Spend the day with her."

"*Oh,* I'll see."

Leaving him by the benches, I chuckled and marched to the other side of the racetrack, about twenty feet away.

As I unzipped my bag on the ground, in my eye's periphery, his shadow picked the flowers and fidgeted from foot to foot. Surreal it was. When another shadow enlarged, I pulled the towel out of my bag and wiped my neck, careful not to intrude, careful to let them have space. No one was happier for aloof Aryan than me. He needed this dash of emotion in his life.

A struggle of the shadows tore through my comforting thoughts for him, and I turned.

She snatched the flowers from his hands and threw them at his face. One by one, the rose petals fell on his shoes as my hand lifted to my chest.

Aryan's face slumped toward the obliterated flowers.

She raised her voice. "Just give me the money. That's all I need. I hate you! Why did you put up all this drama? I only need the—"

He raised his hand, his shoulders low. Slipping his hand inside his pocket, he drew out some cash as she snatched it from his hands and marched away, yelling, "Jerk!"

He wiped the corner of his eye with his index finger.

Oh, the man was my rock, and it was hard to catch him impaled.

When he turned. I quickly swung, too, zipped my bag shut, and started jogging in one place, feigning ignorance. Proud Aryan wouldn't have it any other way.

"Let's go," he said, and we started our warm-up routine, circling the field.

His eyes remained dry, giving nothing away. And I itched to reach for his hand. His daughter had no clue about his good heart. In the moment, I swore I would never leave Aryan.

We spent hours on the track, focused on the prize called the Olympics.

Hours later, when I said goodbye at the parking lot, he held me by the shoulders. "Siana, we leave tomorrow. You are ready. I can feel it."

I hadn't even considered tomorrow. It didn't exist until that moment. And considering everything I fought for, worked hard for, had arrived, chills traveled down my spine.

Good chills. Tomorrow.

A tingly bubbly sensation toyed with me as I brushed my teeth. My clothes were packed. I only had to do my last routine at the stadium. The next time I would brush, it would be in Rio. In my gray pajamas, I had sprung outside into the living room, but my footsteps screeched to a halt. Mamma poured him tea while Sandeep sat across from them. A piece broke in my heart as I stood petrified, staring at the toxic, twisted relationship between Mamma and Tayaji.

When I caught his eye, Tayaji smiled. "Siana, we waited for you. Come and join us for tea."

I don't know why I chose that moment to address my deepest struggle. Twisting my hips, I swaggered to him and grabbed an apple from the table.

Crunching into the juicy Ambrosia, I chomped loudly. "What's going on between the two of you?"

Sandeep dropped his *paratha*. All stared at me as though I was smoking weed.

Mamma's voice quivered. "What are you saying? Your tayaji came here to wish you good luck with your races in Rio. He gave me money for your fees—your expensive stadium membership and your flight—"

"I have already paid for my memberships and flights through the crowdfunding for Team USA, and I'm fine without his money."

My eyes watered, and my heavy voice fought the lump in my throat. "And how do you repay him for his generosity?"

She slapped me across the face and covered her mouth before whispering to Tayaji, "You should go now."

"I'm sorry," he said and plodded to the door.

Sandeep rose from his seat. "Siana, be careful. You can't accuse them without a good reason."

Mamma stuck her chin toward me. "You are as rude today as you used to be when your father was alive, and I'm an old person capable of making my own decisions." She flung her finger at me. "I'm unanswerable to you—especially you—who never learned how to respect her elders."

When she barged into her room crying into her arm, my insides wept, too. Guilty I was, but this was gnawing me inside out—the hand brushes, the smiles, the one-on-one conversations.

Sandeep pointed at my face. "Understand your audience. Do you even realize how selfless and pure her heart is to think this of her?"

"I'm a broadminded person. I don't mind Mamma moving on from our father. But with Tayaji?"

"Sure, you are 'broadminded.' " He marched to the kitchen with his half-full plate.

I clenched the dining chair's back as Sandeep dumped his uneaten food into the garbage and washed the plate. Crossing me, he left without meeting my gaze.

And I squeezed the chair, rocking and staring at the shut door to Mamma's room. My eyes fluttered as I lifted my chin, changed into my sneakers, and bolted out for my morning run. My insulting her, my heart and soul, the only piece of my parents alive, chipped away at my soul.

A dog barked in a side street.

The trucks zoomed past.

When I passed by a deli, the oil and salt aroma grew a stomach growl in me. And I halted my sprint, holding my knees. Two chuckles came from an open window. I glanced above, huffing.

My family was uncomfortable with words.

So was I.

The last time I disrespected a parent, he left me forever. My heart crunched into a ball, and I grabbed my head before dashing to the house. Mamma was all I had, my silent pillar, the unsung hero who always loved. I increased my pace.

🍀

I stormed into my home, where Mamma sat at the edge of a chair. Her hands flew in the air, jumping out and rushing to me, drawing me into her tight embrace.

"We must talk." I tore away.

"And I need to talk to you." She pointed at me through the corner of her eye.

"I'm sorry about this morning. I don't know what happened to me."

"But I do." She tapped my upper chest. "You keep things here, buried. When your feelings get too full, you erupt. You did the same when you were in school. One time, someone ate your lunch in second grade. You didn't say a word to anyone. A week later, I rescued you crying from the principal's office. You *must* speak up more often."

I chuckled. "You're right. I must erupt more often." My shrink could never describe it that well.

"Yes, you see something—you call it out. No thinking, thinking, and thinking about it." She caressed my hands. "Siana, I need to talk to you."

I freed my hands from her grasp and raised them. "If you are having an affair with Tayaji, I'm not ready to face it. Not yet. Let's talk after the Olympics." *What'll happen then to change my mind?*

"Let's go somewhere out and talk now." She adjusted her bangles on her arm. "Take me to the Golden Gate area. I heard they have a beautiful red lighthouse across the bay."

"Ma, what did I just say?"

"And what did I say? Let's escape this home and talk." She swung around me and marched to the front door, sliding her feet into her shoes.

I glanced at my watch. "The Golden Gate Bridge area is an hour away. I must be at practice in half an hour before I fly out tonight."

"You cannot cancel your last practice for your old mother?" She scowled at me.

Her shiny eyes reflected my image, and I whispered, "Of course, I can. Let's go."

"Pick a beach closer than the Golden Gate, as I don't want you to miss your flight. Anything will do as long as we are by the ocean."

Outside, the gentle Diablo breeze hit us, our clothes dancing rhythmically. Unsure if she tested me with scenery change, I stared at Mamma with my mouth open.

When we slipped into the car and rode away, she brushed the dirt off the dashboard. "Now, you can buy a new car."

"And get rid of this gem? It has another ten years left." Papa's car was imperishable. I turned into Mathis road outside our subdivision.

"It sounds horrible, and it looks terrible, too, Siana. Get a bright car. Yellow."

I chuckled for a good minute, most happy about the color of her choice.

"Are you worried about the status symbol?" I winked.

"I grew up in India where status, status, status defined everyone and everything. But if I worried about it, I would have been long gone by now."

"Gone? Where?" The red light halted the car and my levity. Tayaji stroking her hand flashed in front of my eyes. So did his Mercedes.

She tugged my arm. "To God, Siana." She mixed in light laughter.

I hit the gas pedal when the light switched to green. "Besides, I still don't have enough money to buy a car."

She inhaled deeply and thrust her chest forward. "You will, after the Olympics."

Another red light.

"What if I lose?" I whispered.

She pressed on my shoulder tightly. "You still would have run for America—the richest, most beautiful country in the world. No one can take that away from you." She sounded like Papa.

Littered with boats, the marina appeared right then, and I swerved inside the lane.

I pulled into a parking spot before Mamma jutted open the door.

A tunnel of warm, moist breeze stormed into the car as she stepped out, and I unbuckled. Hurriedly, I popped out, dashing behind her. With her *kameez* rustling like a kite wrapped around her, she glided straight to the ice cream truck and handed cash to the seller. I scratched my forehead. When I caught up, she thrust me a chocolate ice cream cone while she licked her strawberry one. Quietly, we meandered toward the beach. How did she bounce from our fight effortlessly?

After we finished, we sat down on the sand as the waves delivered secret, rumbling therapy, and the seagulls squawked and wailed. I closed my eyes and inhaled the moist, salty air, a slit elongating along my lips.

"Siana, have you ever been in love?"

I opened my eyes wide and sat upright. "I've had my share of crushes."

"With Brian?" She cocked her head at me, holding her knees to her chest.

I suppressed a smile. "How did you find out?"

"I'm a mother, Siana. Only love can make you do such silly things. Do you still like him?"

"No, not anymore."

"Good. Brian was a wrong fit, but I would have said yes if you had asked me."

I snorted.

Her voice gelled in with the ocean waves' howls and chalky seagulls' dips. "You used to be so angry at us because we were not modern enough—you know—American." She tightened her grasp around her knees. "I grew up in a tiny village in Punjab, comprising a handful of homes on one road inside endless wheat and mustard fields." She crisscrossed her legs and grabbed my hand. "Our society forbade us to talk to boys. Girls made friends with girls and boys with boys. Some fellows followed the girls, teased them, and made their life miserable unless they wanted the attention, of course." She chuckled and snuck a hair strand behind my ear. "You have so much more freedom than what I had growing up in my village. And yet, you blamed us. If you wanted to date the Brian fellow, I would have said yes."

Did I assume my prison? Or had she separated her philosophy from Papa?

"Really?" I said.

"Really. Do you believe in destiny?" She removed her slippers and pressed her crossed knees to her body, staring at the waves rolling up little children, their chuckles cracking through the atmosphere.

I scratched my neck. "I don't know. Maybe not."

"I do. I believe destiny chose your father for me. Even though I couldn't choose my life partner or go out and experiment with lovers, your generation didn't invent love. We fell in love, too. Our hearts broke, too." Her eyes watered.

"Did you like someone when you were young?"

"I did—before I met your father, of course."

And she told me her story. Her words melted into a black and white film.

Mamma was fifteen. Every day, she had sat in a carriage filled with villagers, and the horse grunted, taking her to school—an all-girls establishment. The horse's knocks against the stony road and the driver's whip's lash accompanied the ride. And every day, their eyes met as he followed her the entire way on his bicycle, his eyes fixed on her, her biting her chiffon scarf. Into electricity poles, villagers, and cows, he had bumped; into animal dung and potholes, he had driven, so what? The ride served as their daily date—Mamma and her lover.

One day, he slyly handed her a love note. Another day, she wrote him a letter.

In this manner, two years passed, and then came the day when a longer note delivered heartbreak.

I shoved my legs underneath me. "He was being forced into an arranged marriage?"

"No. H—"

"He wanted you to elope with him, and you said no." *Please, please, please, be true.*

Mamma rested her index finger on my lips. "Shush. He was leaving me."

"What?" I felt my body sliding into the sand. "Why?"

She smiled sadly. "The note . . . he'd gotten admission in some university in Dallas for mechanical engineering. He'd promised to return."

"Oh, that's not bad."

"Ya?"

"Yes. He didn't leave you. And you didn't leave him. Rather, he requited your love. You . . ." When had I become so desperate for the reciprocation of love?

Mamma brought her face near me, her breaths warming my cheeks. "Do you want to hear my story or your version of it?"

"Yours."

She pulled back, her umber eyes growing deeper as the waves lapped against her bare feet. When she spoke, her voice came out heavy. "I was now alone in a carriage full of people. A year passed, and the village changed. Educated youngsters left for larger towns or to study abroad. A strange dullness survived." She bent her toes, draped in wet sand. "Only drug cartels, gossips, or old retirees sitting under trees remained. When I passed the twelfth grade, two years had passed with no news from him. I still remembered him well. But I'd no choice. The only path forward led people out of the village. My parents, too, picked the best proposal that would get me to America, and I married your father. I saw his face for the first time on our wedding night. Can you imagine?"

"Papa was your lover from the past." I snapped my fingers.

"Oh, Siana."

"No?" My insides shifted in my body, unable to wish away her past.

"You must listen to the rest of the story to find out, isn't it?"

Maybe there's hope.

"But how can you marry a man without seeing his face?"

Mamma smiled, staring at her feet. "Your father's work visa had come through, and he dropped out of college. He spoke so highly about his brother throughout the flight, how your Tayaji worked at a small company that made washing machines in the Bay Area. We landed at the airport, and . . ."

"What?"

"He waited at the airport with red roses in his hands." Her voice quivered. "I'd dreamed of seeing him again for so long."

"Who? Your lover?" She still hadn't told me his name.

"Yes."

I gasped. No, Papa wasn't Mamma's true love. She stroked my wet cheek.

"Siana?"

"Wh-what did you do?"

"I did nothing. I met your Tayaji as if I'd never met him before."

I pushed against the sand and rose. "Was Tayaji your lover?"

Suddenly, the waves lost their comfort. Their laps turned into wails. A child cried in the distance.

Why couldn't I weep like that toddler? A luxury snatched from adults is the acceptance of them falling apart wherever they wished.

She pulled at me for seconds until I hit the ground next to her, and she dried my cheeks with her hands. "It's okay, my darling. These small things happen in life."

We stared at the ocean for a bit before she asked, "Do you want to know more?"

My voice left my body, and I responded with my eyes.

"At the airport, your Tayaji had a fuller physique and thicker beard, but he bore the same ancient longing in his eyes as before." She exhaled, staring beyond me. *"Ah,* how could I explain to the world what never materialized beyond a vision inflicted me so much pain?" A tear fell down her cheek. "Something that never was . . . that never will be . . ."

I grabbed her hand and didn't let go.

"Speechless, I had followed them to the car at the airport."

She chuckled even though her eyes were moist. "On the ride home, your father slipped behind with me. He wouldn't leave me, worried that I cried because I was lonely in a new country. He pointed at every hill, every bridge, every building, trying to make me happy. And he lived his life making me happy. He loved this country—in a way he never loved India."

Mamma caressed my back.

"They—the brothers—had planned to live a 'bachelor life' together: visit pubs and have fun, but their parents had worried both sons would remain single for life. So, they rushed your father into marriage even though he was the younger one." She sighed. "Their want-to-be-bachelor-pad turned into an uncomfortable joint family home."

The bright sunlight dimmed for me as I expected a happy love story, not a tragic one. "How did you cope?" I stared down, unable to look her in the eye.

"I cried myself to sleep the first night, but life kept on going. I had two beautiful children and got over it. Your Tayaji chose to be a bachelor for life. The end." She smiled.

Not the end. Not like this. After a long silence, I asked, "Why did you guys not exchange phone numbers? He could have written to you from here."

Mamma lovingly shoved my head back. "Everything is so simplistic in your mind. We failed to bridge the gap between America and India, and we did not even have a landline then. And today, people carry phones in their pockets. Who knew?"

"So, when did you start meeting alone?" I frowned.

She chuckled. "Tayaji and I don't meet alone, my innocent *puttar*. When your father died, he got concerned. He offers help that I refuse. I lived a happy life with your father, who did nothing wrong. I remained loyal to your father, and I intend to keep it that way. Your tayaji is drawn to us because our past has knitted us together, and we cannot change it. But I want you to trust me that nothing is going on between us. If he offers help, I decline."

"You can move on with your life. Other single men exist out there."

"Really?" She half-smiled.

"Yes."

"Why not with your tayaji?" She tilted her head.

Because he's Papa's brother, the man in front of whom Papa didn't measure up.

She shut her eyes. Every wrinkle on her face was a mark of beauty. "Siana, men are weak. I dedicated my life to your father, willfully forgetting my past. Your tayaji, on the other hand, expressed to me multiple times that he still remembers me, and I ignore him every time."

Pressing on my head, I glanced away at a seagull, carrying its prey in its beak. I whispered, "Thank you for trusting me with your secrets."

Her hand glided against my back. "You, my girl, are free to choose whoever you want to marry no matter their race, religion, or color."

I embraced Mamma tightly, viewing her in a fresh new light. How did I miss this side of her all my life?

She made me so proud.

"You will pick a fine college, finish higher education, find an outstanding job, and always be an athlete who ran for Team USA."

Her pats on my back felt cathartic.

"You are living my dream, Siana. It makes me soooo happy. Who knows what you will bring back from the Olympics? Make your father proud, Siana. Run for him."

I released myself and braced her at arm's length. "Why did you and Papa live your life only for the children? I mean, it's okay to follow your dreams. For example, you can still fall in love and get married. You are young."

"My parents raised me this way. And I'm happy with myself and my children. One day, I may go to college. But I will never—marry—again. Two loves are more than enough for a lifetime."

I noted she said two loves. "Do you want to be with Tayaji?"

She turned me to her. "I brought you here to tell you the story about my true love. What did you get?"

I shrugged my shoulders. "That Tayaji—"

"Siana, think harder."

"That life is unfair."

She tapped my forehead. "No, that I met my true love—your father. I forgot about your tayaji the day I married your father. God tested my commitment in the hardest way by making me live right in front of my old lover if you understand that."

She slipped her feet into her slippers, and so did I. She showed me love differed from my idea of it.

She continued, "I found your tayaji's pride pretentious and your father's heart genuine. I had a—what you call it—a crush, illogical. I fell in love with your father's innocence, sincerity, and dedication with which he loved this country. I fell in love with him with reason."

I stared at my watch as Mamma clapped once and rose. "Let's go. You have a flight to catch."

It took moments to return from her life story to today. My heart thumped, thinking about the Olympics. The entire way to the car, I latched onto her hand. "Thank you. It must have been hard on you. If ever you change your mind about moving on with your life, I will support you. Not that you need my support, but I want you to know I will."

"I know, *Puttar.*"

When we reached the car, I gasped. Mamma, oblivious of me, continued to her door.

Twenty feet away, John Flynn rested on a sedan with only a jeep separating us. His bony fingers' touch hadn't left my neck. Standing behind Mamma, he glared at me.

"What's wrong?" Mamma called from across our car.

I pressed my lips and entered the car, as did John climb into his.

Inside, Mamma clenched my shoulder. "What's wrong, Siana? You look pale."

I smiled shakily. "Nothing."

When I reversed, he swerved out, too.

After I turned, his car, too, appeared behind us. Yikes!

When we reached our home street, I didn't turn into it because he stayed behind me. He had no business in Fremont, far from his home in San Francisco.

Mamma swung behind, eyeing our street. "Siana, you missed our road. Why are you lost?" She pointed at the dashboard clock. "You are running late for your flight now."

I took a sudden illegal U-turn, my throat parching. "Sorry, Mamma." I stared at the rearview mirror. He turned, too! No! He shouldn't know where we lived. No, no, no. And I couldn't leave for the Olympics like this.

I stiffened, but this time, I had no choice but to turn into our road from Mathis street because Mamma was right. I would miss my flight.

"Siana, what's wrong?"

Monitoring the rearview mirror, I pulled into our driveway and jerked my door open before storming outside. After slowing down for a quick second, John sped away.

Mamma tugged on my shoulders. "What's going on?"

The Olympics

"In three words, I can sum up everything I have learned about life. It goes on."

ROBERT FROST

Thirty-Five

RIO DE JANEIRO, BRAZIL. AUGUST 7, 2016

TO THE OLYMPICS, I carried Papa's heart and John's worry. Zoned into a cocoon, I performed the motions—check into the village, register, shake hands with the athletes, in a pearl tracksuit, march and wave our flag—but the moments squirted in and out without leaving an imprint like the damp, earthbound clouds that seldom brought rain. Similar to fumes from hot pavements slaked with water, my minutes melted into the future.

The electric atmosphere blurred the distinction between reality and dreams. During the first two days, I was a walking, talking figment, a speck.

On the third day, I watched a long jump event when the overhead commentator said my name a second before my phone rang. I hurried to the sidelines and answered the call.

"Siana, your photo is live on TV!" Mamma screamed.

"Okay." Scratching my neck, I passed an athlete as I headed up the stairs.

"They are saying you are the front-runner."

"What?" I halted.

"Yes, all eyes are on you, Siana. I cannot believe it. If your father . . ."

I glanced up at the screen, my image filling the big screen, and I gasped. "Mamma, I got to go."

I pressed on end as an athlete approached me. "You are Siana Singh from the USA, right?"

"Yes." I tucked the phone away, glancing around for Aryan.

"You broke a record in your Olympic trials."

"Yes, but just once."

She dashed away, talking to another athlete and pointing in my direction. How did I become a front-runner? To my laughter, Tia, a fellow runner from New Jersey, had told me so an hour ago. Ironic. I headed to the locker rooms as we had a day planned.

When I stared at the price tag, my eyes popped, and I placed the lovely, chiffon, navy-blue dress on its shelf. Disappointed that I could only afford a neck scarf or a sock, I lugged the almost empty basket around. Why did I bother picking a basket, after all?

I halted when a hand rested on my shoulder. Tia pointed behind me. "Do you see the girl over there?"

I swung my face around, where a girl with thick braids felt the fabric of a party gown. "Yes. Why?"

"You do? Wow!" She whispered into my ear, "Then, do you know she's known as the Indian Bullet?"

"No."

We moved a section away from the Bullet, whom I knew as Mina from the IAAF World Championship, the girl who reached out to me and pulled away when she realized I was not Indian like her.

How could I forget her?

Tia swiveled at her, latching on to my arm. "She's a runner from India who grew up in a slum of Calcutta. People say her life was so hard that she is now headstrong and made of steel."

My body tingled into an eerie chilliness while Tia's fingers dug into my shoulder.

How did Mina appear herculean, singularly confident, and not submissive as Aryan pegged Indians to be? He profiled our race, and Indian Bullet defied the stereotype on my deceptively American face.

Tia continued, "She has never come second in a race, always first by a huge margin. Man! The world records she has broken."

With a full cart, Mina strolled to the checkout counter steps away from us.

"She isn't poor anymore." I winked at Tia.

"Well, *duh.* I would hate to run against the Bullet, though. Just look at her muscles."

I swallowed. "Yes, she is intimidating."

"Are you buying this?" Tia lifted a bra off my basket.

Leaving it by the fitting rooms, we zipped out of the store.

The escalators' gurgle led us to the top floor. When I turned, Bullet, too, headed up to the food court. Grabbing our trays, Tia and I joined a small group of Team USA. But as I tossed silverware and swung around, I crashed into someone. As my hand flew to my forehead, a shape materialized in front of me. Squinting at me, tapping her foot on the floor, stood Mina, newly known as the Indian Bullet.

"I'm sorry." I raised my hand. *Oh,* Aryan would cringe right about now.

"Are you blind?" She bared her teeth as quickly as a smirk took over. *"Ah,* the loser from the London IAAF World Championship. What are you doing here?"

"Focus on your braids, not mine." To pass, I maneuvered to the side, but she moved with me, blocking my way as a shadow enlarged behind her.

"Is there a problem?" her companion asked before Tia and the others, too, headed toward us.

"Nah, I got this one." She glanced at me from toe to head. "Has the American standard gone so low that an average athlete like you is in Team USA? Rubbish."

When Tia reached me, I said to Bullet, "Save your insults, and let me pass."

She jeered. "Are you not a little too brown for Team USA?"

"Mind your foul mouth, turtle," Tia shouted.

Bullet's face reddened, and she leaned into Tia. "What mouth? And what did you call me?"

"You heard me right. Listen up. You don't insult my sister." Tia twisted her lips and clenched my shoulder. "I'm black and part of Team USA."

Naomi stepped forward, holding Tia's shoulder, reiterating the slogan.

Hillary: "I'm white and in team USA."

They searched my face, and I rattled, "I'm brown and in team USA."

Talk about political correctness!

Tia glided her arm across my back to my shoulder, as Naomi, the gymnast, grabbed my other shoulder. We embraced one another, shoulder to shoulder, and glared at Mina. She sputtered a non-verbal gibberish and left. As soon as she disappeared, we erupted and exchanged high-fives.

Tia pointed at me. "Don't you let her intimidate you again, Sia, you understand? Why are you crying?"

Swiping at my cheeks, I bawled before hugging her. They had just gifted me an awareness I had abandoned when John murdered Papa, when the court denied him justice, this acute love of my country and a sense of belonging. And the dreams Papa eloquently talked about formed—the American dream. The House of Milk and Cheese became real.

Here, anything was possible.

I grew up listening to the holy scriptures known as *Shabads* that rang out loud from my phone's speaker now. My hands were steepled, my head covered, and my eyes shut, praying for Papa's spirit on his *Barsi,* his first death anniversary.

Today, my back was straight, chest pushed forward, just how Papa lived his life.

Mamma whispered, "It's fitting you are at the Olympics on your father's first anniversary." A kissing sound was audible. "Win the gold, *Puttar.*"

Eyes shut, I rocked. *"Hanji,* Mamma."

"I kept the flowers."

I brought the phone to my ear. "What?"

"Sandeep and I walked to Mathis Street, where your Papa died to keep roses, but a mountain of flowers already lay there." Her voice quivered. "Siana, your father's spirit lives on."

I rose and paced my room, a tingling sensation sparking inside my heart. The path to justice was winding, indeed.

Thirty-Six

SAN FRANCISCO, CALIFORNIA. AUGUST 12, 2016

RHONDA drew open the drapes. Holding banners and chanting, people gathered outside. One poster displayed a picture of Siana's father and said: *Hardworking, peace-loving American killed this day last year across the bridge.*

The second sign said: *Justice for Tejpal Singh.*

The third sign said: *Sikhs are Sikhs. Don't confuse with Muslims or Arabs.*

The fourth: *I love my Muslim neighbor.*

The afternoon sun high, a fifth sign glinted: *For Sale.* Shutting the drapes, Rhonda rested against the wall, her core misplaced. The last yard sign belonged to her. Not a Sunday, an ordinary, regular Tuesday except for one detail from a year ago when she had bailed John out of jail, this day etched into a death-like permanence. Death-like life. The police ignored her complaints, educating her the protestors could legally snatch her peace, her home. Why? Because of a license, a piece of paper.

She clumped into the living room, glancing around. "Where is John?"

Jacob jumped out of his seat. "Sorry. You startled me. John is out." He flipped through the TV channels.

She gripped the couch's backside. "Did you talk to John about rehab?"

"I did."

"And?"

"Nothing."

Rhonda tapped his arm. "Are you going to continue to play this question and to-the-point answer game?"

He slammed the remote on the coffee table. "What do you want to hear—John is beyond our help? Let him go, Rhonda. He is on his own." Heaving, he pressed on his forehead. "It breaks my heart to face the fact we had two children, and both are beyond our reach."

Oh, he would bring up Grace now. Staring at the TV, Rhonda pressed her lips. "When is her race?"

"Whose?"

"Sia's." She revolved her eyes.

"For God's sake, Rhonda, we need to move past this episode so John can restart his life."

She craned to reach his ear. "Is he starting his life anew?"

Flipping through the channels, Jacob settled on one. "The one-hundred-meter races are about to begin here."

When the garage rattled, Jacob rose, both gawping at the door.

John marched inside, frowning. "After we leave, these people can move into our home. Did you see the crowd out there, a—" He turned to the TV. "What are you watching?"

"Olympics. Come watch with us." Jacob sat.

John waltzed over to Rhonda behind the couch.

"Here they come," Jacob said.

Leaning forward, squinting, Rhonda used the couch for support as Sia's picture flashed on the screen.

The commentator said, "All eyes are on this budding athlete from San Francisco. She broke a record in her hundred-meter trials. Pay attention to her and Mina from India, the front-runners."

The steady clink from John rotating his car keys irked Rhonda.

As the crowd's pitch grew, she pointed at the screen. "Is she limping?"

"I'm afraid I noticed that, too." Jacob rubbed his mouth.

The NBC commentator continued to praise Sia, the runners kneeling at their positions, Rhonda tightening her hold on the couch.

The shot fired, and the runners dashed forward. The crowd's roar ratcheting, Jacob and Rhonda straightened.

Her breaths amplified, focusing on Sia's frame, but they all appeared like dots. When her cell phone rang, she scrambled and silenced it, facing up. The race had concluded. "What happened?"

John mock laughed.

Jacob shook his head. "I doubt she made it."

"What?" The phone almost dropped from her hands.

The scorecard flashed on the screen.

First was India, second Jamaica, followed by Canada, the UK, and the USA.

Sia was an abysmal number five.

Rhonda's voice quivered. "Does this mean she failed to qualify for the semifinals?"

"I'm afraid so." Jacob stroked his forehead. "She was the front-runner, certain of a spot in the top three. Do you think—"

She raised her hand. "No, I don't think that anymore. Please turn off the Olympics."

John fidgeted on his feet, rolling his eyes. "You're looking away from the facts, Mother." He pointed at the TV. "That girl is trouble. I can see it in her eyes."

When Rhonda swung away, John grasped her shoulder. "Mother, she is not good."

"I have no soft corner for Sia, John. None. And it matters not to me what is in her heart." She jabbed her finger at the TV. "She does not matter."

"No? We have to move because of her. Does that not matter?"

"It does." She brought her hands together as Jacob frowned. "We are moving because of you, John, you."

"Rhonda." His face ruddy, Jacob rose.

She oscillated from face to face as though enlightened. "It all started, John, when you pulled the trigger."

Her extended finger stiffened at John. "How dare you feel it's okay to shoot anyone, no matter what!"

John's chin lifted as he scratched it, and his voice quivered. "Rhonda . . . so you blame me, too."

Aware that John had enjoyed her unparalleled and steady support, a guilt tormented her if she encouraged him.

She tugged on her hair. "John, Jesus Christ as my witness, I have rallied behind you." She tackled him by the shoulders repeatedly. "I have had your back, but you, my dear, darling brat, have only threatened me with warnings of running away from home."

"D-do you want him to?" Jacob fidgeted.

"Yah!" She released John. "I would like to see you go. I have had it with your anger and your refusal to let us help you. We are on your side. God damn it! You want to leave us and be with those men whose ideas I didn't teach you? Go right ahead, mister." She crossed her arms and lifted her chin.

John's cheeks were red as he stared at his feet, his lower lip shivering. His entire frame jittered before he moped along the picture wall to his room in the same posture before Rhonda marched into her office and slammed the door shut.

Thirty-Seven

RIO DE JANEIRO, BRAZIL. AUGUST 12, 2016

I PULLED on my hair, lumbering away from Aryan. The wind gusts slapped my moist cheeks.

Aryan caught up to me in front of the women's locker rooms. "It's okay."

"Nothing is okay." I flung the door and marched inside where he couldn't follow me. Ten steps in, I halted and swung around, staring at the shut door. I imagined Aryan on the other side, and my eyes burned with anguish. The last time a man waited for me outside a locker room after a failed race was Papa. I slid down to the chilling floor, cupping my hand over my mouth. A bathroom stall creaked open before an athlete emerged and frowned at me. Two others swiveled at me through the mirror.

My forehead dropped to my palms, filling with salty moisture. Athletes here were ironclad. Their feet were feathers upon which they soared. I didn't measure up in this crowd, same as London's IAAF World Championship. So what if I sprained my ankle the previous day? So what if I hadn't heard from Mamma since Papa's *Barsi?* So intense was my misery that when my phone rang, it flew out of my hands.

Recognizing Mamma's ID, I scrambled to answer. "Mamma! I have called you twenty thousand times."

Heavy breaths were audible. Four days of silence from Mamma was like snow in Death Valley in summer.

"Are you there?" I rose.

"Yes, *Puttar*. I've been busy."

"With what?"

She sighed again. "Don't worry about me or your race. You will win the next one."

"I called Sandeep yesterday when you didn't answer your phone. He said you weren't around, but I heard you." I paced around, ignoring the surrounding athletes.

"I'm sorry, Siana. I was busy—"

"We used to talk daily, and you would harass me with your calls, especially before my races. You didn't even call me before my qualifying race today."

"I'm so sorry." She choked.

"The last time we talked was four days ago. Where have you been?"

Please tell me the truth, Mamma.

"The phone lines were busy. My calls weren't going through to you."

I chuckled and leaned against the wall. "Not going through? You don't have to lie to me, Mamma. Just tell me one thing."

"What?"

Wetting my lips, I straightened my posture. "Has anyone tried to hurt you?"

"What do you mean?"

"I don't know. A white boy, blue eyes, goes by the name of John Flynn."

She chuckled. "No, *Puttar*. Who is this person? And why would he wish to hurt us?"

An eerie silence followed, and no athlete was in my immediate vicinity by the sinks as I whispered, "He shot Papa."

Silence threaded the static for seconds.

"Why would this person hurt us again, Siana? Don't be funny." On the face of my affliction, she laughed.

"And don't mind your loss in your race. You have the two-hundred-meter race."

Tears flew out of my eyes now. My lips curled, and I hung up on Mamma, my rock. I pretended to throw my cell phone away, except it stayed in my hands. An athlete emerged out of a bathroom stall and rolled her eyes on my wet face. I wiped it with my sleeve and called back Mamma. "I'm sorry I yelled and shut the phone on you, Mamma, but please promise me, John—"

"No white boy has contacted us or harassed us. I speak the truth, Siana."

I ended the call quickly afterward, unable to witness Mamma's forced levity. My foot throbbed in excruciating pain as I drew out a heaping pile of tissues, wet them, and stuck them onto the mirror. Only after ensuring I couldn't look myself in the eye, I washed my hands. A group of athletes entered the lockers, stared at the tissues on the mirror, and jeered, *"Weirdo."*

Ten minutes later, I took my tear-stained, defeated face outside where Aryan paced the hallway. "Save the lecture." Raising my hand, I passed him.

He marched alongside me. "You have one more chance in the two-hundred-meter race tomorrow."

I halted, peering into his dense eyes. "Aryan, this is what I do. I build it up, and then I break it apart. I did the same to Papa, and I'll pack my bags to save any further humiliation."

Aryan's fingers dug into my shoulders before he spoke with clenched teeth and a fierce whisper. "An athlete learns to face defeat and victory with dignity. I forbid you to run away."

"Try me." I wiggled out of his grasp and bolted into the night. When a cab drove up, I hopped inside. "The nearest bar."

I glared at the flickering night lights of Rio. Soon, the cab pulled up to a small, shady joint, and I barreled inside, my heart pounding.

Loud music blasted from the giant speakers, and I sat under the large screen monitors. Every digital display covered the Olympics. Sugary, alcohol-rich whiff consumed me whole, just like the coffee beans aroused me. Drooling, I licked my lips and heeded the bartender's approach.

Drumming the table, unable to wait for another second, I hastily ordered a Chardonnay, Brian's favorite. I had spent months craving a drop of beer. Today, Chardonnay would do, drowning my sorrow once and for all.

When the bartender thrust it in front of me, I pressed down on the table, my palms spread. Staring at the twirly, shimmering, deep gold liquid, I couldn't get my hands to lift the glass. My lips pouted and twisted, shutting the images floating inside my drink: Brian's home where I'd mock Papa, his sad eyes, my barking the last spoken words at him, his eventual departure. What did Papa think about on his final grocery trek? Did he look up rehab centers around San Francisco to admit me into? The night before the final test was when I messed up. Always. Like tonight.

A stream of warm, salty guck plowed down my face before I slammed money on the counter and stormed outside, dashing to the Olympic village. Chardonnay, untouched.

Aryan waited for me in the lobby of my building. Seeing me, he rose.

Holding my legs, I heaved at first before rising to be at his eye level. "Aryan, I refuse to quit. I'll do everything in my power to win."

Color returned to his face. "Good. That is the Siana I know. Come here. Sit."

We sat down on the wicker couch.

"I want you to think positive thoughts and understand all runners are as human as you. They aren't God and can err, too, and they may carry bigger baggage than yours, even if you can't see it. All it takes is one race and one millisecond. It's far from over."

He clenched my shoulders. "I have full confidence in you, your perseverance, and your abilities. You twisted your ankle, that's all. Minor injury. Allow it to heal tonight."

"Will it heal tonight?" My eyes watered.

He smiled. "That's all you have, Siana. One night to heal."

The next morning, the sitar music rang, delivering a dollop of calm. Without wetting us, a moist mist sprayed while a circular, rotating fan whirred. At the campus meditation room, Aryan and I sat on the ground in the yoga position. An instructor faced the room and instructed us to visualize not a meadow or a beach but an elevator descending seven rainbow-colored floors until we entered a violet room containing an idol of our choice.

My idol oscillated between Aryan and Papa, settling on Papa.

Instant words rolled out of my imagination. "Papa, I'm sorry."

His eyelids relaxed, his wrinkles gone, his face serene, a faint smile flitted across his lips. "You have nothing for which to be sorry."

"But I'm so scared."

He curled his fingers. "Be fearless, Siana. I'm proud of you."

I missed him so much that seeing him, hearing him, but not touching him was unbearable.

"I let you down." My stomach knotted.

"Rather, you make me proud. Be fearless, Siana. Run with abandon."

"How do I not be afraid? I sprained my foot. The competitors are better than me, and I could have trained harder in the past four years."

His eyes widened. "Worry not, my child. You are where God wants you to be. It's no coincidence. Stay calm as destiny has been pre-written. Go where the wind takes you, Siana. I'll leave you with a quote of Gurbani."

"Don't go."

"As is the order of your command, so do things happen. Wherever you keep me, there I stand.[1]"

When his image melted, I swiped at my cheeks and glided outside, feeling liberated. Papa used to share this quote with me often. No wonder it echoed through meditation.

Aryan joined me soon, and we didn't share our idol, heading for the racetrack.

Unlike the hundred-meter qualifying race when the commentators sang my praises and the cameras traveled with me, today, I inconspicuously took my position for the two-hundred-meter semifinal. Invisibly, I ran.

And my lifeline in the Olympics extended with a second-place finish. I veered away from the cameras this time, Aryan patting my shoulders. Speaking no words, we slipped to the low-profile corners of the audience. Even Indian Bullet ceased to pick on me and found other targets.

Aryan believed we'd done all we could, and I needed to rest my injured foot because sprains were a serial killer of dreams. So, my leg bouncing, watching others perform, I sat with the audience while Aryan talked with other coaches. I smiled at strangers and drank only a sip of water at a time, my bottle staying full. Glued to the racetrack's vicinity as though that would shorten the wait, I gulped burps and suppressed a tingling sensation throughout my body.

Half an hour before my final and last race, Aryan joined me. We spoke zero words. He understood, for once in my life, I had internalized my life lessons.

Twelve minutes before the race, he asked, "How's the pain in your foot?"

"It's there, but I feel nothing." I blew air through a circular opening in my mouth.

[1] Guru Granth Sahib Jee, Aug 523, Fifth Mehl, https://i.pinimg.com/originals/19/9d/af/199daf7aeb5405f1773cb27ead77fc76.jpg

"Good."

When he left for the restrooms, I called Mamma. She picked the phone on the first ring. Again, that hesitation lurked in her voice.

"Mamma, is there anything you need to tell me? Please prove to me all is well with you."

"Siana, my child, I'm fine, sitting in front of the TV, waiting for your race. San Francisco is just as you left it. Boring."

Somehow, her assurances fell short. Never left my mind, the image of John speeding outside my home.

At the dining table, across from each other, sat Rhonda and Jacob.

"I snapped at John," Rhonda said.

She had calmed down and worried that her boy, who wrote about his guilt, harmed himself even though he was brash on the outside, may have taken her outburst badly. But before she confronted him again, she had to collect herself.

"You can't keep this going—yell at him, then apologize, and then yell again. He is in a delicate state of mind. And he depends on you for support."

She nodded. John had disappeared into his room, again skipping the meals. But he didn't party since the fight. Neither did he start studying or talk to her.

Jacob continued. "I know I disagree with all the support you give him and have asked you to leave him to his devices. But . . . there's such a thing as too much."

Just then, she felt a shadow in the periphery of her eye and instantly turned. But no one was there except for one clue. The window curtain on the front door was swinging. Bolting to the door, she stepped out. No one was around.

When she reentered her home, Jacob asked, "What happened?"

"I thought I saw John."

"He is in his room. Rhonda, you can't—"
Rhonda dashed to the base of the stairs.
"John!" she shouted.

They called our names, and we rose at once, but when Aryan and
I reached the steps leading down to the racetrack, my footsteps
halted, and I grabbed my chest.

Aryan turned, extending out his hand. "Siana? Let's go."

I said no, and a smile flickered on his face as he dropped his
hand, staring at his shoes. *Come on, Aryan, give your lecture.* But
he said nothing. Teetering, I toddled down the steps, and my
knees threatened to buckle before I latched onto Aryan's limp
hand. Together, we marched to the racetrack.

On the grounds, Aryan helped me with the last of my stretches,
staring into my eyes without blinking. Even I couldn't tear from
his gaze.

Words weren't a necessity when eyes said it all.

The whistle blew, and I wobbled, my chilly breaths bursting in
and out while Aryan pressed down on my shoulders. "You got this
one," he whispered.

I scrambled toward the start line as a tingling pulse traveled
through my torso out to my limbs.

Indian Bullet bumped into me and croaked, "Watch out!"

Gently, I patted her shoulder, smiling. I bet she vindicated her
poverty-stricken past just as I avenged Papa. Our demons. Our
Gods. My stomach fluttered, my chest expanding. I prayed,
reciting all the verses I had memorized. A player stared ahead
listlessly. Music from the far corner of the stadium rang through
the stillness of the air. His arms folded, his face ashen and
expressionless, not a blink escaping his eyes, like a statue, Aryan
stood on the sidelines.

The judge pointed up the gun.

To ward off the vivid sights, I closed my eyes, kneeling. I
chanted, inhaling deeply like a woman in labor.

"As is the order of your command, so do things happen. Wherever you keep me, there I stand.[2]"

I opened my eyes and searched for Papa, who was always present during my races, but he wasn't here today. Instead, I saw the tease in John Flynn's eyes.

Caressing a pistol, he adorned an ugly smirk.

Rhonda climbed the stairs and flung open his bedroom door. "John."

He wasn't there.

She peeked into the bathroom, Jacob trailing her. Not there, either. She shouted his name everywhere: nothing.

Her hands dropped to her sides. "My baby left. He's gone. He left me."

Jacob held her from falling. "He will not just leave like that."

"I challenged him to do so. I broke him down." Yanking her phone out of her pocket, she dialed his phone number.

It rang.

She thanked the lord that he hadn't turned it off. Rather he answered. She opened her mouth to speak, but noises on the other side dried up her voice: A door creaked open.

"Yes," a male voice that wasn't John said.

John stuttered. "T-tejpal Singh?"

Hearing the dead man's name, a tremor shot inside her, her hands turning limp.

The phone dropped to the floor.

[1] Guru Granth Sahib Jee, Aug 523, Fifth Mehl, https://i.pinimg.com/originals/19/9d/af/199daf7aeb5405f1773cb27ead77fc76.jpg

John shot at me, and I charged toward him with every ounce of drive in me. His face reddening, his fingers firing, he was unstoppable.

At arm's length, a rope curtailed my reach, landing me on my face.

Darkness erupted into a wild roar, the claps bursting through the stadium. Aryan's firm hands lifted me off my feet.

Indian Bullet was bawling.

Coming in at the second position wasn't a habit she had cracked.

My hands flew to my face, drenching in my tears while Aryan twirled me in the air.

When he set me down, he whispered, "Sia, you have vindicated your father and proved yourself."

Although I nodded at him, reality hadn't punched me yet. I just followed the commands and trotted to the pedestal, where they flung medals around our necks.

And so it was, years in the making, years in the faltering: stitched-up voids, woven wounds, faded shoes, twinkly, persistent dreamy eyes—Papa flowed through the notes of the American anthem, in every corner, just not where I could touch him, see him, and tell him he was right in believing in the United States.

It took Rhonda one minute to stabilize. When she retrieved the phone from the floor, John wasn't on the end of the line. Return calls didn't ring; they beeped as though he had no line waiting. Jacob behind her, Rhonda stormed downstairs.

He implored, "You might have misheard. We don't want to spook him that we're always panicked f—"

"Jacob, I'm going for my son. I should have helped him yesterday. Are you coming with me, or am I going alone? I know where he is."

"Coming." He raised his hands in the air and followed her into the car.

Saved on her phone for exactly this day, she entered Siana's address into the GPS.

Neither did Mamma call me to congratulate, nor did she or Sandeep answer my phone. I strode around my room when the door flung open.

Aryan entered with a bottle of champagne and two glasses. "We can still go to Rio Scenarium and have a party."

My phone between my lips felt icy, solid, and silent.

"What is it?"

"I can't reach my family."

He rolled his eyes, placing the bottle by the TV. "They are probably busy celebrating."

"No, they would talk to me first. I won the freaking gold! They'd call me."

Aryan opened the bottle, filling two glasses with it. "Give them an hour, at least."

My bottom plummeted, and the bed hit against me. "When do we fly back?"

"Day after tomorrow." He sat next to me, handing me a glass as I shoved it away.

"You got to be kidding me, you addict. Drink."

He placed the glasses back and played with the fingers of his hands. "Let's sit here and wait for the phone call. Yay!"

No other option existed for me. My heart boomed like a bomb, and under his steady stare, I goggled at my phone in my lap. *Please, please, please ring.* All horrendous possibilities crossed my mind.

"Try the phone again." He elbowed me.

I did. But only the empty rings threatened my sanity.

"No answer?" Aryan frowned.

I slammed the phone on the bed while he lifted his hand to my back, but he didn't touch.

"It's endearing how you worry about them."

When he finally rested it against me, the tightness of his grasp spread tingling currents, my back the only comfortable part of my being.

I always reacted the same way to Aryan's touch, my back uncurling and hands reaching for his stubble. But he snuck away from the bed.

Whatever remained of my core, escaped with him, even if separated by only a step.

His head bent, he massaged his forehead with his thumb and middle finger. "I'm sorry. Someday, I can explain to you why you and I can't get together like that."

I leaned over my knees, an icy tear gliding down my cheek. I refused to look him in the eye. If he mocked me or pitied me, I couldn't say. A mountain of shame and pity buried me.

Through the peripheral vision, his blurry shadow turned and headed out the door.

He slammed the door shut in what seemed like an explosion, leaving me alone, helpless, and hungry—so hungry for love, it crunched my heart.

Half an hour later, I packed my bags and slipped out into the darkness of midnight like a criminal, not an Olympic medalist. Via a text, I informed Aryan that I had gone.

Life After Destination

"Forgiveness is the fragrance that the violet sheds on the heel that has crushed it."

MARK TWAIN

Thirty-Eight

HOME. AUGUST 15, 2016

I CLUTCHED the gold as the cab whirred, steering into my street. When the multi-colored lights danced on my face, I shot up. But it was just police pulling over a car: a mundane occurrence. It must be the neighbor's son, a learner's permit in hand but not permitted to drive out of the subdivision.

As the cab swerved into our driveway, it jerked to a halt, its headlights illuminating a corn-colored construction tape blocking the way. Every muscle in my body tightened, my stomach knotting into a million tangles. Dashing out of the running car, I jumped over the tape onto the porch, where dried blood had stained the concrete. I screamed and fetched my keys from my pocket with one hand and pounded the door with the other, shouting, "Mamma!" A dim light, probably our ever-lit emergency light, emanated from the windows. For the cop car, I glanced around the street, but it had driven away. So had the pulled-over car. Wrenching the keys, I flung open the door to my home.

The cab driver hollered, "Everything okay, miss?"

I barged inside, gaping at my empty home, a dark void. Halfway into the living room, a voice thundered from the outside, and I shuffled to the door.

Our neighbor, Mrs. Patel, grasped the bushes between our homes. "They are at the hospital."

"Hospital?"

"Kaiser Hospital."

I plodded to her. "Is everything all right?"

"I don't know, Siana." She sighed, looking at our scarlet patio. "We arrived from India this morning, and no one has been at your home. The neighbors told us there was a shooting."

I swirled around and stormed to the cab.

"Can you take me to Kaiser Hospital?" I clenched the open backdoor.

When I entered the cab, Mrs. Patel shouted, "Siana, we are so proud of you!"

My head hot, my palms sweaty, I dashed into the ER. I surveyed the area: the front desk attendant checked in a patient. People filled the seats in the lobby, turning magazine pages. An overhead TV spitted out hygiene tips, the iodoform odor nauseating. My vision darted from face to face, settling on one, no, two of them. Bandaged in a cream dressing, dispensing an item from the vending machine, Dr. Rhonda Silverstone talked weakly to her husband.

Through the buzz of the crowd, I marched toward them with purpose at first. But when her eyes fell on me, I halted four feet away while her husband stroked her shoulder. I opened and closed my mouth as a baby cried in the distance, and a nurse wheeled an elderly patient past us. Her face didn't give away a reaction as she rubbed her hand with the dressing, drops of blood visible on one side. Leaving her husband by the machine, she lumbered to me, extending her healthy hand as though for a handshake. I grabbed it. Was the blood on my porch hers?

She wrapped her hands around mine, her dressing rough. "I can take you to your mother."

"Is Mamma okay?"

Dr. Silverstone moved her head. I wanted to think she said yes as she stared at her husband, who didn't follow us. With belabored breaths, the doctor plodded along the hall, and I was darn scared to ask her why.

An ascent of two floors in the elevator later, she led me down a corridor past the ICU into a section of wards.

In one room, Mamma sat upright, the IV needles inserted and taped into her arms.

Her arms bore bright blush scratches, and I shrieked. So did she as I landed on her, holding her tight, wetting her cheeks with my tears.

Dr. Silverstone took a step back.

"Where is Sandeep?" I tore from her embrace.

She didn't answer.

"Mamma?" My pitch matched my heart rate.

"Beta, you texted us you are coming home earlier a—"

"Where is he?" I turned to Dr. Silverstone, wondering if her killer son had hurt us, heat rising. The blood droplets on her meager bandage were too small to spatter the giant puddle on our porch.

"What time is it?" Mamma asked.

"Ten." I pointed at the giant wall clock right in front of her. "Are you going to tell me what happened?"

Mamma glanced at Dr. Silverstone. "Yes. Grave injustice happened, *Puttar.* Grave injustice."

"Please, just let it out. Why are you here?" I rose from the bed, grabbing its cold steel handles.

"Heart disease. Irregular heartbeat. They admitted me for checkup a week ago. Then now again for what they suspected as a mild heart attack or symptoms before the heart fails—so not a heart attack—frankly, I don't quite get it. But I'm stable now, just awaiting some test results. Th—"

"You are fine now? I want to talk to a doctor."

She blew out air. "With the grace of almighty, everything is under control. I didn't want to worry you, so didn't tell you all this was going on. And I'm—"

I crossed my arms, knocking on the floor with my foot. "Well, your plan failed. You did worry me crazy and still aren't telling me where Sandeep is. Why is there a construction tape around our home? Whose blood is on the porch?"

Mamma's lips fluttered, and she pulled me to bed, her cheeks wetting. "Your race was about to start, but Sandeep kept looking out the window. I got angry. He told me that a car was circling the neighborhood."

I stared back at Dr. Silverstone, who now rocked on the chair. "Did your son again hurt my family?" I hissed, and she burst into tears. "Where is John?"

Mamma's fingers cupped around my face, and she swiveled my head to face her. "Do you want to know what happened?"

Why couldn't she tell me Sandeep was okay? Maybe he wasn't.

"Then Sandeep said," she thickened her voice to mimic him. " 'Here, he comes.' And he slammed his teacup on the table before the bell rang. I was busy with TV. At first, I ignored him and kept watching. But when I heard the boy say your father's name at the door, I ran, but Sandeep shut the door from the outside and wouldn't let me open it."

"Did he hurt Sandeep?"

"Sandeep said that it's just telemarketing and asked me not to miss the race—strange. But I put my head against the door and listened."

Dr. Silverstone joined us on the bed as though to hear the story more closely.

Mamma followed along with the conversation through the door.

"You don't wanna do this, man," Sandeep had said. "Listen, we can sort out the matter. Say something, for God's sake!"

When sobs tore through the door, a voice croaked, "You t-took everything from me. Everything! You have ruined my life." He wept.

"You are robbing my friends, my beliefs, my family, and now my home."

Sandeep's voice came deep, too. "No, man. Listen to yourself. How could we take all that from you?"

"By targeting my home with your marches, that's how."

"Please, John!"

John? The name had sounded familiar to Mamma.

"You shot my father, bro. Do you have any idea what I'm feeling right now?" His voice wobbled, and that's when she connected the dots. John: the boy who shot her husband, who worried me. She hit 9-1-1 but stopped when she heard the boy say, "Do you know what happens in the afterlife?"

She reattached her ear to the door.

"I'm so sorry," John said.

My vision darted from Mamma to Dr. Silverstone bawling. Mamma had yet to tell me how many people died.

"Can you please cut through the chase?" My voice came barely above a decibel.

"Siana, I ran to the TV. You had started the race. All my children's lives depended on that moment. You were fighting for gold, and I had no idea that Sandeep was fighting for his."

My hands fisted and teeth clenched.

She continued, "My eyes had glued on your frame leading the race. I saw you get farther and farther ahead while I said a prayer. But I knew when you started the race, and I saw your determined eyes that this girl had arrived—she was going to win. And you did. I'm so proud of you."

Dr. Silverstone patted my back, still sitting on the bed. "You did good, Sia."

"Thank you. Then what happened?" *Tell me what happened to Sandeep. Now!*

"I dialed 9-1-1 and ran out. This time, the door opened—a pool of blood splashed under my feet outside."

I cupped my mouth while Mamma burst into a sob.

"Two bodies lay flat on the ground—a vase broken into a million pieces next to them. A crowd had gathered, and I, too, collapsed with this weak heart of mine."

Mamma took the long route to tell me Sandeep had died. I couldn't lift a finger, a brow. In the room's stillness, my spirit sank into a dark hole of misery. I'd lost everything the day I won everything. Mamma's voice interrupted my sadness. "Sandeep is fine, my darling."

Tingling life sprung back into me. "What?"

"He is just a little hurt and has a stitched-up and bandaged gash on his forehead." She pointed at her ear. "A bullet grazed his ear, but he can still hear from the other one." She elbowed me.

A thousand prayers left my mouth as I involuntarily chuckled. Only Mamma could joke on such an occasion. Well, her and Sandeep. "Where is he?"

"He went to the airport to receive you with the *bhangra* dancers from Stanford University to put up a show at the airport, but clearly, we missed. We are so proud that we didn't want this tragedy to reduce what you have achieved." She leaned forward and slid her hand across my head. "Siana, you have fulfilled your father's dreams and completed his life."

She pointed at Dr. Silverstone. "A mother has lost her son. John shot himself and died of his injuries this morning. This mother has lost all her children, and I can't explain to you about a parent's grief o—"

"It's okay, Mrs. Singh. John died a year ago. Whatever remained of him departed today." She rose and slid back into the rocking chair.

I wiggled my toes, unable to look her in the eye.

"He died the day he murdered your husband. It was a curse for him to pass seconds of his day. I believe he's at a more peaceful place now. The kid never learned how to live in this world. His ideals drove him to insanity." Dr. Silverstone leaned forward. "Mrs. Singh, I had enough time to hold him this morning, and he died knowing we loved him, and after listening to your story, I'm so happy that he got to repent, too. I can live with that truth."

Mamma brushed wrinkles off the bedsheet. "It's not okay, Doctor. I forgave my husband's shooter in the first week itself. My religion teaches me to forgive else we live a miserable life. If I knew my children were marching in front of your home, I would have discouraged them as little actions result in big changes and to spread awareness without taking from you your peace. Siana, you could have marched for peace anywhere in the world. Why in front of their home?"

Her unblinking eyes were crimson.

"I'm sorry," I whispered.

She was right. Had I killed John in my pursuit, too?

Dr. Silverstone's voice broke through my guilty thoughts. "Last year was like a super volcano threatening to explode. I'm glad it's over."

I wondered if her office paintings now delivered shudders because she was now broken like me. And I rose and sat on the couch next to Dr. Silverstone's rocking chair. She stayed at ease with Mamma. Grief and tragedy conjoined us together, but somehow, we had all lost.

My phone beeped. Aryan: *Is your family okay?*

I brought my phone to my lips, staring ahead listlessly, where Mamma prayed on her rosary. A moment later, Dr. Silverstone's husband joined us, and Mamma discussed life and John's funeral, so only mistakes didn't define him. Mamma, my hero.

And in no time, Sandeep barged in. "Here you are!"

We hugged and shed tears. I pulled out my gold medal and flaunted it over his bandaged face. "Compete with this, always-better-than-Siana, bro!"

He laughed so hard that he had to stop and hold his head, cringing. When he asked Mamma what she wrote in her notebook, she lifted her chin "We are making a list of things to give the boy a proper funeral. Tejpal would have wanted us to move on."

"Who?" Sandeep asked.

"John, the boy." She shrugged.

Thirty-Nine

OUTSIDE ARYAN'S HOME. AUGUST 16, 2016

THE SUNBURNT light danced through his window, and I stared at the ground, taking one step forward and two back. Having run out of reasons to see Aryan besides those buried deep inside the heart, I worried he wasn't my heart's keeper and would turn me away with a flick of a finger.

I lifted my chin and climbed the three steps, and instead of gliding over to the window and watching him crack eggs, I raised my fist at the door and stared at its shadow before knocking. An anguished wait etched in a manufactured clock ticking inside my head.

Wearing checkered pajamas and a burgundy woolen sweater over his white shirt, he opened the door. My heart raced. Suddenly, I fought the desire to flee.

He pursed his lips as though hiding a smile. "Hi, Sia. How are you? What brings you here today?"

His curt response fit. Aryan, how about a: *oh,* Sia, how nice to see you after the Olympic Gold we won together! Come inside.

He rotated the doorknob.

Far away, a bird chirped, the traffic buzzed, and a stray honk hooted.

My fingers played with each other as it was a Brian-please-love-me all over again. I didn't stalk Aryan. Not even close. But his expensive behavior turned him into a sought-out celebrity. And I hungered to hear his life's story and his troubles instead of our worlds rotating around me.

"Sia, you haven't spoken."

I lurched upward. Say something. "I-i-are you busy?"

"Yes."

"I miss you, Aryan."

His expression softened, only by a fraction, before he stared at my sneakers. Suddenly, his muscles tightened. "I got to go. You did well at the Olympics. Talk later?" He slammed the door shut as my mouth opened.

The shadow of his feet fastened under the door, and I glared at it, shoving back tears. Pouting my lips, I saluted the chilly air between us. When I climbed down the steps, the evening's cherry colors had brightened, and so had my remorse. "Why did I come here" clawed at me like a thousand daggers.

In front of my car, I paused, motivating myself to learn how to live my life the way I used to before I met Aryan. I continued to fall for the wrong men—the cute drug addicts or the older men with a terrible taste in women. *Eh.* I shut my ears, exiled my thoughts, and banished all words. And still, his voice tore through: "Sia?"

Changed into his track pants and a jacket, he locked his front door and marched to me with his hands in his pocket. "Do you have a few minutes?"

"I thought you were busy."

"Yes, I am, but it's important we talk now. Do you want to grab dinner?"

Staring at my sparkly new shoes, I whispered, "Okay."

I played with the water in my glass with a straw. "I leave for university in three days."

"I know." He crossed his arms and stared past me like I didn't exist. "Sia, everything I invested in my life hasn't materialized. When I was young, my father dreamed of me joining the air force and fighting for India, but I failed the vision test." He uncrossed his arms and folded his hands on the table. "So, I applied to the universities in the United States to study law and pursued sports back home. That, too, ended because I injured my leg and couldn't compete with the younger athletes. The doctors termed my knee a 'Runner's Knee,' and I was in constant pain. Anyway . . ." He gulped his water.

Listening to Aryan ramble, I felt like I was floating outside my body, looking for a place to crash.

"What I'm trying to say is, I'm forty-six years old and haven't settled down." His eyes watered, staring at his folded hands. "When I married Safia—it was an arranged marriage—she got along wonderfully with my parents and morphed into an ideal daughter-in-law, who everybody loved except for me." He chuckled. "After she left me in the United States, and we divorced, my family adopted her and haven't spoken a word to me."

Having witnessed his daughter's wrath, I ached for him. Life was unfair. But where he led this conversation worried me. *Get to the point quickly, Aryan. You are giving me heartburn.*

"I have achieved nothing in my life. I—"

"Aryan, you are a successful lawyer and a brilliant coach. Why do you negate your accomplishments?" I left out the part that I loved him and that I needed him.

"It's not about material possessions. And you won because of your merit, not mine. Rather, you inspire me." He leaned back, smiling with his eyes. "And now you are about to start a new chapter of your life. The way you fought for your father . . . if I had a daughter like you, I would be so proud."

I had to look away. Aryan had compared me to a daughter. I hadn't even told him I chose Criminal Justice as my major, not business. The way the court denied Papa justice, I didn't want that happening to someone else.

He continued, "Sia, you rebuilt yourself, bit by bit, and that gives me hope, but it also takes it away."

"What?" I frowned.

The server came with our salads, and I stared at his face. His hands vibrated rapidly, too hard to ignore as a random occurrence since his childhood. He was vulnerable and sick. My body turned limp.

He rotated his salad plate. "I don't want you to come to my home anymore."

"Because I take away your hope? How do I do that, Aryan?" My cheeks burned under a gush of embarrassment and adrenaline.

"I'm in the early stage of Parkinson's disease."

The party next to us burst into bubbly laughter, and the restaurant's chatter grew a headache in me.

"It's why my hands shake," he whispered. "I'm progressing quickly and on heavy medication. The doctor visits have kept me away from my job since your father's trial. I'm on a sabbatical, but quitting may be my only choice."

He pursed his lips, and my heart tore into pieces. My fingers curled, dissatisfied I couldn't punch the table in a pleasant restaurant.

"I think it's better if we stay away from each other."

A plate shattered inside the kitchen. My nails dug into my palms. "Why?"

He cupped his hands. "Seeing you makes me want more out of my life than what I had settled for—you know: going with the flow, using women for sex, and wishing nothing more. When I'm with you," he fisted his hand, "I want more, and it's wrong. I have tried to distance myself from you, but you keep—coming—back, challenging my resolve. Do you understand?"

Aryan wants me, too. That's all I heard. "Do you like me?" I whispered.

Seconds thundered.

He flung his hands. "Yes, okay, I like you. But I don't want you to be with me."

I glanced away, hiding my smile as a load evaporated off me of being unwanted by Aryan. A small family of four chattered in the faraway corner while I blew out air bubbles to calm my nerves.

A young parent escorted a crying baby out of the restaurant. Having waited so long for an ounce of affection from this stubborn man, I shut my eyes, still facing away from him.

When I turned toward him, I enunciated every syllable. "Don't tell me what to want or what not to want, okay? I must learn to figure out my feelings and make my own decisions for a change." My voice came out heavy. "First, Papa used to decide on my behalf, and now it's you. What do you fear will happen if we continue to meet?"

"I can't fight myself any longer." He shut his eyes.

I held his hand on the table, keeping it from vibrating. "Don't. Go with the flow. Forty-six is young enough."

He was unwell, but we overrated illnesses. People without a named disease could be sicker. I was a witness.

He freed his hand. "But the twenty years of age gap is enough of a barrier. It's the right thing to do. And I'm not asking you, Sia, I'm telling you for the last time why we will meet no more."

I leaned forward. "It's not your decision to make alone. I get a say."

"You are stubborn. Let me help you choose the simple path." He flung his cloth napkin on the table.

"Aryan!"

He raised his hand, rose, pulled out his wallet, and dropped some cash on the table.

I rose, too. "Let me help you. You say you have this serious condition. We can skip labeling our relationship, and we will be the pathetic people who fit into no mold, who thrive on one another, who lift each other when we are down—how you helped me."

Two fat tears carved down his face, and my core broke into pieces.

"You make your decision, but I have made mine. I wanted to inform you why you will not be seeing me again. Don't internalize it as your fault." He pointed at me. "It's not your fault."

He grabbed my hand and pressed on it and suddenly removed it, charging away. Where once his warmth comforted, now chilly air raised shivers, my hand still extended.

The server returned, and her stare traveled from me to the uneaten salads and the cash at the table. "Are you not planning on eating?"

"No."

Four Years Later

"But love is like a dam:
if you allow a tiny crack to form through which only a trickle of water
can pass, that trickle will quickly bring down the whole structure,
and soon no one will be able to control the force of the current.
For when those walls come down, then love takes over,
and it no longer matters what is possible or impossible;
it doesn't matter whether we can keep the loved one at our side.
To love is to lose control."

PAUL COELHO, BY THE RIVER PIEDRA I SAT DOWN AND WEPT

Forty

FOUR SEASONS circulated like the blood in my body. Drought. Wildfires. A city burned down completely. A pandemic raged through it all. Yet, the Diablo winds continued to howl. And the clouds continued to flirt with the Golden Gate Bridge. After John's funeral, Dr. Silverstone didn't have to leave her home, but she did. I never saw her again. I often thought about the Talking Room: if the new tenants had converted it into a parlor. But as Mamma advised me that it was useless to dwell in the past, I had to look forward. Especially today. Especially now. I sat in front of my laptop over a virtual ceremony. Not only had I passed in honors in Criminal Justice, but I was also giving the keynote speech at the graduation as my mind wrapped around the journey that led me here.

I spoke: "My father always said, 'Siana, this is America, the land of dreams. Here, anything is possible.' It took me a while to learn the meaning behind his words because the road to your aspirations is often winding, complicated, and filled with misunderstanding. Mine sure was. It'll be easy to trust in your failures when all you have is a dream."

I cleared my throat. "What's a dream, but a series of images knitted together. It's not real. And one dear loss can shatter imagination and replace it with something hideous. Like Covid-19."

Behind my laptop across from our coffee table, Mamma wiped tears as a smile plastered on Tayaji's face.

Tayaji visited us less often long before the pandemic lockdown. Mamma convinced me that I hadn't forced her out of any relationship. But she stood steadfast on focusing the rest of her life on herself instead of seeking to love again. Behind Mamma, Sandeep hid behind a camera.

I continued, "I learned to believe from my father. Without fail, he focused on the bright side, a quality that made him an incredibly joyful man. He could ignore the rip on his pants because he put his faith in dreams. He would most certainly look past the hardships caused by this pandemic. And he was right." I smiled and spread my arms as my father would. "No bigger purpose exists in life than pursuing a dream that gains shape when you believe and sprouts wings when you work toward it. But don't wish for an uncomplicated life. The complexities hide the thrill and joy. I hope this is the beginning of your dreams. My father was right to dream and love this country. I'm proud of the opportunities I received as an immigrant. God Bless America!"

After the ceremony ended, I high-fived Sandeep, planted a kiss on Mamma's cheek, and elbow-bumped Tayaji. With past grudges buried behind me, Tayaji no longer existed in my evil book. He only attempted the impossible to fill Papa's shoes. No one could do that. He realized the same, and that's why I suppose he pulled back. That and the lockdown.

Hurriedly, I excused myself. Mamma opened her mouth, but she shut it immediately. She knew I had to be somewhere important today. She said, "Go on."

As she explained to the others, I hid in my new car that made no noise I was used to my entire life.

Instead of my rental in the city, I drove straight to the rehabilitation center. Through the double doors, I pulled up my mask, badged in my annual pass, and headed up the stairs.

In one corner of the empty cafeteria, he sat playing chess with a patient. Our eyes met, his glinting in return. Rushing to him, I handed him the bouquet.

"These flowers belong to you, Sia." He adjusted his face mask.

"No, they are yours now."

And yes, I would never leave this man, no matter how stubborn he could be.

He moved a piece on the board, and his opponent killed his king, celebrating. And Aryan winked at me. "Not all battles won are visible. And not all defeats are failures. Get me out of here."

Aryan rehabilitated at the center, but now and then, I got to take him home as if I shared his joint custody with the center. His health deteriorated fast. Without putting my life on hold, I lived it forward through lockdowns and openings.

This man was my pillar during my hardships, and I refused to abandon him when he needed the most help. I clawed my way into his "pathetic" life, as he called it, and I took care of him. We didn't know if we had one day together or a month or several years, but we lived our lives like children—blowing bubbles, staring at clouds, listening to the ocean waves, cracking jokes, and playing tic-tac-toe. We didn't label our love. But I was tied to him till death did us part.

The End

ACKNOWLEDGEMENT

To everyone who shared their personal stories to support my research, I owe you. To everyone who critiqued, edited, beta read, proofread, shared difficult feedback, you have etched your place in the history of this book. Bleeding from my heart, Siana's story rings close to me. And it's a privilege to share it with the world. Inspired by unprovoked attacks on Sikhs, I sat and wrote this. Fiction, it may be, but the inspiration behind it is true. No matter her struggles, no matter her setbacks, no matter her race, no matter her country, a woman can achieve anything when she makes up her mind. This book is about those dreams that beckon us, keep us awake at night, and busy during the day. Until next time, keep on dreaming.

About the Author

MARS D. GILL is a mother, a coach, an IT professional, and an author of the well-received *Letters from the Queen*. *House of Milk and Cheese* is her second novel. Her third book is about a superstitious scientist, even though science and superstition don't mix. It transports love from interior streets of New Delhi and the US to the outer space, providing a glimpse into the author's geek side. Stay tuned for her future releases by signing up for her newsletters at: **www.bookofdreams.us** and connecting with her on YouTube, LinkedIn, Facebook, Instagram, and Twitter at handle MarsDGill.

She is also open to select readings and lectures. To inquire about a possible appearance, please contact her at bookofdreams.us@gmail.com.